Of Murder, Muses and Me

Claudia Chibici-Revneanu

JACARANDA

First published in Great Britain 2017 by
Jacaranda Books Art Music Ltd
Unit 304 Metal Box Factory
30 Great Guildford Street,
London SE1 0HS
www.jacarandabooksartmusic.co.uk

A CIP catalogue record for this book is available from the British
Library

ISBN: 978-1-909762-39-8
eISBN: 978-1-909762-40-4

Jacket Design: Rodney Dive

Printed and bound in Great-Britain by
CPI (UK) Ltd, Croydon CR0 4YY

To Gonzalo and Ana Lucía

Foreword

The meaning of life? Who knows. We'll all die. This isn't a particularly nice thought. All's bad that ends badly. So you see, I needed to do something about this. Create a better ending for myself. Through words. Through her, so obsessed with him. And now enjoy reading my attempt to defeat mortality.

Yours,
Me.

Chapter One

It was early morning on the 5th of May and the air buzzed with the promise of spring. Rosalind hid behind the fortress of books she had built for herself in the crowded library of her Midlands university. Undergraduate exam time was approaching and countless boys and girls passed by her desk enveloped in the morning's sunshine. Some read; some chatted; others laughed. On the table behind her, a couple kissed and she could hear their careful sighing, their mouths separating and finding each other again. They all seemed so immersed in life; filled with an electric joy.

And although her existence had been devoid of electric joy lately, there was always Mark Drubenheimer, subject of her thesis and focus of her life. The wonderful Mark Drubenheimer. A personification of hope, value and truth.

Since 8.30, this very morning, she had been steadily working on an article about him that was destined for a Caribbean journal. She knew that if only more people read Drubenheimer's work—touched upon his novels' messages of a deep joy underlining life's pain—the world could be a far happier place.

She would read through what she had written so far, then take the afternoon off and treat herself to a classic. A ray of sunlight fell into the library window and onto her face.

Rosalind shut her eyes for a second, feeling the warmth on her skin. When she opened them again, she surreptitiously glanced at the kissing couple. They were both immersed in their studies, now. She took a deep breath and started to read.

Introducing: Mark Drubenheimer

The novelist Mark Drubenheimer, currently one of England's most acclaimed writers of fiction, is considered the star author of the prestigious publishing company Flow. His first novel, *Seabound*, tells the story of Frederic, a depressed man in his fifties who goes on a beach holiday to recover from the loss of his wife. Intent on fulfilling a half-forgotten dream, he learns to dive. During a particularly hazardous descent, he encounters and falls in love with a mermaid. From then on, they meet every day in the depth of the Caribbean, kissing, making love—the exotic, mermaid way—and speaking about the secret workings of the world. She teaches him many comforting truths, among them the existence of a hidden light behind life's darkness and pain.

Drubenheimer's second work, *Story*, is about a young woman, Anette, who guiltily lives for reading. One night she decides to sleep at her local library, where she is seduced by another woman sharing her hide-away, the beautiful violinist Gwen. They become lovers and Gwen, at first, urges Anette to expand her experiences beyond stories. To face "life as it is". To Anette's surprise and Gwen's joy, this proves impossible. Hungry for experiences, Anette ends up tumbling in and out of "real-life" narratives (quests, tales of redemption and love) and learns that life never leaves story-mode, that the world is a multicoloured chaos of tales. Anette's path to fulfilment, apart from marrying Gwen, becomes the conscious creation of her own, unique mixture of these stories—her life-plot—from now on.

Rosalind smiled. She hadn't achieved more than a summary so far. And yet, it delighted her that Drubenheimer's and her writing were mysteriously intertwined in her notebook, now. Also, if the article happened to get accepted, it might give her the confidence to finally ask her father—his literary agent—to arrange a meeting with him.

To the high-pitched sound of birds chirping away outside, she dreamily rested her head on her hands. Separated by two cups of coffee, Rosalind Waterloo and Mark Drubenheimer wouldn't only talk, they would think together. The connection between them would be immediate, magical. Mark Drubenheimer would make her feel infinitely special. Like a person who mattered at last.

She blushed ever so slightly, then made herself read on:

Mark Drubenheimer's allure is not limited to his writing. Literature lovers all over the nation are fascinated by the few facts known about his personal life. He arrived in England as an infant after his German parents—about to give their lives for the anti-Nazi resistance movement—put him unaccompanied on an airplane so he may survive.

Perhaps it is this dramatic formative story which has given his writing—with its colourful treatment of life and death—its wisdom and force.

More sunrays played shadow-games on Rosalind's body. The library grew warmer. The couple kissed, again. Her heartbeat quickened—she loved this heroic story about Drubenheimer's parents. It contained such poetry it seemed almost invented, unreal; it linked the author's life to her own. Her mother's parents had also come from the continent—they were Italians—to England during the war. Although her father had always taken pride in the fact that her mum was the most un-Italian of all the world's Italians he knew.

At the thought of her father, Rosalind felt her throat tighten. Yes, he was none other than Drubenheimer's agent. And yet, he had never helped Rosalind to establish contact with him; nor had she ever asked. Although cheerful and sociable on the outside, he was a very private person, never revealing much about work—or anything. This wasn't the only problem. But she really didn't want to think about this now! She hadn't even discovered Drubenheimer's work through him. No, Rosalind had come across *Seabound* of her own accord, shortly after her mother had died. She had walked into a bookshop, utterly bewildered and confused, looking for something, anything, to comfort her.

She had begun with the self-help section, a place she would usually avoid, leafing through books with titles like *Easy Grieving* and *Death for Beginners*. Immediately frustrated she had hurried back to the fiction department—her world. There she had come across him. Mark Drubenheimer, whose *Seabound* was on special display. For Rosalind this arrangement had not been created by a shop manager (or whoever held the responsibility for such things), but by fate itself. Then, just as now, Drubenheimer's writing whispered some secret knowledge that both thrilled and soothed her.

She stood up and shoved her notebook into her bag. Oh, Drubenheimer! But enough dreaming, enough past! Hadn't she been planning to indulge in one of her favourite past times now—browsing through a literary classic? As always, she would only flick through the pages, to refresh her memory. Which one should it be?

Rosalind slowly demolished her readable fortress and returned small piles of books to the library cart. She felt in the mood for a novel unrelated to her thesis. Some famous book full of colour and intensity that would momentarily bring back her mother, to her. Their bookshop visits together had been one of their few bonding activities. She still remembered their last trip. Her mother's belly had already shown and they had enjoyed the fact that an adult daughter and a pregnant mother would go book-shopping together. Her mother had picked up Dostoyevsky's *Crime and Punishment* and called it the best novel in the world. Dark and real. She had adored classics throughout her short life.

Crime and Punishment, then. In a few moments, she would return to the story of Raskolnikov, the student—about her age—driven wild by lack of space, food and delusions of superiority. She would be transported to Russia, and witness the young man haunted by coincidence until he murders, twice. The book's darkness would be set against the relentless sunlight of the student library.

Accompanied by the sounds of other students nervously scribbling or quietly talking and giggling, she moved towards the Russian literature section, bent down and looked at the neat line of books on the bottom shelf. Although the "Secret Committee Against Superficial Affairs", or SCASA (her internalised voice which provided strict guidance as to which thoughts and behaviour were acceptable) objected, Rosalind chose a glamorous blue paperback volume published several years ago by Subtlety as part of a Classics series. The cover showed the picture of a star-sprinkled city at night, the shadow of a man haunting its streets.

Respectfully balancing the book in her hands, Rosalind walked towards one of the wooden chairs next to the window overlooking the lake. She sat down and glanced at the view of sun-dappled water, lost ducks and lush trees. Filled with anticipation—a lightness in her neck and her chest—she started to read.

The beginning followed the young Raskolnikov trudging home, desperately trying to avoid his landlady. The young man was in a terrible state:

It was not that he had been terrified or crushed by misfortune, but that for some time past he had fallen into a state of nervous depression akin to hypochondria. He had withdrawn from society and shut himself up, till he was ready to shun, not merely his landlady, but every human face.

There was only one face, one body that may have broken his loneliness. The body of a woman now dead. He vaguely remembered her beauty. Light caught in her hair and her eyes; the hypnotic power of her voice. Now she was gone, there was nothing left but vague memories and fierce poverty.

Rosalind stopped reading, taken aback. She didn't quite remember Raskolnikov's dead girlfriend appearing so early on in the novel. Why did she have a feeling that she had been described differently, as a sick and frail creature, without much importance to either the poor student or the plot? Still, here she was, mentioned on the very first page and in such praising detail. As if Dostoyevsky had crawled out of his grave and re-written her entire character! Surely this was her mistake? She must have imagined someone else instead.

Bewildered, Rosalind shut the book. Maybe it was time to go home.

By the time she arrived at the entrance to her home, Rosalind had already forgotten about Dostoyevsky and the celebrated dead girlfriend she had discovered. Instead, she fantasised about taking a bath. The mere thought of warm water and huge bubbles which smelled of lavender and reflected the light gave her a pleasant sensation. It was her comfort. Her way of hiding, or at least resting, from a threatening world.

She unlocked the door and stepped inside her small flat, consisting of one living room and one bedroom—both usually dark. She made herself stand entirely still, and breathed in. Coffee. Tea. Stale air.

Since her mother's death, she had become more aware of smells, perhaps because they might help her predict another disaster. She had always been shy. For a while, she had woken up every night in a state of panic, afraid she too was about to die. Afraid of a world that contained too much misery. Missing her mother's body. The sights and smells and sounds of it. As a result, she had dived into literature with more dedication than ever. Books were more stable than human beings. Novels contained the vanishing essence of human bodies and thoughts, captured on reliable matter. And yet the very quietness she had craved for had begun to irritate her.

Immersed in a reflection on this, Rosalind almost stepped on a white envelope on the brown floor.

Odd—someone must have slipped it beneath the door. Hoping it wasn't a bank statement or something as impersonal and dull she picked it up. She found no addressee, no sender. Her heart started beating faster. Maybe it was a secret message for her? Better yet: a letter from a secret admirer! Wouldn't it be beautiful if someone had surreptitiously observed her all along, watched her read and think and live and found her utterly special and wonderful? If there had been a benevolent eye on her, attached to some beauty or spark she herself couldn't see, liking her, loving her?

She broke the seal enthusiastically. Something was about to happen. Something exciting was about to begin.

Her hand reached into the envelope and pulled out a tiny blue card. "Hello, my Rosalinda," it began. Before she could check herself, every muscle in her face moved to express disappointment. It came from her boyfriend, Mat.

Passed by on a surprise visit. Will come again tomorrow with some wine.

Seduce you.

For: I love you and love you and love you.

Mat.

(Who can also be literary, as you can see.)

Mat! Well, it was a nice card. And he said he loved her, thrice. That classified as very romantic. How lovely that now, several years into their relationship, he still made such original gestures. Unfortunately, Rosalind didn't quite manage to feel how nice and romantic this was. Instead she just felt a tightness in her throat; a sensation she couldn't and didn't want to name.

She sighed and sat down on the floor, putting the card back into its envelope. It was terrible sometimes, being twenty-three. There was always this sense of duty to enjoy every moment of this odd, insecure time called "youth". Perhaps because everyone insisted that life got progressively worse with age.

But enough! What about her bath? She would take it a little later. Right now she craved a cup of tea.

She walked into the kitchen. After distractedly placing the envelope on her faded grey side-board, she switched on the kettle and put a teabag inside her favourite cup, decorated with the image of a mermaid which she always associated with *Seabound*.

How thrilling it would be to be loved by someone like Mark Drubenheimer rather than Mat. How different it must feel to be adored by a creative mind. Would he compare her to sunshine and rain? Find a beautiful line for each of her faults? Write her into one of his novels? Take away some of that insecurity and desolation from her?

Unfortunately, he didn't even know her and he loved Mrs. Drubenheimer. This was beyond dispute. In the only proper interview Drubenheimer had ever given, he hadn't only spoken about his heroic parents but also declared her the absolute love of his life. He had even explained that they didn't want to have children because they couldn't possibly share their love. Bad luck for Rosalind! Her daily confrontation with the sublime would have to be limited, as always, to her analysis of other people's stories.

The kettle clicked and Rosalind, a little sadly, poured water and milk into her cup. It spilled over and—accidentally—onto

Mat's envelope. She quickly hid it inside her bag. As her hands moved to take two slices of toast from the freezer, the telephone rang. It was probably him.

A bit more slowly than she should have, Rosalind took her tea and walked towards the phone.

"Yes, thanks for the card, it was very nice and-"

"Hello, Rosy," her dad's voice came, energetic and secure, like a game-show host.

"Oh hi, Dad," she replied, trying to sound happy.

"Rosalind," Frank Waterloo went on, with a sudden, complete change of tone. "I'm afraid something terrible happened."

She felt an immediate pain on hearing this sentence, because he had said it once before. *Rosalind, something terrible happened.* When her father had called from the hospital. When along with the gaining of a new life—her little brother's, Othello— there had been the loss of another: her mother's.

"It's about this writer of mine you're obsessed with, Mark Drubenheimer," he said. She couldn't believe he was speaking to her about him. "I'm afraid he killed himself."

The teacup fell onto the floor, exploding into a fierce mass of liquid and splintered china. She hoped that the world would follow. Rosalind's face turned into a grimace of pain.

She hung up the phone and let herself sink into the mess on the floor. There was no point now, anyhow. Her beloved Drubenheimer was dead.

Frank Waterloo put down his transparent phone and leaned against his cool office window. *And if the little golden stars knew my pain, they would come down from their heights to comfort me*, he thought as soon as Rosalind had hung up on him. It was a sentence from a song-cycle he loved. "Dichterliebe und Leben"—a poet's life and love—by the Romantic composer Robert Schumann; his favourite.

Underneath his building was a quaint little square with a tiny, Italian-style, café. He stared at the tourists filling its aluminium chairs and tables. With its sensual red signs advertising hot drinks, its constant production of noise—chatter, clatter, the clashing of wheels against the ground—the café summed up Soho, even London, for him. Teasing the senses; occasionally exhausting them with overload.

Should he call Rosalind again, to check on her?

Although she had never explicitly told him, she didn't seem to have too many friends. She had always been bookish and shy, and had become even more withdrawn after Eleonora's death. She had a boyfriend but when they had met once—or was it twice?—he hadn't struck him as the overly sensitive type. He could do the "good dad" thing and ask her if she was OK, even though it was clear she was not. There had even been a sound of her smashing something; probably a cup she had been drinking from.

He sat down at his desk, glanced at his computer and put on his headphones. He felt sorry for Drubenheimer. If one life was all one had—one's only appearance in the overwhelming vastness of forever—how could he have chosen to leave so early? Especially given the extent of his fame and his ever-growing wealth? A dull, dark sensation invaded him.

He quickly searched for some new music, the Schumann song cycle his mind had quoted to him a moment ago. He found it in one of his music apps and in one smooth gesture switched it on. There came the first song—"In the Beautiful

Month of May". Gentle, dreamy piano notes. The soothing voice of a tenor. The music travelled like light up and down his spine.

Rosalind. Should he tell her she would be fine, even though he wasn't sure if this was true? Fine, in what way? Luckily, his daughter had never caused him any difficulties—he wouldn't have been able to handle it. She was no druggy, or school drop-out. And yet, she wasn't a daughter to be particularly proud of, either. Not good at sports; not good at (or interested in) business, not glamorous in a way he—Frank Waterloo—considered himself. Good at getting high grades and surfing through one expensive degree after another. A functional way of maintaining her in dream-world for just a little while longer.

He had tried to shelter her from the world's horrors, its fleetingness and instability. For Rosalind couldn't cope with death. After the tragedy of his wife, he had managed to keep his act together. Look after Othello, move on fast to survive.

But about a month after Eleonora's death, Rosalind had arrived on a surprise visit from university and found him kissing Othello's attractive wet-nurse, Suzy, in the kitchen. Just one, passionate kiss with a woman whose breasts he had been exposed to every single day.

Rosalind having not inherited his strength, had not been able to handle it. Like a jealous madwoman, she had screamed at them, sent them to hell, then run away. Back to university. Without even greeting her little brother, asleep in his cradle, at all. They had never spoken about it—except once on the phone, when he had called her hysterical, immature. He had taken his distance from her. He had enough to cope with, himself!

He felt suddenly angry. Heat rose from his chest into his throat and into his face. Death, the ultimate truth! What was the big deal? He should write his own book about it, one day. People died and then they were gone. Only people with illusions they spent a lot of energy on maintaining had to worry about death.

Death, he mentally explained to an imaginary, uncomprehending audience—was the benchmark for life. The universal end of humanity's messy plotlines. Unexciting for most of the rich (at least at this present, over-fed time in history); filled with rather nasty tragedies for most of the poor—a real problem, to be sure, but certainly not his own. Boredom, trouble, boredom, trouble: the end. Even the ridiculous plots some aspiring authors were unashamed enough to send to his agency were, usually, better than that. The fact that so many people couldn't understand this exasperated him.

Frank Waterloo sank into his office chair and attempted a smug smile. The trick was—but one had to be strong enough for that—to just accept that all humans were bound to be worm food and get on with that. Be realistic, not emotional about it. Enjoy life. Make money. For, to make the most of one's time on earth, one needed financial resources. As an agent, he prided himself on being one of the few with an unashamed interest in money. In an industry stuffed to the brim with intrinsic motivation—endless love of literature—his business acumen had always been one of his unique selling points. This, and his decision to retain a certain distance from his authors, to not become too involved in their private life. He knew about their financial affairs, but very little about their personal thoughts, obsessions and fears. That was certainly how he had attracted Drubenheimer initially. Sadly, it might also be why he hadn't foreseen his death.

Chapter Two

The sky was cruel enough to be radiant. Rosalind stared out of the window, watching the sun's reflection on the pond in the park beneath, the way the shadows of the trees danced on the lawn.

This showed another clear advantage of literature over life. In books, one usually found some correspondence between incidents and the weather. Parties were held in the sunlight; people were killed in the rain. The day Frederic's wife died in *Seabound*, it hailed so ferociously, the bereft man ran outside, hoping to be killed by a hunk of ice falling onto his head. But Drubenheimer's death was a warm-weather tragedy.

And, life, indifferent life, would just go on and on and on. Even she, Rosalind Waterloo, who had adored him without knowing him, would still eat and sleep and read. Within an hour or two, Mat would arrive, wearing his Saturday smile. And meanwhile, she wouldn't be able to grasp, really grasp, that her barely defined dream had been lost. That she would never meet Drubenheimer; that they would never have their magical talk.

How would she go about grieving for him, saying goodbye to a person she had never met? How could she let go of someone whose body she couldn't trace with her hands, whose smells she wouldn't recognise even if he were to haunt her at night, in her room? She held no imprint of him in her mind.

The sun still sparkled, the tree-shadows danced.

If only she knew where to place Death. If she knew whether some form of heaven, or moving of energies, or reincarnation existed. Or maybe her father was right and, as he had often told her, life just ended, game over, for all eternity. Which one would turn out to be true?

How she longed for a sense of certainty. About life or death after Death. About everything! It was like staring at the most important book in the world, without being able to open it. And knowing that one's entire life somehow depended on its contents.

The message of *Seabound* had helped her so much after her mother's death. The idea that death didn't really exist, that beyond life everything was simply: light. But, at the moment, she felt far too depressed to be able to take even this wonderful piece of Drubenheimer's wisdom seriously.

Rosalind got up, went into the bedroom and slipped on her shoes. She needed to do something. She would go out and look at the papers. There had been nothing in them about Drubenheimer's death the day before, she would check again today.

She ran downstairs to the entrance and stepped outside into the neat line of white houses that made up her small-town street. As soon as she reached the shop on the corner, she entered, and blushed as the man at the counter greeted her with a greedy stare. She nodded shyly in response and hid away between a row of messy papers, crisp packets and chocolate bars. She quickly inhaled: dust; pungent male perfume; the smell of onions frying. Strangely, these smells comforted her.

At last focusing her attention on the newspapers, she started to slowly, almost languidly, scan them for information about Mark Drubenheimer. One paper after another had no news coverage of his death. But finally, on opening the *Guardian*, she found the longed-for headline: "Mark Drubenheimer, critically acclaimed author of *Seabound* and *Story* dies."

Her throat tightened with a new wave of pain. Pressing her fingers against the folded newspaper, she walked towards the counter. There, she had to confront the shopkeeper's display of an uneven set of teeth, and approximation of an alluring smile.

Forcing herself to be friendly Rosalind said, "What a sad thing about Drubenheimer, isn't it?" and quickly placed the necessary coins into his bony, pink hand.

"Sad thing about who?" the man replied and looked at her blankly, any interest in her instantly vanished.

Rosalind's sadness mingled with something close to excitement as she sat cross-legged on her couch opening the paper so it covered the lower half of her body like a newspaper-skirt. She sensed a fluttering lightness in her chest; some force lifted her cheeks to almost resemble a smile. It was, perhaps, the old habit of admiring Drubenheimer and feeling a little in love with him; and knowing she would know more about him soon, even if this time it would be about his end.

Her eyes keenly sought out the article. When still alive, Drubenheimer had refused to have his photograph printed on book covers or in the press. To Rosalind's initial pleasure, the piece included an actual picture of him. Unfortunately, her delight soon faded when she realised how worn out and pale he looked. And this wasn't even the worst of it. In strange contrast to the deliberate elegance of his black suit, something in his eyes scared her, as though even dejection had been drained from him. They reflected a disconcerting lack of passion and vitality, the two features she had perhaps most expected to find in his eyes.

Who knew how writers worked, those priests of hidden worlds? Above all, who cared what they looked like?

Rosalind moved on to the article itself and read it fast and eagerly: Morning of the 5th of May, hanging out of his studio window on a rope… Suicide… The police found nothing suspicious… A volume of Romantic poetry lying on the floor… Typical for a man who had struggled with his art and died early. Then followed statistics about writers and other artists who had killed themselves. There existed, it stated, a thin line between genius and madness. Many an artist had crossed it and been lost along the way. Mark Drubenheimer's suicide was the following a long tradition… Art hurt… He was dead. Luckily, he would live on in his books.

Rosalind put the paper aside for a moment, with tears not yet in her eyes but all over her mind. If only she had met him! If only they had been able to have their encounter! Maybe she could have reminded her beloved author of the messages of his own novels, the deep and light-filled importance of existence, the possibility of self-assurance, of creating one's own story. She could have taught her teacher how important life was. Or at least, she might have convinced him to stay alive for a little while longer, stay *in a* life, in hers! But no, they had never met and now he had killed himself.

And now? She would finish the article. With a weak gesture of her hand, Rosalind picked up the paper and read on. After a few more details about depression and the creative process, she suddenly—and a little unexpectedly—came to the exclusive presentation of Drubenheimer's suicide letter.

"This," the paper announced, "is the letter, or rather, the poem, the great writer left to the world."

Rosalind started. A poem? A poem by Mark Drubenheimer,

the master of prose? She struggled to understand. Hadn't he even made the protagonist of *Seabound* declare that "poetry was dead"? Did Drubenheimer himself not believe in this declaration? Or was it the very reason he used it now, a moment before his own annihilation? A dead medium for a dead man? Confused, yet fervent to find out about his last words, Rosalind jumped over a few lines probably explaining the poem's significance to the non-expert reader and began to take it all in:

> When I have fears that I may cease to be
> Before my pen has glean'd my teeming brain,
> Before high-piled books in charact'ry
> Hold like rich garners the full ripen'd grain;...
> When I behold upon the night's starr'd face
> Huge cloudy symbols of a high romance,
> And think that I may never live to trace
> Their shadow with the magic hand of chance;
> And when I feel, fair creature of an hour,
> That I shall never look upon thee more,
> Never have relish in the faery power
> Of unreflecting love;—then on the shore
> Of the wide world I stand alone, and think
> Till love and fame to nothingness do sink.

What a poem! So sad and so beautiful! Full of a longing for life, a fear of death! The language and style so far removed from the lack of clarity she often struggled with in more typical contemporary poems. Now she understood why he had chosen poetry. Now she really... Rosalind couldn't think any further. Tears rolled down her cheeks, down her throat, wetting her chest. She made no noise and yet she could hear herself sobbing inside as she grasped, for a second, the horror of his disappearance, the horror that Mark Drubenheimer and her mother were dead.

A knock at the door interrupted the onset of complete desperation. For a few seconds, Rosalind just sat there and listened. Then, as if on command, her tears stopped flowing and she jumped up to get a handkerchief to hurriedly wipe her face. The fear of being seen in such a state gave her a new rush of energy—she hastily hid the paper in a drawer of her desk, took a deep breath and went to open the door. Despite her efforts, he caught her out straight away.

"Rosy! You haven't been crying?" Mat asked, winking at her as he walked inside. "How tragic this thing about that writer of yours! I felt quite shocked when I found out. I just don't see why people would want to kill themselves." He tried to gauge her expression. "Anyway, here's the wine I promised." He waved the bottle in the air. "Did you like my mysterious letter? Didn't you find it quite impressively poetic for a young corporate star like me?"

"It was such a sweet gesture," Rosalind answered with a forced smile. She received a kiss on her cheek and watched, wordlessly, as Mat, without losing time, went into the kitchen, and started fumbling about with the bottle he had brought.

She took in the perfect symmetry of his face, as if an exact line ran through the centre of his body, separating the mirror and its original. He had a very handsome face. She was lucky to have such a boyfriend. It was her own fault if sometimes she didn't feel so lucky.

He stepped out of the kitchen again and handed her a glass filled to the brim with red wine.

"I'm not sure I want a drink," she objected, carefully. "It's only noon."

"Oh Rosy, don't be so boring again!" Mat protested, making her wonder when last she had been so boring.

He shook his head at her with the somewhat unconvincing playfulness that characterised him, then walked into the bedroom, where he lay down on the mattress and comfortably stretched out his legs.

Rosalind followed him hesitantly, stopping in front of the bed. So he wanted to have sex immediately. She didn't mind. She liked being near him, being able to feel his body. And yet all the crying had worn her out and she would have liked to talk to him, talk to anyone, just for a while.

"Mat," she began, but only inside of herself, as he started drinking his wine in fast, appreciative, gulps. "You know, I feel so sad about Drubenheimer. I think I'm still in a state of shock. Can you imagine that I spent yesterday morning in the library, writing my article about him, unaware he was already dead? And that he wrote this poem, his goodbye poem and–"

Should she say all this out loud? It would make his eyes glaze over with boredom or produce an irritated sparkle in them. So instead, with a sigh of resignation, Rosalind also took a sip from her drink and sat down next to him on the bed.

"Rosy, don't drive yourself mad worrying about this man," Mat instructed her, in an evident attempt to interpret the emotional content of her sigh, and started to take off his shirt.

Rosalind worried she might start crying again, aware of Mat's expectant glance on her.

Her mind started to recite Drubenheimer's poem: *And when I feel, fair creature of an hour, That I shall never look upon thee more*. Yes, this was so very true! Every hour was precious.

Hours were the only thing one really possessed, in life.

"Hello?" Mat asked. "Anyone home? Can you not stop dreaming for once and come a little closer?"

Rosalind barely heard him by now, immersed in the lines and meaning of the poem. It was a little odd that Drubenheimer had written this before committing suicide. Yes, it explored death and dying. But didn't it speak of someone afraid of death and worried that it may tear him away, rather than someone choosing to die?

Half-naked Mat, still sitting on her bed, got rather impatient. In a moment, he would start pulling at her shirt. If only she could discuss these doubts with him! Would he understand? Well, perhaps she could at least give it a try. Maybe it was unfair to think that he couldn't share the workings of her mind. She should simply attempt to open up. Let herself be surprised.

"Mat," she began, toying with the glass in her hand. "Did you read that article about Drubenheimer in the *Guardian*? Did you see the goodbye poem?"

Mat rolled his eyes at the ceiling and stretched out his hands.

"Oh, whatever, Rosy," he said, as though he were a teacher reprimanding a naughty child. "You won't start with any of your 'artsy-fartsy' business again, will you?"

Rosalind shrugged. Her experiment had failed. At least, she could still lie next to him, make love and capture the hour by capturing Mat.

Determined now, she put her glass onto the floor and cuddled up to him. He smiled at her. He fiddled around with his trousers, unbuttoned them and lowered his boxer shorts to his knees. He squeezed her tightly. Even without having to convince herself, she liked the touch of his muscles, his skin.

His smell of aftershave and cleanliness grew stronger as he

rolled onto her body, flattening himself out. He stroked her hair, quite tenderly; he kissed her nose.

"So, finally I caught you," he exclaimed, aroused.

Soft rays of light fell in through the curtains. Rosalind smiled too, feeling a little more relaxed. Maybe she thought too much. Maybe she was too intense. She made herself listen to his breath, rhythmical in her ear. He moved off her for a moment and they undressed her, together. Soon, she felt his body clash against hers; slowly at first, then faster.

For an instant, Rosalind's brain seemed void, emptied of all restlessness and doubts regarding her grief about Drubenheimer's death. Then, as Mat slowed down his rhythm once more, unhappiness returned with new strength, gripping her entire being.

Mark Drubenheimer stared at her from inside of her mind. The man with such vacant and disenchanted eyes. The body that used to contain his brilliant brain was now in the process of decomposition. Had worms already started to eat away at his skin and his—what a terrible thought! He was gone forever and there was nothing, nothing she could do. She hated the word nothing. It made her feel scared.

Mat sped up again.

"Rosalinda," he sighed, as always in moments of great arousal. "Rosalinda, my beautiful rose."

She looked at him, in panic.

Mat lifted his body, put his hands on her back and twisted her around. Apparently, it was her turn to go on top; she managed to function, somehow. His graceful, hairless body beneath hers, Rosalind rocked up and down in her own, uneasy rhythm. *When I have fears that I may cease to be.* She bent forward and pressed herself against his chest. *Before my pen has glean'd my teeming brain...* Enough, enough! She moved harder and harder to make the words go away. But it didn't work.

Suddenly, as Mat's excitement tightened, it began to dawn on her. No-one would have written such a poem before committing suicide! No-one, attacking death, fearing it, would moments later choose it, invite it in. One could not fight death by dying. Her speed became frantic. Writing offered a better way out.

Mat's orgasms were as reliable as a Swiss cuckoo clock. The second he came, certainty exploded in her head. Drubenheimer had never committed suicide. It might be absurd, but it was the only explanation. The writer must have been threatened. Somehow, he must have been murdered.

Rosalind sat on her bed, looking at Mat, now fast asleep. She had opened the curtains and watched the afternoon sun on his skin, illuminating his face's faultlessness. She reminisced about the closeness they had once shared. There had been a time, shortly after what had happened to her mother, when having a body near her, a body whose muscles, whose strength she could hold onto, had been enough.

She slowly got up, wrapped a light-blue bathrobe around her naked body and—leaving the bedroom door open—walked towards the living room. She still felt a little giddy, as though she had not slept for three nights in a row.

Had she been crazy to think all this? That Drubenheimer had been murdered?

Yes. Maybe. But should she really distrust the one thing she could easily do, analyse and find hidden meanings in texts?

Her dizziness increased; not only due to the shock of the discovery itself, but because she feared she could do nothing about it. She found no room for rebellious reactions in her life. For what could she do, even if she were right?

Nothing. Finish her PhD. Publish articles. Become a university professor. Do research. Read books. And hopefully one day she would forget about her doubts.

Rosalind closed her eyes for a few seconds, as if to rest from life. She craved for a sense of protection. She felt as if someone stabbed her, with a flashing knife, from the inside. She could almost picture her own worthlessness; a blue and threatening cloud of pain.

Then a thought made the cloud lift a little. Perhaps she could do something about this, after all. A very frightening thing. She could call her father and let him know. Her beloved author was dead. And there was some hope that if her father found out that his star might have been murdered, he would start scratching at the separation that followed her wild screams after she had found him kissing another woman. He might make phone calls, speak to important people and perhaps even cause an investigation of some kind.

Through the open door, she quickly glanced at Mat. He lay on his stomach, his bum left uncovered by the duvet, fast asleep. What would he say about her suspicion? Should she tell him? Would he surprise her this time and support her belief, her idea?

Quickly before her determination could falter, Rosalind went to the phone and dialled her father's home number. No-one picked up. She tried his mobile. Still no-one. Finally, she called his number at work.

"Dad?" she asked, sudden excitement pushing aside her nervousness.

There was a tinkling laughter.

"No," said a woman. "Wait."

A woman, again.

Frank Waterloo's voice appeared, a moment later. "Is that you, Rosalind? Have you any more functional cups in your flat? I mean, of course, are you feeling better now?"

"Yes, I'm much better," Rosalind uttered, unsure. She swallowed. Her saliva passed what felt like a large stone in her throat. "But I'm calling because I made a strange discovery."

Her dad chuckled.

"What is it, my darling? Some unprecedented academic insight?"

Rosalind could hear suppressed laughter in the background—that tinkling laugher again. Had it been a mistake to call? Maybe she had interrupted her dad and he would be irritated with her?

Still, she had to speak on. She owed this—this phone call at least—to the memory and legacy of Mark Drubenheimer. She knew that her admiration for him would give her strength.

"Dad," she continued, bravely. "I need to talk to you about your work, I'm sorry. But I have a feeling that Drubenheimer didn't commit suicide after all. To be honest, I have a suspicion that-"

"He's alive?" her dad cut her short.

"No," Rosalind replied, struggling to ignore his playful tone and fearing that her words would sound entirely ridiculous. "Dad, I think he was murdered."

"Rosy," her dad pronounced, quite earnestly. "I'm afraid, once again, you've gone mad."

By now, of its own accord, Rosalind's imagination produced more background laugher. She winced.

"But Dad," she said very quietly, in an enormous effort to

maintain her voice steady and calm. "I'm not joking. You must have read Drubenheimer's poem in the *Guardian*, today, his goodbye poem. Didn't it make you suspicious?"

"That poem? Of course it made me suspicious!" He paused for a second. "But only of Mark's authenticity."

"Of his authenticity? Why? I thought it was beautiful, so very, very moving!"

"Rosalind, wait. Are you sure you are doing a Lit PhD? Didn't you-"

"And that's the problem, you see," Rosalind interrupted her father, too emotional now to stop. "He's scared that his life might come to an end unexpectedly! It isn't a poem about someone embracing death. It's an expression of fear. Drubenheimer's fear that he might be murdered!"

Her father's sighed demonstratively.

"Fine. Inter-textuality and all that. Nothing new under the sun. You see why I never employ people with more than a BA? You postgraduate students all turn crazy eventually!"

"Dad, please! Please believe me. What if I'm right and Drubenheimer really was murdered?"

"Oh, Rosy. What are you reading these days? Murder, ha! But if it's of any comfort to you, a delightful friend of mine and I actually spoke to the police yesterday. Helped them do their paperwork about our good old Mark."

"And?" Rosalind asked, expectantly, trying to ignore the reference to his "delightful friend", most probably the woman now near him.

"And? Nothing. Absolutely nothing."

He pronounced "nothing" with an Italian accent, a mock memory of her mother, his wife.

"There isn't the slightest doubt that our beloved

Drubenheimer jumped out of the window out of his own free will. With a rope tied around his neck. A double suicide, if you think about it. Very creative. A piece of art."

Rosalind asked, very, very quietly, "Do you not care that he died?"

"Of course I care," Mr. Waterloo answered, probably still showing off to the laughing woman in the background. "But he killed himself and it's a personal choice one has to respect."

"But, what if it isn't true!" Rosalind protested, with sudden vehemence. "A person who's scared of death just doesn't go and cure his fear by dying."

"Why not? People get over their fear of spiders by–"

"But it's death we're talking about. How can one heal anything by dying? What would be the use of that, if one doesn't return–"

She could tell from the way her father cleared his throat that he had become impatient.

"I'm sure he managed to get rid of all of his fears, Rosy," he cut her short, as though talking to a slightly deranged child. "In fact, unless Mark tumbled straight into hell, he's now probably free of all kinds of problems. Unlike the rest of us, who have work to do. Someone has to pay your outrageous university fees, I'm afraid."

He emitted a dry laughter to indicate their conversation was over.

An old, dull sensation of anger welled up inside Rosalind. Her hand wound itself tightly around the telephone. A second later, it loosened its grasp again, as if it had already resigned itself and was about to hang up. But something about Drubenheimer's death had instilled her with a new sense of (still fragile) power and purpose.

"Wait!" she pleaded, with forced self-assurance. She was a grown-up woman. She had a master's degree and a naked man in her bed. "What if I call the police and tell them what I know?"

She could literally hear her father's eyes rolling at the ceiling.

"You'll call the police? And tell them you had an intuition? Rosalind, you are deranged!"

"Yes," she replied, still trying to sound firm. "I mean, no, I'm not deranged. But yes, I will call the police."

"Well, then..."

"Wait, Dad, just one more moment! Whom did you speak to? From the police, I mean."

"You're not serious, are you?"

Was she serious? No, of course not. Well, maybe, yes.

"Oh dear, at least don't say that you know me. I think his name was—something aggressive. Puncher. No. Pincher, that's it. Pincher, from the Metropolitan Police. A tall and not very happy man. He'll be even less happy if you call him on a Saturday afternoon."

"OK, Dad," Rosalind said, feeling a little strange. "Thanks very much for your help."

It was a warm day, but Rosalind felt suddenly cold. What was she getting herself into? Was she really so sure that Drubenheimer had been murdered? Well, almost. What she knew with sudden certainty was that she couldn't continue her life as before. She desperately needed some small revolution. She no longer wanted to feel... What? Today's stabbing sensation; the cloud of pain. A sense of emptiness, loneliness, of having to hide away, deep inside of herself, lest something might happen to her. She needed to act. She had already tried to talk to her father about Drubenheimer. And now she would... call the police!

She walked into her bedroom to check on Mat. He was still asleep. Their love-making happened a little more than half an hour ago; and yet so much had happened to her since!

She quietly returned to the living room and switched on the computer. It struck her as important to ignore her hesitations from now on. She would fight for Drubenheimer. Perhaps her feelings for him would help pull out a new Rosalind, somehow.

She opened up the Met Police website and searched for a contact number. Shaking ever so slightly, she scribbled it down, got up from the computer and walked to the phone. She hesitated, despite her good intentions. Maybe her dad had been right to laugh at her. She didn't have any evidence, other than the poem. And yet, couldn't she at least try to inform the police? It was really the least she could do for her lost and beloved genius.

Her heart pounding frantically, Rosalind dialled the number. Even though it was Saturday afternoon, getting to the crime department was easy. A woman's voice mumbled some professional greeting.

"Good afternoon," Rosalind said, trying to sound as polite as possible. "Could you put me through to a man called Pincher, please?"

The female voice murmured something else to the effect of communicating that she should hold on. Then Rosalind heard a click followed by the sound of a man clearing his throat.

"Yes?"

He had evidently been disturbed. Rosalind immediately felt guilty.

"Hello, Mr. Pincher? I'm sorry to bother you. My name is Rosalind Waterloo and I would like to-"

"I'm Detective Pincher, yes. What can I do for you?" He

pronounced the question like an insult rather than an offer to help.

"I'm calling about the Drubenheimer case. Mark Druben-heimer, the writer."

"Yes, yes, I know who he is," the man responded, impatiently. "What about him?"

This was more difficult than she had expected.

"Well, Detective Pincher," she went on, struggling to suppress an urge to hang up the phone and forget all about this. "You see, I'm a PhD student on Mark Drubenheimer and, a little ironically, I'm writing about the theme of death in his work, so-"

"Oh, so you're an expert," he interrupted her, with careful sarcasm. "And?"

"Well, I'm sure you read his goodbye poem in the *Guardian* today? This may sound a little odd, but it gave me the strong impression that Mr. Drubenheimer didn't actually commit suicide. Instead," she took a deep breath, "I believe he may have been murdered."

"That's quite something to insinuate," the man responded, dryly. "And you think that because of that poem?"

"Yes," Rosalind admitted. How she wished this Mr. Pincher was a little warmer and more encouraging! "I know it's strange, but—really—why would a man about to kill himself write something like *When I have fears that I may cease to be*? You see, it just doesn't make any sense! Take the word 'may' for instance. Why would someone use it who knows he's going to kill himself? And then there is the word 'cease', so unaggressive given the way he…"

Rosalind stopped. She sensed the detective didn't even listen properly.

Indeed, he simply said, a second later:

"Well, excellent. I congratulate you on this profound literary insight. So that's why you think he used that poem. Excellent. For the moment, I can assure you, there's little doubt regarding the nature of Mark Drubenheimer's death. Naturally, we're still waiting for the results of some standard procedures. Literary analysis is usually not one of them. Still, if you could leave your name and address with my secretary in case we have any questions, I'd be ever so grateful. Thank you very much for your call."

Without waiting to speak to the secretary again, Rosalind hung up the phone and sank down on the floor. She put her head onto her knees. So no-one took her discovery seriously. Worse, everyone appeared almost indifferent about Drubenheimer's death. Although her father had been his agent for years, his cheerfulness already seemed restored—just like before. And as to this Mr. or Detective Pincher, Drubenheimer represented clearly no more than another "case" to him, another writer who had trampled on life's fragile limits, then fallen off.

It was evident the police would do nothing. So it was probably best if, from now on, she would do nothing, too. At least, as far as Drubenheimer's death was concerned.

Rosalind gazed out of the window. The morning's sun had disappeared. In the distance, she could see clouds racing, faster than usual, as if anxious to get somewhere else. The water of the pond had turned a squalid grey. A strong restlessness took hold of her. It was as though she had unwittingly started something, stepped onto some internal train that she couldn't simply jump off again. No! She wanted, she needed to keep on moving! Only, where was she to go?

She slowly got up, walked to the desk where she had hidden the poem, took it out and read it again. She really had no doubt about it. It was everywhere, squeezed in between the lines, an emerging red light. Murder! Mark Drubenheimer had been murdered! But why? And how? And by whom?

She went into her bedroom and sat down next to her sleeping boyfriend.

"Mat!" she whispered, pleadingly. "Mat, could you do me a favour?"

"What's it this time?" he grumbled.

"I'm really sorry. But could you give me a lift to the station? I have to go to London right now."

Right now before she could change her mind.

Frank Waterloo let himself fall into his favourite armchair and on his legs accommodated a thin manuscript and his laptop. Made of expensive brown leather, the chair could expand in various directions as soon as you pressed little buttons, to accommodate a body or—as his girlfriend Berlina had shown him the other day—even two. He planned to pick her up later to spend a quiet evening at his flat.

Othello was fast asleep. While Frank had nipped into his office, Othello's nanny had taken him to a playground nearby and he had come back exhausted, and happy.

Frank Waterloo loved a quiet Saturday, in his own flat, in his own library. Sunrays enveloped his body, soothingly. His headphones had shut out all sounds other than those of a symphony. It would have been a perfect moment. Unfortunately, Rosalind was on his mind again.

He wasn't usually a worried father, else he might have ended up like Drubenheimer, throwing himself out of the window, on a rope. How could he have coped with being left—just like his own dad, except for different reasons—a single father?

But now Rosalind had turned hysterical all over again. She claimed that Drubenheimer had been murdered. How utterly ridiculous! If only Rosalind's imagination weren't just wild but also disciplined, he could get her to write best-sellers from the ideas she cooked up on occasions. She could replace Drubenheimer, his great author lost!

Murder! What a thought!

Well, she would grow up, eventually. He needed to focus on another, urgent issue: his income. After emerging from his initial shock and, possibly, denial, he had realised what the death of Drubenheimer would mean to him financially. His clients included other well-known writers such as Loren Benjamin and Sunny McHay, but none as lucrative as Drubenheimer. His clever mixture of literary elegance and wacky optimism couldn't be easily replaced.

For a short while, sales would increase due to his death. But the author had died too soon after the release his first novels to think about re-publishing them. And, despite his popularity and the critical acclaim, he hadn't quite made it to the status of modern classic author yet. In other words, he would soon be forgotten and things wouldn't be easy, financially.

But Frank Waterloo was a man of action. He had already written both to Benjamin and McHay asking if they were ready to deliver their new novels soon. Loren—a woman in her mid-forties with three small children—who had planned to finish her next book in a year from now, had gently told him to get lost. But Sunny McHay had sounded enthusiastic about the attention and promised to send something in very soon. He explained a little manically that he had met a new muse and spent the past weeks writing in a state of ecstasy. Also, he was probably relieved that his rival was gone and thought this the first thrilling after-effect of his death.

Frank Waterloo had told his assistant to take another close look at the slush pile—maybe the ever-growing mountain contained a jewel of some kind. The young man had almost immediately picked out a promising novel which he would have a look at right now.

He scratched his right arm. His neck muscles tensed. Why did the man have to die? Could he not have given a moment's thought to those he left behind? Luckily, Mark Drubenheimer had had no children, but what about his wife, his publisher (although Berlina seemed unfazed), his agent? Those who depended on him somehow?

Then again, "dependent" wasn't, couldn't, be the right word. Frank Waterloo was a free and outstandingly capable man. He already had an impressive list of authors, enough to cover his overheads. And as to the extra luxuries such as a beautiful retirement home and enlarged retirement fund he needed (he was already fifty-eight) he would find a brilliant new-comer soon.

He looked down at the manuscript, his laptop serving as a portable desk. He glanced down at the author's name: Susan Gold. That, for a man looking for jewels, was a promising name.

Frank Waterloo held his breath for a few seconds, trying to feel a sense of anticipation. Really, he had seen too many uninspiring works picked out by eager assistants and interns to feel much real hope.

His eyes ran over the synopsis. He had been right. It was... nothing. A blah, blah, novel about a British women poet's personal crisis on the beaches of South India; falls in love with, etc. Discovers writing as a way of healing and self-connection, of releasing her anger, without hurting anyone else. A pitiful attempt at writing something deep, when in reality it was one more stereotypical love story with a mass-therapy message, set in "exotic" India. This really wouldn't do.

"Next," Frank Waterloo exclaimed, too loudly, before he remembered that Othello was asleep. Carelessly, he threw the manuscript onto the floor. Luckily, he would see Berlina soon, and they could laugh about this, together.

He looked forward to rejecting it on Monday.

Chapter Three

By the time Mat and Rosalind arrived at the station, her grief about Drubenheimer's death had become mixed with something akin to enthusiasm, the thrill of—at last—embarking on some kind of adventure. She had been like Anette at the beginning of *Story* for too long. For the past years, her stubborn need for events that emotionally moved her had been mainly covered by books. Now, excitement pulsated all around her.

Short of breath with anticipation, she purchased a ticket from a cross-eyed attendant and walked towards Mat, who waited for her on a bench. She smiled. The station's smell of cigarettes and sweat formed a warped harmony with its dusty windows and walls. Rusty signs not only displayed information about trains—they teased a new life.

"Will you tell me why you're going?" Mat asked when she reached him, breaking the silence that had accompanied them throughout their journey.

She looked at him a little confusedly, as if his voice came from another world; one she had already left behind.

"I had an intuition," she summarised, a fragment of the complex account her imagination had already provided him with in the car. "I think Mark Drubenheimer was actually murdered. So I'm going to London to find out by whom."

She sat down next to him on the bench.

"Great," Mat said.

He couldn't help grinning. He took her hand and patted it with acted concern.

"This is called denial, you know. But then, I suppose this is a normal stage of the grieving process."

"Denial?" Rosalind asked, more than a little taken aback.

Why did Mat have to see her in such a negative light? He kept on calling her boring, complained she was too dreamy, and now he turned her insight into "denial"? There was a loving way and a dark way of judging other people—the choice between them almost arbitrary. And Mat, although he claimed to love and love and love her, usually chose the latter. Couldn't he just be proud that she embarked on a search?

"Yes, denial! Why don't you just accept the fact that this writer of yours wanted to die? Some people do. Especially artists, you know what they're like. They get crazier and crazier from just sitting around all day, doing nothing..."

He made his last statement with a teasing smile, perhaps —to his credit or not—attempting to lighten up the situation. Still, Rosalind couldn't help feeling angry even if this had been his only intention. Should she try to express this emotion? She took a deep breath.

"Hmmm," she muttered (which was unfortunately as much direct unconformity as she could muster).

Mat, misunderstanding this altogether, thought he had managed to change her mind.

"But you're going anyway?" he asked.

"Yes," she replied, shyly.

"Oh, whatever, Rosalind!" Mat snapped, clearly without any inhibitions about voicing his anger. "Oh, whatever, whatever, whatever! Just go, it might even be good for you. Or good for me, if you carry your temporary madness somewhere else."

Fine! She would carry her temporary madness somewhere else. To her father, who was about as willing as Mat to receive it. To his flat in St. John's Wood. To find him kissing a wet-nurse or nanny, again.

"I'm sorry," she said. Although what she was sorry for she wasn't quite sure. "I just really feel I'm onto something, you know?"

"Oh well," Mat conceded, slightly appeased. "As long as you don't think you'll bring him back to life, this way. I know what you're like, Rosalind."

An old lady walking past them with a shopping basket showed an interest in Mat's little speech; he went on, evidently pleased to have an audience:

"Besides, even if you were right—which you're obviously not—no-one could have murdered Mr. Writer without leaving a trace. And if he had left one, the police would be looking into this, by now. This is what they're here for, after all."

Rosalind sat next to the train window and watched as a waving Mat receded until he fully disappeared. Oh Mat! What was she to do with him? Love clearly was a complicated business. So if she didn't feel so happy with him at the moment, was this just one of its many, necessary complications? Surely there was something superficial about couples who were always deeply in love or, at least, content?

Unconvinced, Rosalind looked around the almost empty carriage, taking in the blue seats, like rigidly lined-up bodies, facing her. A vending cart passed by and she bought a cup of black coffee and a cheese sandwich. Suddenly realising how hungry she felt, she bit into the sandwich with great appetite.

But it tasted bitter, like sadness squashed between two slices of bread. She dropped the remains into the metal bin by her side.

She had barely taken her first sip from the coffee, when she recalled Mat's objection that no-one could have murdered Drubenheimer without leaving a trace.

Rosalind shifted in her seat uncomfortably. It was a shame there weren't more passengers on the train. There would have been smells to list, faces to analyse. Instead, now it was difficult to avoid thinking about Mat's reservations. He might have a point. Really, how could anyone have simply tied a rope around Drubenheimer's neck and hurled him out of the window? Wouldn't he have resisted, fought back, and this would have left its marks on poor Mark?

Rosalind glanced out of the window. A number of farmhouses replete with cows and sheep sped past outside. What should she do? She didn't even have a theory as to how her beloved author's death had been brought about. And this wasn't even the worst of it yet! For, quite apart from possessing no more tangible proof than the poem that Drubenheimer had been murdered, she wasn't in the least qualified to look for a killer. Of course, she felt incompetent about many things—apart from literature—rather frequently; but wasn't her lack of knowledge and ability serious in this case?

She played around with the paper cup in her hand. The train's rattling struck her as menacing. She listened to its rhythm until she became used to her fear and, strangely, grew calmer. For, as childish as this may sound to her father or Mat, she had read a lot of Agatha Christie and PD James novels as a child and they had provided her with some of the basics of detective work. She would have to identify suspects. Then (and this, for a moment, sounded almost easy) she would have to question them, find out about their motives and—what were they called?—alibis. Finally, from all these talks, she would gather enough information to piece together the truth and present it to everyone, well to someone at least, and rectify the wrong done to Drubenheimer's memory!

Rosalind felt oddly detached from reality. Maybe she was in denial? Rather than face life itself, had grief generously pushed her into an Agatha Christie fantasy-land? Was she becoming a female Don Quixote about to interview windmills?

Reality was a messy pile of stories. She had only just embarked on her own. As the farmhouses outside turned into shiny office buildings, she started to smile.

The train pulled into Euston station. It impressed her how quickly the mere idea of going to London had turned into the reality of a noisy and crowded platform. She jumped off the train, walked into the main station hall replete with bakeries, fast food stores, travel agencies and people milling about like ants in a colony. Her body felt light; almost suspended. And she was a fish darting through a sea of colourful activity.

A few minutes later she arrived at Euston Square tube station and got onto the Circle Line. There, duly transformed into more of a canned fish stuffed among countless representatives of her own species, she couldn't help feeling excited. It was London, it was her hometown. Still, with her growing sense of purpose, she saw herself as a stranger. In a good way.

As the tube rattled through narrow corridors, likewise her mind rattled along. She glanced around. Within an hour, this train must transport people from every single nation on the planet, excluding North Korea, perhaps. This disconcerted her.

How, from among the city's vast multitude was she to find some suspects, let alone the killer?

Rosalind sighed, breathing out dusty air. Her doubts returned. Was she—as everyone had been trying to tell her—actually crazy for doing this? Should she simply spend a few days at her dad's to recover from her grief?

Luckily, at Great Portland Street station, a young man stepped onto the train distracting her from the rather gloomy direction her thoughts had been taking. She found him immediately attractive. Straight brown unevenly cut hair emerged from a black baseball cap that read "Fuerte Ventura—Surfing is my life", and made him look just a little bit wild. At the same time, he held himself very upright, emanating a cheerful and unshakeable confidence. This wasn't the only reason why Rosalind kept staring at him. Impossible as it seemed, the young man began to read nothing other than Drubenheimer's *Seabound*. On the sparkling, enticing cover was the mermaid with a smiling Frederic—the novel's protagonist.

Rosalind watched, intrigued, as his dark eyes wandered across the first page. Aware of her stares, he shifted his position.

The train pulled into Baker Street station and Rosalind felt nervous. What if she spoke to him? Yes, it was ridiculously daring. But wasn't this too important a coincidence to do nothing about? And, quite apart from that, hadn't she decided to ignore all hesitations from now on?

No, this was crazy. No, it wasn't. After all, she only wanted to exchange a few words about Drubenheimer, a passion they apparently shared.

Anxious, yet determined, Rosalind got up and almost lost her balance as the train departed again. She knew she had little time. She needed to act. In fact, she would make it clear that her interest had been directed at the book, not at him.

Telling herself to be brave, she took one step towards him. Her heart duly started racing. She feared she might start stuttering any moment.

Luckily, when she blurted: "Isn't the beginning beautiful?" her voice shook only a little.

The young man took his time to look up at her. Rosalind had once read that when a man is attracted to a woman, his pupils are supposed to widen in appreciation. She carefully scrutinised his eyes. Although they didn't notably dilate, they at least didn't shrink in horror at the sight of her.

"Maybe," he retorted and grinned. Then he turned towards the book again.

Heat rose into Rosalind's face. This hadn't gone all that well. She felt a little silly. Well, a little more than a little. She felt, she had to explain.

"It's just," she said, "that I'm writing a PhD about him. About Drubenheimer, the author. Who's now dead."

Mortified, Rosalind hoped that the mentioning of his death had saved her; that it had given weight to her words and could excuse her behaviour as symptoms of her grief.

He glanced at her again, his pupils widening, at last. With a half-smile that wasn't entirely derisive but almost proud of the author's achievements, the young man commented:

"So they're even writing PhDs about him."

Rosalind nodded. She smiled back, a little awkwardly. She thought of something else to say but decided she had done enough. If he wanted to add anything, it was his turn to speak now. But he didn't. He just read on, though the half-smile on his face had not yet entirely disappeared.

The train entered Edgware Road station.

"Goodbye," Rosalind mumbled and got off the train, dutifully minding the gap.

Rosalind arrived back on street level. What a useless coincidence! First the universe itself seemed to make an effort, perhaps to signal that she was on the right track. And then, she had only managed to squeeze the exchange of a few, insignificant words from this opportunity. This often made her sad about life: the walls between people. The meaningless things one had to say. Perhaps most of all, the fact that she often felt so very awkward, so very insignificant, saying them.

Trying to shrug off these thoughts, Rosalind walked fast towards her father's flat, passing shops and blocks of flats gradually disappearing into the twilight. She turned into Church Street, where rotting flowers and vegetables lay on the pavement, left-over from market day. She hurried past the street's familiar mixture of small cafés and antique shops. A doll, wearing a faded red dress, stared at her from one of the windows, blinking her enormous blue eyes. Rosalind nodded at her. They talked of ever-changing London. Yet she could swear the doll had been in the exact same place fifteen years ago.

When she came to Lisson Grove, she let out a sigh of relief. She recognised the same old elegant houses; the entrance to the canal; the church. At last, she arrived at the red-brick building that contained her father's—and her former—home.

She entered the flat and smiled a little wearily. The luxury still managed to surprise her, it was a kind of game her parents played to near perfection. It had always united them: the love of beauty, not of a wild and natural kind, but one that was expensive and seemingly deliberate.

Still, even though her mother had helped to create all this, over the years her presence had become less noticeable, her absence increasingly real.

Rosalind's body felt threatened by old pain. She hurried into the kitchen. The place where her father had kissed the beautiful wet-nurse. She had never seen her again; but there must have been many other kitchen-kissed women since. Now, it looked as if nobody had made more than coffee or tea there for days. Should she call Mat to tell him she had arrived? Somehow she couldn't face speaking to him again, so soon.

Instead, she stepped back onto the hallway and walked down into the flat's library. There, she finally felt calmer and more at home.

From the main wall filled with contemporary English literature, the shelves had been organised according to nationalities. To the left were the Russians, Germans, Italians, French; to the right they ventured to more far-away places; Latin-America, Japan and even the odd Chinese writers she had never dared to read.

Rosalind let her eyes glide over the bookshelves scanning them for new titles, especially any new acquisitions of the classics she so depended on for her peace of mind. Moving closer to the European section, she smiled at a type of glossy cover which had by now become familiar to her. It was the Subtlety Classics edition of Alessandro Manzoni's *The Betrothed*. She had gone through half of it during her undergraduate degree and should probably finish it sometimes. After all, her mum had always insisted that this slightly over-catholic tale of a pair of lovers separated by uncountable obstacles was Italy's first and one of its finest novels. But for the moment she would choose something more appealing that would help her relax.

Rosalind walked on towards the English section, where, almost instantly, her eyes were caught by another sparkling Subtlety cover. Did they haunt her? Were they little book-angels sent to entertain and comfort her? This time it was *Mrs. Dalloway*, a book she had also read only once a long time ago and fallen in love with straight away.

She stroked the cover more tenderly than she had recently stroked Mat. It showed a lady, standing inside a door frame, lit up by radiant sunshine that made her glow like a saint. Rosalind let herself sink onto her father's enormous brown armchair, opened the book and eagerly flicked through its pages. Soon, she came to a passage about the depressed Septimus—a character deeply traumatised by his war experience—listening to his wife and the doctor downstairs:

Then he heard a whisper. He was almost certain the hushed voice was hers. He strained his ears to hear, and the effort brought tears to his eyes. Was she, his wife, betraying him? His beautiful, beautiful wife?

Did she not like what he had written? Did she despise his revelations, the truth? Or was it her absence in his writing she hated? Had she wanted to be his muse—a real muse—and he had let her down?

This then was her revenge.

A pleasant, light warmth travelled through Rosalind's body. She liked the book's side plot—the story about Septimus and his Italian wife—almost better than the one about Mrs. Dalloway's party. Wasn't it tragic and at the same time so very beautiful the way he spent his last moments writing and writing, scribbling down revelations no-one wanted to hear? And now, the poor man would kill himself. She hadn't quite remembered that in his madness he blamed his wife for his suicide, or that she had wanted to be a muse. Funny how twice now, a classic had managed to surprise her; how they contained elements she, somehow, recalled differently.

Still, this time it didn't worry her too much. She breathed out, a little wistfully, and read on:

Holmes was coming upstairs. Holmes would burst open the door. Holmes would say, "In a funk, eh?" Holmes would get him. His wife would get him. But no; not Holmes, not his wife. He had failed her and he would pay. But no Holmes, no. Getting up rather unsteadily, hopping indeed from foot to foot, he considered Mrs. Filmer's nice clean bread-knife with "Bread" carved on the handle. Ah, but he mustn't spoil that. The gas fire? But it was too late now. Holmes was coming. Holmes was at the door. "I'll give it you!" he cried, and flung himself vigorously, violently down onto Mrs. Filmer's area railings.

Rosalind looked up, amazed and terrified. Where did this secret power of books come from? Why did she end up picking a novel—a passage—that spoke about what happened inside of her mind or in her life? As if books were a layer behind the world, its wisdom; and to access it, one only had to open their covers and read.

Weren't the similarities between Septimus and Drubenheimer striking? Two sensitive geniuses at odds with a cold, rigid world who fell to their deaths through a window. The only sad difference (apart from the rope tied around

Drubenheimer's neck), was that her beloved author had never chosen to die.

A sudden whirlwind of noise announced that her father and her little brother Othello had arrived. She heard rapid, tiny foot-steps racing along the corridor, followed by the sound of glass being smashed.

"What's it this time, Othello?" her father asked, jovially.

His comment was received with the same tinkling laughter that had accompanied her last conversation with her father, many hours ago. Rosalind strained her ears, to listen.

"Oh, isn't he just a small version of you!" the female voiced responsible for all that tinkling declared, apparently delighted.

"I'm not sure that's a compliment, my angel," he responded.

Angel? So she had been right. Her father had a new girlfriend.

"Of course it is. How can he not be a little destructive, with that name?" the female voice meanwhile went on. "Oh, I so love it! It's so original."

"My late wife chose it," Mr. Waterloo explained, flirtatiously. He must have told her at least a million times.

"In that case," the woman countered with sensual determination, "I don't love it quite so much."

Her mother had chosen her brother's name badly, considering she had died during his birth. Yet she wouldn't think about this now. There was to be Drubenheimer and Drubenheimer only on her mind.

The small group moved into the kitchen. The moment for her own noiseless appearance had come.

Standing timidly in the doorframe, she watched her father (as well as Othello clinging to one of his legs) beaming at the woman who leaned against a wall, handling a bottle of wine.

She was the first to feel Rosalind's gaze, look up and smile at her. Rosalind blushed and felt something close to awe at the sight of this imposing and beautiful creature.

Her bright red dress fascinated Rosalind. Tight at the top, its fabric reaching the floor, it looked like a costume from an Elizabethan play. Her long and curly blond hair reflected the kitchen light and flowed around a face no longer young but subtly and perfectly painted. Her large blue eyes glowed with a charm Rosalind found a little unsettling, yet impossible to resist. Beneath the dress, she could guess at the curves of a sensual and well-proportioned body, with ample breasts and a small, delicately shaped waist. She felt her own skinniness like a headache.

"Frank, there's a girl staring at us," the woman declared, flashing her eyes at Rosalind and tilting her head to one side.

Only now did her father, closely followed by Othello, look up at her.

"Rosy," Othello shouted, and run to hug her.

"What on earth!" her father cried out, getting up.

Rosalind gave Othello a kiss and picked him up from the floor. She wanted to hold him a little, but her brother immediately wiggled in her embrace and she put him down again. Rosalind observed, smiling, as he turned around and started playing with a small box of eyeshadow which he produced from his trouser pocket and presently used to create a tribal design on his cheeks and nose. She knew her father did not pay much attention to him. Othello spent most of the time with his nanny, across the road.

"I'm sorry," Rosalind said. "I should have called to let you know I was coming."

"That might have been a nice idea, you know," her father

replied. "Or are your thoughts caught up in such lofty PhD-student-heights they don't allow you to focus on such minor details?"

"Now, now, now-" the woman intervened.

Mr. Waterloo took the bottle from her hands, uncorked it and poured red wine into two crystal glasses, stopped for a second, then reached for another. He filled the third glass and offered it to Rosalind.

"Before I forget," he grumbled, turning towards the stunning woman. "I'm afraid this is Rosalind, my daughter."

"Your daughter!" she exclaimed, mock-scolding him with one hand and sending another one of her beaming smiles into Rosalind's direction. "I'm so happy to meet you at last. I'm Berlina. Berlina Marrowing."

"Very nice to meet you," Rosalind said and looked at the floor. Then, she forced herself to add something. "So you work with my dad?" was the only thing that came out.

"Work with your dad?" the woman asked, winking cheerfully at her. "Well, we do often work together. But I'm an editor at Flow Publishing."

Rosalind started. An editor at Flow? Was this possible? Well, yes, her father was an agent. It was his job to work with publishers of all kinds, even to bring them home. And yet, wasn't this another strange (almost spooky) coincidence, like the man reading Drubenheimer on the tube? If only this one would turn out to be more meaningful and of more consequence than the last!

"That's incredible," Rosalind cried out, unable to conceal her excitement. "That means you also know—knew—Mark Drubenheimer!"

"Of course," Berlina pronounced, dramatically. "He was one of my authors."

Rosalind looked at her father, as if asking for permission to speak on.

"Here we go again," he complained, shrugging with ostentatious boredom and rolling his eyes to the ceiling. Rosalind interpreted this as a good sign. "Can't we let the poor man be?"

"Not be!" Berlina corrected him.

A second later, the woman shook with sobs which sounded a little more like sexual excitement and a little less like pain.

"Oh Mark!" she said reproachfully, as though telling him off for dying. "It's terrible, Rosalind, isn't it? Shocking, exhausting and terrible!"

"Let's go to the living room, shall we?" Mr. Waterloo pleaded. "And leave Rosalind to unpack her things or analyse novels or whatever she wants to do, as long as she does it alone? She's doing her PhD on Mark, so don't get her started. Believe me, she just goes on and on and on. Her most recent madness is that, apparently, Mark didn't commit suicide, but that he was murdered."

"Murdered?" the editor asked, widening her eyes and mouth in utter surprise.

"I don't know, I just had an intuition," Rosalind murmured, looking at the ground.

Berlina stared thoughtfully at Rosalind, who became more embarrassed by the second. Then she smiled, apparently enchanted by the idea.

"This is fascinating! My God, Frank, what an interesting daughter you have." Berlina poked his belly as if to say and look at you. "Have you told the police about this?"

"Yes, she has," Mr. Waterloo muttered. "At least she threatened to when I last spoke to her."

"And?" Berlina's eyes were lit-up with admiration.

Rosalind glanced at her dad, a little sheepishly.

"They didn't believe me," she explained.

"Oh, what a shame!" Berlina absently answered, as she had just spotted Othello's face paint. She walked towards him and gave him an exuberant kiss on the cheek. The little boy instantly wiped it away.

"How wonderful!" she said. "Othello, you look stunning. You haven't stolen my make-up box for this?"

Othello didn't reply. He retreated again to his father's leg.

In the meantime, Rosalind's mind raced. Her doubts came once more; a sense of the ludicrousness of her actions. Still, what was it Gwen had told Anette in *Story*, quoting Newton, no: Einstein? The world will not be destroyed by those who do evil, but those who watch… without doing anything. Something along those lines. So, she might make a fool of herself; but what was new about that?

Rosalind would cope. She needed to act, and fast. Make use of this wonderful coincidence, now. For standing right in front of her—if she was at all serious about her mission—was the first person she would have to call a "suspect"; someone who might have murdered Mark Drubenheimer. Or, at the very least, provide her with vital information about the author's private life.

Rosalind stepped from one foot to another.

"If you were Drubenheimer's editor," she spoke quickly, telling herself to ignore all hesitations (as well as her father's deriding smile), "do you think I could maybe come and speak to you sometime? I'm actually looking for people who could help me find out more about him."

Berlina looked at Frank Waterloo, questioningly.

"But what about your dad?" she asked. "Can't he tell you more?"

"Well," Rosalind began, embarrassed.

"I won't," Frank Waterloo declared. He could hardly mention the wet-nurse to her. "I refuse to get involved with my authors' private lives. It's what makes me special as an agent. I believe it's why our dead friend chose me in the first place."

Berlina smiled and winked at Rosalind, a gesture of complicity, as if to say: "Aren't all men mad?"

"Well in that case," she then half-sang with joy. "I'd love to be of some help. I've always wanted to meet Frank's daughter. More so now that she turns out to have such interesting theories. Are you going to try to find the murderer? Or is this just for your PhD?"

Rosalind threw a worried glance at her father, who shook his head at her, entertained.

"My PhD," she mumbled, forcing herself to lie.

"You really don't have to do this," Mr. Waterloo told Berlina.

"But I want to, Frank. This fascinates me. Here's someone who's thinking against the Flow!" She giggled, enchanted by her word-game. "Seriously now, my darling. Just come to my office on Monday. Your father will give you the address."

"Thank you so, so much!" Rosalind said, effusively.

"You're ever so welcome," Berlina replied, winking at her flirtatiously, as to a lover. "I can already tell we'll get on brilliantly."

Chapter Four

Rosalind felt nervous. She had held the image of Berlina in her mind for the rest of the weekend, confident that their encounter had been a sign, an indication that she had chosen the right path. Now that she pushed her way through a feverish Monday morning crowd at London Bridge station, she was overwhelmed by a sudden, almost painful awkwardness. To make things worse, she instantly associated the shabbiness of her surroundings with the last minutes she had spent with Mat, waiting for her train.

She quickly took out her mobile and dialled his number. Then—before it had even started ringing—she hung up again. No, she just couldn't do it yet. It would connect her with his critical voice. She was about to have her very first interrogation and he would only discourage her and make her go to a bookshop instead.

Slightly shaking her head at herself, Rosalind left the station and entered the narrow and gloomy streets surrounding it. Eventually a bright-orange building emerged in front of her, a flower in a field of dust. It announced "Flow Publishing" on a silver plate.

Rosalind wanted to create an inventory of the smells around her, but her heart throbbed so insistently, she could no longer concentrate. She pressed a little button on the wall, at which the glass door sprang open and she stepped inside.

For several seconds, she just stood and stared—everything around her had such a soothing sparkle to it. The walls of the entrance hall were adorned with glamorous photographs of authors and books; there was a strong odour of perfume and flowers. This sanctuary of words had been Drubenheimer's literary home!

Right by the door, a girl about her age sat at a desk, reading. Instinctively, Rosalind checked the name on the attractive book cover and was surprised by what she saw: not, as she had expected, some new novel published by Flow, but a Subtlety Classics edition of *Don Quixote*. Was this destiny, teasing her? Hinting that she was about to interview her first windmill? Rosalind covered her face with her hands, squeezing her skin tightly. Then she revealed her slightly reddened features again. It only meant she wasn't the only one incapable of resisting the beauty and glow of these covers.

"Don't they mind if you read books from the competition?" Rosalind asked, when the girl at last managed to detach her glance from the book and gave her a friendly smile.

"I don't think so," the receptionist responded, shaking her short, braided hair. "Some editors at Flow used to work for Subtlety, so I don't think it bothers them, on the contrary. The editions are addictive, don't you think?"

"They're almost irresistible," Rosalind agreed.

"Well," said the girl, smiling some more and getting ready to outline a basic SCASA, anti-superficiality principle: "Of course, one shouldn't judge a book by its cover. But anyway, how can I help?"

"I've come to see Berlina," Rosalind announced quickly, then realised she had forgotten her surname. "She's one of the editors, but I'm afraid I-"

"You mean Berlina Marrowing," the girl told her, untroubled. "Let me just call her assistant for you. What's your name?"

"Rosalind Waterloo," she almost whispered, hoping the girl wouldn't recognise her surname, all too well known in literary circles.

But the girl didn't seem in the least startled by it. She simply picked up a pink receiver and said: "Hi, this is Lin! Rosalind Waterloo's here to see Berlina."

"Her assistant will be here in a moment," she declared after hanging up the phone, pointing towards a couch of brilliant gold, purple and blue in a corner, before she turned to her novel again.

"Thanks," Rosalind murmured and sat down on the couch. It was a dream of India, turned into furniture.

Trying to control her ever increasing nervousness, Rosalind picked up one of the magazines from the glass table in front of her. It was the company's most recent catalogue, announcing upcoming authors and novels. She started flicking through it, automatically searching for a new book by Drubenheimer. But when, an instant later, her consciousness caught up with her, she sadly shut the catalogue and let it sink back onto the table. There would be no more Drubenheimer novels. Never again.

The assistant arrived, a girl so plain, she seemed to have worked on her features to make them disappear into nothingness. She nodded timidly at Rosalind and indicated that she should follow her.

They passed through a glass door into a space flooded with light and books. Rosalind held her breath in amazement. Unfortunately, before she had time to look at any of them, the assistant led her into another, much smaller, room.

Berlina sat at the centre of it, a receiver in her hand, her long legs stretched out on a desk overloaded with manuscripts. The assistant muttered something towards Rosalind, a sudden flicker of intelligence in her eyes, then disappeared into the beautiful chaos of books outside.

"I don't think it's terrible. It's just incoherent," the editor sang into the receiver, while Rosalind stood there, waiting for her to finish, fidgeting around with her hands. "You have a book about madness, you need a mad cover. Remember, I'm brilliant with covers—as with most things, of course. And yours is sensual, I agree, but the girl's crazy, so sensuality isn't what we need!"

Trying not to listen, Rosalind let her eyes wander around the room; yet they were soon drawn back towards Berlina, her legs and down—the length of them—to her feet. She wore dark-blue and turquoise shoes with an entire underwater world painted onto them. Rosalind could even make out a tadpole's face.

Berlina chanted on until the person on the other end seemed to agree.

"OK. Whatever you do, make it beautiful, do you understand? Extraordinary. Sparkling," she merrily winked at Rosalind, "just like me. Alright then, my darling. Byeeee!"

With the grace of a flamenco dancer, the editor waved about the receiver before slamming it down. She lowered her legs and made two full turns on her white leather chair. When she stopped, she looked straight into Rosalind's eyes.

"Frank Waterloo's daughter!" she cried out, festively. "My dearest of all Rosalinds. Please take a seat!"

"Thank you very much," Rosalind stuttered, awkwardly. She caught sight of a wooden chair in a corner, shifted it towards her and sat down.

"So you're writing a PhD about Mark! In English Literature, your father tells me. What a beautiful subject, indeed! But I'll confess I've always had some reservations about literature PhDs. Books are such lively things. Don't you kill them by studying them in such detail? I mean, don't you end up analysing the symbolic meaning of someone's shoes?"

Rosalind felt all the heat of a blush, inside. She looked at Berlina's underwater footwear.

"Sometimes," she confessed, wondering whether this woman had ever heard of or applied any anti-superficiality principles to her own, undoubtedly charismatic, self.

Berlina followed her glance and laughed.

"Oh these!" she giggled. "They're incredible, aren't they? I so love shoes! And, to be honest, I have such a way with them! I bought these when *Seabound* was launched. So inspiring, don't you think? In any case, has my assistant offered you tea?"

Rosalind shook her head.

"And would you like some?" Berlina fluttered her eyelids at her.

"Yes, please," Rosalind replied, a little overwhelmed.

"Milk and sugar?"

"Just milk."

"Oh," Berlina exclaimed, enthusiastically. "You're just like me!"

She called out for her assistant. The girl appeared almost instantly, her eyes fixed onto the ground.

"My lovely," Berlina said, reproachfully. "Did you not offer my guest tea?"

"I'm sorry, I didn't want to-"

"We'll have two, with just milk!" Berlina cut her short.

The girl nodded, frightened. She walked out of the door and a satisfied Berlina threw back her abundant blond hair and smiled.

"So," the editor continued, "you think Mark was murdered. How very extraordinary! How did this even occur to you?"

Was it wise to share the cause for her intuition so openly with this woman? Then again, her father wouldn't have any qualms about telling her anyway; and being honest might help break the ice. Indeed—after she had briefly explained about the phrasing of the poem and what it made her realise—Berlina stared at her, more evidently impressed than ever.

"So it was the poem, was it? Oh, I would have never noticed myself. Like most people, I was just too preoccupied wondering about the intertextuality, the homage. But you really are an extremely intelligent young lady! I just thought it was a wonderful poem which spoke right to my heart. *When I have fears that I may cease to be...* You see, I'm so terrified of dying myself. Aren't you?"

Thankfully, before Rosalind had any time to even think about an answer to this question and why everyone mentioned the word intertextuality in connection with Drubenheimer's wonderful poem, the assistant returned, placing two cups of tea on opposite sides of the desk. The editor pronounced a dramatic "thank you", dismissing her with no more than a slight movement of the head. Then—clearly not remembering that she had asked a question—she just smiled at Rosalind and, as though in some half-ecstasy, went on:

"So what was I saying? I'm terrified of death! I even had a cross, a statue of Buddha and of some Hindu goddess in my office until a few weeks ago just to make sure that one of them will take me on when my time has come—until my boss hinted it might scare some of my authors away. Oh, death is just shocking, disgusting and terrible. Poor, poor Mark! Now, you know, I try to seize the day, live every day as though it were my last and—well, in any case, I thought it was incredible to hear Mark express all of this so well in the poem he chose. And to now hear you say that it was the poem that made you think he was murdered... But anyway, enough about that! Do you have any idea who might have done such a horrible thing? I mean, murder him?"

"Not yet," Rosalind admitted, grateful to finally have a chance to steer the conversation into the direction she desired. "Actually, this was one of the things I wanted to ask you about."

"Oh?" Berlina uttered, not very meaningfully, perhaps just in order to encourage her to speak on.

"Well," Rosalind said, taking a sip from her tea and gathering courage from its warmth. "I'm sure you know a lot about his personal life, who his friends and enemies were."

Rosalind stopped. She felt so very silly saying all this. And the worst part was still to come. She took a deep breath, then burst out, quickly and shyly: "Do you know if there's anyone who might have had an interest in murdering Drubenheimer?"

Rosalind could barely believe she had actually said this out loud. To her relief, Berlina's eyes widened, gently and charmingly.

"Your dad really has been useless, has he? He hasn't told you anything about Drubenheimer's life?"

Rosalind shook her head, nervously.

"Well, I'll tell him off for you. And before I answer your other questions, tell me one thing. This isn't just for your PhD, is it? Are you trying to conduct a proper search? Like a detective? Create a, let's say, plotline about this whole incident?"

Rosalind nodded, proudly.

"Well, that's absolutely wonderful, my darling. How utterly thrilling! You're like a protagonist of some sort of post-modern detective novel. You're fascinating. Life is fascinating! So full of surprises to enhance the paths of those who choose to create!"

"Yes," Rosalind stammered, unsure what Berlina was talking about. Still, she liked the reference to a post-modern detective novel. She recalled her thoughts on the train; that she tried to act out stories. In her own mind, it had been a source of embarrassment; a worldly sin. But Berlina made it sound glamorous. Like Anette, she would move out of predetermined narratives and create a more exciting life-story for herself.

Now, how could she get this woman to actually speak about what she needed to hear?

"Like the path of Drubenheimer," Rosalind went on, blushing. "Deeply fascinating, until he was murdered. So about the people in his life..."

"Oh, yes," Berlina remembered. "Of course, my darling, of course! There weren't that many, you know? There was his wife, Alicia Drubenheimer. You must have heard about her! She's such a beautiful woman. She had dreams of becoming a pianist, I think. And there was his best friend, Lisa Croydon-Bay. According to Mark, they were extremely close. So close that Mark's wife was chronically jealous of her. But I doubt this would have led the poor woman to murder him. They loved each other so much! And if this Lisa had any reason or desire to kill Mark, I have no idea. But you'll probably meet them all at the funeral tomorrow, and then you can judge for yourself. You are coming, aren't you?"

"The funeral?"

"Your father hasn't mentioned this either?"

Rosalind shook her head. She felt ashamed to admit this. Couldn't she just have a normal relationship with her father?

One where they actually spoke and told each other things? But their distance was her fault, too.

"Oh, I really will have to tell him off for you," Berlina assured her. "But to return to our poor Mark, I believe he had some other friends, too, although I don't think he was particularly close to any of them. You know what writers are like. Not as glamorous as one might think. Not as interesting to the crowds. They tend to be a bit antisocial. But probably I should say shy. Mark was such a sensitive man."

A malicious sparkle lit up in Berlina's eyes, but Rosalind felt too saddened by Berlina's words to pay much attention to it.

Yes, Drubenheimer must have been very sensitive to perceive and be able to communicate the kind of things he had written about! Rosalind tried to pull herself together, for the worst of this conversation was yet to come. She would now have to ask Berlina about her own possible motive and "alibi". Alibi! The word itself sounded like an invasion from a different world. Like a blinking UFO in Rosalind's reality.

"Were you close to him?" she asked, avoiding Berlina's eyes: "And, by the way, what were you doing the night Drubenheimer died?"

"Oh my god! You want to know my alibi?" Berlina cried out, immediately discovering Rosalind's motives and turning her bright red with shame. "Am I one of the suspects? Of course, I must be! How very exciting! Do you want me to answer your questions in order of their importance or appearance? In fact, they might coincide. Let's see. Were Mark and I close? We loved each other, with the deep—how should I put it?— platonic bond of a writer and an enabler. Of course we were close. Mark was my best writer!"

Berlina looked down at her eccentric shoes, her lips forming the tiniest smile. Then, suddenly, the editor became tearful again and made some fluttering movements with her hands as if trying to chase her emotions away.

"About the question of what I did the night Mark died," the editor stated, "I'm afraid I spent it with your father. Although, of course, not in the way you might think."

Rosalind had inadvertently wrapped her hands around her cup of tea and struggled against a pressure in her throat, when all of a sudden the editor leaned towards her and announced, with an air of complicity:

"To be honest, my darling, I wanted you to come to my office, because there's something I really need to tell you. I know what happened the night Mark died."

"What?"

Rosalind's heart started beating so fast, she felt its rhythmic pulse in her neck. Was this the end of her search, already?

Berlina's face took on a serious expression.

"Are you ready?" she asked, licking her lips.

Rosalind nodded, expectantly.

"Well, then," Berlina continued. "Mark said: 'Rosebud' and then he expired."

The editor laughed out loud at her own joke.

"You're too young to understand," she added, merrily. "But do tell your father. He'll find it very funny."

Chapter Five

Sitting next to her father in a cab heading to the funeral, Rosalind's mind replayed—for the fifth time at least—yesterday's scene, when Berlina had proclaimed there was something special she wanted to tell her. How she had felt all excited at first, thinking that her search had already been resolved; and how—a moment later—the editor had made her joke and burst into delighted laughter. Her dad (when she had stupidly told him afterwards) claimed that this was very funny, indeed. That Berlina had turned their bizarre encounter into something like a scene from a novel. That it served Rosalind right to be made fun of like this, if she was ridiculous enough to go and question people about Drubenheimer's death.

Rosalind was almost too used to her father's dismissive attitude towards her to take notice of it. Now his girlfriend had joined in the game of putting her down. Well, at least her talk with the editor had made her find out about Drubenheimer's wife and his friend. Really, her search wasn't going so badly. She just needed to push on and things would happen; especially today, when she would probably get to know more people from her beloved author's life and be able to arrange meetings with them.

Unfortunately, the first thing she would have to do was to check on Berlina's alibi.

Rosalind looked at her father. Dressed in an elegant suit, his legs stretched out, he had closed his eyes, enjoying his time off work and Othello who had been left with the nanny, again. Would she really have to ask him if he spent the night with Berlina? Confront him about being with another woman, again? Well, maybe it would be her chance to prove how very respectful she was of his life, of his moving on. But not now, not yet. She needed at least a few minutes to gather her strength.

A series of similar colourless houses sped past outside, half-disappearing in the morning drizzle and rising fog. The polyrhythm of the taxi's restless roaring, people shouting, cars honking outside, lulled her into a kind of half-sleep. Memories started to well-up inside of her; as dense and grey as the weather outside.

After her mother had died, Rosalind really had gone to a very dark place. There was the inevitable pain of losing her. The fact she would never see her again, that she had simply been sliced from the unfolding of their everyday lives, cut her from all photographs of the future. Apart from their bookshop visits together, they had never been truly close. It had been hard to be close to her mother. With the exception of her love for classics and her enthusiasm for India, there had always been something cold and distant about her. She had been kind, never cruel, always "proper". Yet Rosalind had missed motherly hugs and smiles. To know that she would never have these now, that nothing would ever melt the ice inside of her mother, that instead she had melted away as a whole, was terrible. But it wasn't even the worst for Rosalind.

The worst wasn't the direct grief—difficult but somehow logical, understandable. The worst were the phantoms it had unlocked. The sleepless nights not only crying about her loss but also suffering from shortness of breath and a heartbeat, frenetic and wild, at seeing the world turned irremediably dark. She had seen human hell wherever she went, physically or in her mind. People starving. People diseased. As if some incurable cancer had spread across the insides of the globe.

The human condition.

After a while this got better. She found things she liked again. The classics, connecting her to her mum. Drubenheimer. And the idea, especially in *Seabound*, that somehow, perhaps idiotically, everything was actually good. Life was light. Death was light. And we were just too absorbed in our struggles to see.

Rosalind stretched out her arms suddenly, as if craving for help and shook her head. Why had she allowed herself to think about all this? It was time to question her father about Berlina.

Trying to run away from her mind made running towards her search—even this deeply uncomfortable part—easier.

"Dad," she began, very quietly. "Can I ask you a question?"

Her father opened his eyes.

"Thanks for waking me up," he complained. "But do what you must, oh daughter!"

He smiled, which puzzled her. He performed for the taxi-driver who observed them through the rear-view window.

"You know, Dad, I was just wondering, generally, what you were doing the night Drubenheimer died?"

Rosalind feared he might make one of his snide remarks. Instead, her father just waved his arms theatrically, his palms turned towards the car ceiling as if imploring it for help: "Oh, dear me! How old are you, five? Playing detective? Rosy, I know you're prone to attacks of full-blown loony madness, but I thought that was over by now?"

To her unpleasant surprise, Rosalind's eyes filled with tears. It must be because of Drubenheimer's funeral and the memories of her mother's death it had evoked. That much for her display of maturity!

She made an enormous effort to swallow them down again.

"Oh dear," her father added, almost tenderly. "I'm afraid Mark really must have been quite a star in Rosy-world. But then I think you already know what I did the night he died. She has told you, hasn't she? Well, we couldn't have known, could we? That Mark would choose that night to end his days? And by now, Rosy, it really has been a long time since your mother died, so I hope I don't deserve to rot in hell, yet again."

He laughed.

"Thanks, Dad, thanks," Rosalind mumbled, quickly, before she had a chance to become tearful again. "That was all I needed to know."

By the time they arrived at the cemetery Rosalind felt a little more composed. A crowd of no more than twenty people had gathered outside the cemetery's iron gates. She looked at their variations of black designer dresses and suits. Did any of them seem like the kind of person who could have hauled Drubenheimer out of the window, on a rope?

She shivered a little, inwardly. Though this assumption was, in some way, the basis of her search, the thought was almost too scary to even be a thought, direct and conscious. Fortunately, most of the people looked rather innocent, their faces—emerging from so much black fabric—all softened and blurred by the morning drizzle and their uniform expression of grief.

The only person she recognised was Berlina, her head gravely lowered to the ground. She wore a short and simple dress, her curls tied back in a ponytail. On feeling Rosalind's glance, she lifted her eyes and—for about a second—smiled at her. Rosalind automatically smiled back, then felt a twinge at remembering their conversation and the editor's Rosebud joke for the sixth time (at least) since its occurrence.

A sudden heaviness took hold of her, again. She had never attended her mother's funeral. Caught by a sense of uncontrollable panic and desperation, she hadn't been able to face saying goodbye to her mother's body and stayed at home.

And now? Would she actually be able to bear becoming a witness to Drubenheimer's body being offered to the unforgiving earth? And what about his soul? Was there such a thing? Had it gone to some sort of heaven, or was it still able to travel from country to country, observing those who stayed behind?

This reminded her of Berlina's claim, during yesterday's conversation (if one could call it that) that she was utterly terrified of death. Rosalind shook her head at herself, feeling slightly dizzy. She could understand the editor a little bit better, now. Maybe she too should invest in a cross, a statue of Buddha and a Hindu goddess; just to make sure someone would take her on, when her own time was up. Maybe she too should try to live—whatever that meant, precisely—as though every day were her last.

The appearance of six men dressed in dark suits carrying Mark Drubenheimer's coffin interrupted Rosalind's thoughts. Something about their behaviour—their stately walk, their faces so well-composed in their seriousness—almost made them seem like actors in a play. This comforted her, a little. Perhaps she just had to pretend she was watching an innovative performance of, say, *Romeo and Juliet* and she would be alright.

A procession formed behind the men and together they passed through the gate which separated the realm of the living from that of the dead. Rosalind started walking very slowly, at a slight distance from the others.

Continuing to calm herself with the thought that "never was a story of more woe, than this of Juliet and her Romeo", she finally dared to look around. The cemetery had a chilling atmosphere. It was made up of about a hundred rows of graves that wound their way through bushes and weeds like sculptured snakes. Indistinct words of hushed voices reached her; somebody sang sadly, and out of tune; a few pigeons shared their ominous, warning sounds. It smelled of moss, smoke and rain.

Two small hills marked the end of the space. On top of one of them stood a single tree, half-dead and without leaves. Though it was May, it seemed locked in eternal winter. Rosalind could make out a figure standing next to it; but distance, and the thickening fog, wouldn't allow her to see properly.

Rosalind slowed down even further and let her eyes wander to the gravestones surrounding her. They were all so similar and simple they looked like rows of semi-detached houses for the dead. Only eventually did she come to a grave that attracted her attention, adorned as it was with the statue of a muse: a tall, gold-plated woman, holding a harp in one hand and smiling at the corpse beneath.

How beautiful! Rosalind had always liked muses, these wonderful creatures who inspired great artists and who—effortlessly, by their sheer beauty, wit or charm—flowed into immortal works, glowing there for all eternity. Although her chance of becoming Drubenheimer's muse had now turned from slight to non-existent, she would enjoy playing that role one day. Acting as the inspiration of a wildly creative mind.

She sighed, dreamily. If only someone would genuinely celebrate the fact that she was alive. It would make her feel so very special! And, somehow, this would allow her to cross an invisible threshold to a place inside, where she could celebrate herself.

So was an artist buried here? Some great and well-known writer who had recently died of old age? Rosalind glanced at the inscription:

Mathew Melloby 1980—2004

On impulse, Rosalind hugged her body. Poor Mathew Melloby! She felt almost guilty she had never heard of him. What was even worse, he not only had the same name as her boyfriend, but had also been about her age!

This was so terrible it almost made her cry. No-one ought to die so young. There ought to be some sort of divine prohibition against it. One should rest assured, when tiring oneself out to feel the "electric joy" of youth that one could never die halfway through it. Rosalind hoped it had been suicide; that this young person had at least decided to die. Was this perhaps, why everyone tried to believe that Drubenheimer had killed himself? To restore an element of choice to his tragedy and pretend that the same couldn't happen to them? Maybe, in someone's death there really was always a double pain. That of the person lost and, as if a corpse were a mirror, the confrontation with one's own mortality.

The procession turned on a corner and the back of her father's head changed into his demonstratively grieving profile.

Rosalind started to walk faster. The group had already come to a halt and gathered around a hole in the ground. Immediately, the sensation that she was in some sort of play returned. Most members of the crowd took out their handkerchiefs and started sobbing or crying with such intensity yet composure, they had probably practiced for years. "O brother Montague," Rosalind thought, in an effort to lighten her own mood. What if Drubenheimer watched them from above? How well she could picture him (looking more charismatic, of course, than on the not very flattering picture she had seen) with paper and pen in his hands, observing the crowd and taking notes. Did he look at her too? What would he write down?

If he simply saw her, perhaps very little. A creative comment about her skinniness, perhaps? But what if he could glimpse right into her mind? Wouldn't he discover the intention of her search and be delighted, or at the very least relieved that someone tried to find out the truth about his death?

Rosalind just began to warm towards this idea when she noticed a frail woman with an elegant black hat who dramatically clasped her hands together in prayer, before raising them towards the sky. Then, as though she wanted to make sure she had been watched by her intended audience, she turned towards another woman and shot a fiery glance at her. Desperately trying to ignore this, the other woman lowered her eyes to the ground. Only once did they desert the cemetery floor, to look up at Rosalind's father. There they remained for a moment until, saddened, they wandered down again, avoiding another aggressive assault of stares.

This wordless eye-battle intrigued Rosalind. What passion and rage! And what a powerful contrast between the two women! Whereas the lady with the black hat oozed a compelling beauty, the other looked worn out and almost deliberately plain. Really, one was like dimmed stage light during Romeo and Juliet's love scene, while the other reminded her of the wiry sponges used to scrub the dirt off sticky frying pans. Could they possibly be the two women Berlina had mentioned? Mark Drubenheimer's wife and his friend, Lisa Croydon-Bay?

Eager to find out more, Rosalind scanned the crowd for Berlina and discovered her standing next to her father, emphatically staring at the gravestone behind the hole. Maybe this wouldn't be the right moment to ask her about this.

Although it frightened her a little, Rosalind made herself look at the white stone that would be Drubenheimer's new home. She had expected instant misery to overcome her, but— to her surprise—she felt almost calm. Had she gone through so much pain and confusion by now, there simply wasn't any left? At least, this momentary absence of grief encouraged her to go one step further and scan the grave's inscription. It read:

Fritz Drubenheimer
Aurelia Drubenheimer

Fritz and Aurelia! They must have been Drubenheimer's heroic, anti-Nazi parents! Yet why were their bodies here? Had Drubenheimer asked for them to be shipped from Southern Germany to England? And why were there no birth or death dates next to their names?

Almost comforted by the return of her confusion, Rosalind let her eyes wander towards the hill with its tree. She instantly lost interest in the ultimate fate of Drubenheimer's progenitors. She had been right, someone really stood next to the tree on the hill! What was more, the figure looked strangely familiar. It was no-one other than the young man who had been reading *Seabound* on the tube.

Was this even conceivable? Why was he at—or rather, near—the funeral? Had he come hoping that he might find her, here? This wasn't all that likely. But then, what? Had he finished reading *Seabound* and loved it so much he wanted to pay his last respects to its author? Or was he Drubenheimer's secret enemy in which case he was a suspect and needed to be interviewed?

The solution was clear: Rosalind needed to go and speak to him straight away.

Her body (and mind) had already turned almost entirely hill-wards, when a man in a cloak stepped out of the crowd and ceremoniously cleared his throat. It was a priest—Drubenheimer had been a non-practising catholic—with an eternal grin of surprise on his face.

"Dear friends," he began. "We have gathered here today..."

Rosalind shot nervous glances at the man next to the tree. What if he would hurry away before the end of the ceremony? Would she ever find him again?

"We all know that in the case of Mark Drubenheimer's decision to leave this world, he should not be granted a place on this cemetery," the surprised priest merrily declared, "nor, for that matter, a place with God. However, recent developments within the Church have made some of us more tolerant, and an exception has been made. Now we can only hope," his grin grew larger, "that God, too, has been modernised in this way."

Rosalind's eyes jumped restlessly from the grave to the hill and back again. What a strange speech! She felt no resonance within her. No fresh onset of tears. Perhaps Mat had been right and she was in denial. Instead of greedily soaking in the priest's words, she simply craved for him to finish so she could run towards that young man she had met on the tube. Regrettably, the priest continued without the slightest hurry, as though he had been begged by the people attending to recite the whole of *Anna Karenina*, at a speed that would allow them to indulge in every word.

Although Rosalind was ashamed to admit this, she felt more than a little pleased when the man of God finally announced some words of goodbye and the crowd began to disperse.

Rosalind felt all the muscles of her body tighten and her emotions come to life again. She was, at once, terrified and excited. Her moment to act had come!

She hadn't taken a single step towards the hill, when she was again interrupted, this time by her father approaching her.

"Let us go then, you and I," he said.

Rosalind looked at him, alarmed. Surely chance wouldn't be that patient with her? Surely, within seconds, the young man would disappear?

"Let's go where?" she asked, quickly. "Not home, already?"

"Are you deaf as well as mad?" her father countered. "Mark's wife—Mrs. Drubenheimer—invited everyone to her flat."

"Oh," Rosalind voiced, nervously observing the hill. Since she hadn't yet managed to arrange a meeting with the people Berlina had mentioned, this was good news. Also, it was surprisingly nice of her father to invite her along. Still, she couldn't possibly leave now!

"Dad, I'm sorry, but please wait for me for a few minutes. I just noticed a friend from school and, anyway, bye."

Rather proud of this short but effective speech, she hurried off through the lawn muddied by the rain. Her father looked after her, startled rather than annoyed.

The young man was dressed in a black jacket, his arms crossed on his chest, looking so sexy he was clearly suspicious.

"Are you following me?" he asked as soon as Rosalind reached him, a little out of breath.

"Following you?" she repeated, timidly. Maybe this coincidence wasn't as wonderful as it had at first seemed. "No, not at all."

"Not following me, then. So," he pointed—somewhat dismissively—towards the thinning crowd beneath. "You're one of them?"

Rosalind looked at him, with an expression probably akin to that of the astonished man of God.

"I mean are you one of those," he clarified, "snobs who sobbed over Drubenheimer's grave?"

"Snobs?" Rosalind asked, bewildered. Were they snobs? Was she a snob? Of course not! She shook her head vigorously.

This seemed to appease him. He instantly relaxed. Rosalind thought—but wasn't quite sure—that he eyed her up and down; in a very manly way.

"Oh, good," he replied and even smiled. It was a nice smile. "Not a snob, then. You're a student, aren't you?"

"Yes, I'm doing a PhD on Mark Drubenheimer," Rosalind replied, flattered and relieved. "You remember that?"

"Obviously," he said, his eyes now sparkling with a malicious charm he appeared to be able to switch on and off at will. "I don't get chatted up on the tube every day."

Rosalind blushed. She felt the urge to explain that she hadn't tried to chat him up at all. That she had been trying to do her duty, and had been assisted by a strange and possibly wonderful coincidence. But she found no way of saying all of this without, potentially, increasing her embarrassment.

"So, did you know him personally?" she made herself ask, instead.

"Who? Drubenheimer?"

Rosalind nodded.

His face darkened a little, which made him look even more alluring.

"Not really. Did you?"

"No," Rosalind admitted, wistfully. "I always wanted my father to introduce us. You see, my father was his agent. I always dreamed of having this meeting with him, but somehow—well, it's a rather long story—it never worked out." The sadness which had been so strangely absent during the whole ceremony suddenly returned and Rosalind found herself adding, almost in tears: "And now it's too late."

The young man—he seemed barely older than 27 or 28—smiled at her with a strange complicity and intensified interest.

"Yes, I know. Now it's too late to get to know him. This annoyed me too, believe me. But maybe it's a good thing. Anyway, your father was his agent? The one who controlled his finances, I mean contracts and everything?"

"Yes," Rosalind retorted, not sure what this had to do with anything. But she definitely liked this young man's smile.

He turned away from her to look at the cemetery beneath them. Meanwhile Rosalind—a tingling lightness in her face and chest—frantically thought of a way to arrange a meeting with him. She really didn't want him to disappear into London's anonymous crowds yet again. He was another suspect to interview.

Yet how could she possibly go about this? She had never—ever—asked a man to meet up with her. She was only with Mat because he had been very drunk and proactive one night. How should she do this? How could she do this? There was only one way. She would have to ignore her body's tingling; and her hesitations, of course.

"This may sound a bit forward," she began, almost whispering, her heart jumping wildly inside of her. "And please, don't get me wrong. I have a boyfriend and all that. But do you think we could, maybe, meet up sometime? To talk about Mark Drubenheimer?"

The young man laughed. It was a nice laugh.

"It is a bit forward," he said, revelling in his own attractiveness. "But if that's what you want, that's fine with me."

A sudden wave of happiness—unexpected on such a dismal day and occasion—washed over her.

She quickly tried to hide this by the very "professional" manner in which she reached into her bag for her notebook, opened it and ripped out a page. She produced a pen and wrote down her mobile phone number.

"I'm Rosalind," she introduced herself, exhilarated she had been able to pull this off, even with something that resembled grace. She handed him the pen and notebook. Accidently, she beamed at him.

He responded with a cheerful twinkle in his eyes. Then he bent his head sideways and scribbled onto an empty page.

"Well, nice to meet you, Rosalind," he declared. "You're definitely a sweet stalker! My name's Gabriel."

Chapter Six

Frank Waterloo relaxed into the taxi seat. They had just left the funeral and he now gratefully listened to Schumann's violin sonata in D-minor, indulging in the work's misleadingly gentle beginning, soon overshadowed by what he felt was the melody's dark power. Once, he had heard that the piece had been hidden away and recovered thanks to no less than the appearance of Schumann's ghost during a séance and that of the violinist it had been dedicated to. Berlina would love this! Also, he should get one of his authors to write a novel about that, one day. The participation of ghosts in the creative process!

Frank Waterloo glanced over at Rosalind, who leaned against the cab window and appeared to be lost in her own world. He had watched her talking to a young, handsome man on the hill. Who was he? Rosalind had seemed very excited to see him. A friend? A new boyfriend? Frank Waterloo wasn't a jealous father; on the contrary. Always a little doubtful of Rosalind's powers, he felt almost glad when someone showed an interest in her. He could perhaps ask who he was. But he couldn't be bothered, really. The funeral had exhausted him.

Death had exhausted him. It had brought back memories, as if one funeral secretly contained many others. His mother's (they had returned her body to England, against her original will); his boarding school friend Walter's, who had died of cancer at the age of 27; his wife's.

He had been so very much in love with her once. When he had met her—a woman much younger than him—ironically at a party of Walter's who died three years later, as if early death had been their secret companion, from the start—she had seemed so beautiful and ethereal to him, half woman, half sea-creature. So tall, so slender, so elegant. He had been a womaniser until he had met his Eleonore; but very soon into their relationship, he had become willing to give all of this up for her. It wasn't just passion he had felt for her—although that, too, had been part of it—she had also perfectly fitted his image of the life he had always wanted. She had the lightness and beauty of luxury. Decades of marriage had eroded much of the original intensity of his feelings for her; but she had still been the person he had felt closest to, so close he did not constantly have to think about her. She had become a subconscious necessity, like breathing, perhaps. Then, suddenly, she was gone. It had been his life's biggest shock. One day he had a quietly fed-up pregnant wife; the next a corpse and a new-born son.

If only he had—what was the right word—honoured her more when she was alive. Knowing how fleeting her presence was to be, he should not have become so annoyed with her for small things; he would not have pitied himself, as he occasionally had done over the past few years, over the imprisoning side-effects of marriage. He might have worked on a way for them to be free together.

Frank Waterloo fidgeted around in his seat. How uncomfortable cab seats—and life—could be. He would not think about all the "could haves" now—or ever. It was as if the soul of a third-rate self-help writer had momentarily possessed his well-shaped, though aging agent body. He made himself grin.

He glanced at Rosalind. She had closed her eyes now, perhaps even drifted off to sleep. A look out of the window revealed nothing interesting. Just endless London roads, noisy, dark, elegant or appealingly wild. He switched off his music. Schumann depressed him now.

He stared at his iPhone for a few moments, then opened his email account. His assistant had already forwarded about ten new submissions to him. Frank Waterloo looked through them with renewed eagerness. It wasn't just a financially promising writer he wanted to find. He would have also been grateful for the embryo of a beautiful story, something uplifting, that would improve his post-funeral pondering, his edgy mood.

But there was nothing. He quickly went through the covering letters. As usual, he was hit by waves of stories where too many things happened (aliens made love with stray elephants and their off-spring tried to save the world) or bored by the low-tide of slow stories about being an inspiring teacher, rejected writer or lover. How tiring his job could be!

Frank Waterloo felt rejuvenated, but not in a nice way. He re-experienced a long-forgotten sense of neediness, this wish to control other people's minds and make them produce mind-blowing pieces. How smug Drubenheimer had made him!

If only he had noticed earlier how depressed the man must have been. He could have perhaps convinced him to go on anti-depressants, or to therapy. Or, instead of being kinder to his author, perhaps he should have been harsher, more focused on him getting his act together and writing a decent new novel.

What was wrong with him today? Life was a short path into the future; walking into the past promised nothing, at all.

The cab dropped Rosalind and her father off outside the enormous block of flats that made up Campden Hill Court. Throughout the trip, Rosalind had been wondering whether to be upset that the mysterious man—Gabriel—had called her a stalker, or elated because she was "sweet". Sweet, indeed! She would be just a little happier than upset as she needed the energy happiness provided for what was to come. In fact, she already needed it right now to cope with her father. She had pretended to be asleep in the cab, because he seemed to get increasingly restless about their somewhat delayed arrival.

As soon as they got off the taxi—and to the discordantly cheerful sound of birds performing their overlapping solos— Frank Waterloo urged her on with an impatient gesture of his head. Rosalind tried to steal a few glances at the building with its magnificent white walls, glaring in sudden sunlight.

Balconies and windows sprinkled the walls, adorned with flowerpots and voluptuous statues. Rosalind felt almost faint at the thought that Drubenheimer had disappeared from the world through one of them. She tried to identify which one might have been the one he had been hanging from. But the windows all struck her as alike in their pristine cleanliness. All smudges of death had already been wiped away.

Rosalind finally realised that she had come to a complete halt, staring at the building, while her father waited again, at the entrance, cursing her. She quickly joined him, at which he cried out "Thank heaven" with exaggerated relief and demonstratively pressed a small gold button.

"It's open!" a voice declared.

They entered and found a porter sitting behind a white desk, welcoming them with an expressionless smile.

Rosalind's father had just announced where they were heading, when his impatience was increased by the gold-framed door leading to the corridor opening and three men who had attended Drubenheimer's funeral coming out. So people were already leaving! Frank Waterloo put his hand inside the door before it shut and shook his head at Rosalind. Then, indicating that she should follow him, he pushed it open again and walked quickly inside.

The corridor's display of glorious wealth amazed Rosalind. Her parents had been quite rich for as long as she could remember and she had grown up in elegant, even glamorous, environments. Yet here, the decoration appeared more subtle and at the same time more dramatic than any she had previously come across. It was more like striding through a carefully arranged film setting, specifically designed to evoke a mood of inner grandeur. As if it weren't the room which (with its red carpets, countless gold-framed mirrors and gentle light) was special, but the person passing through it. Luckily, today herself.

So although she tended to avoid mirrors, this clever interior design now encouraged her to benevolently greet—almost salute—her own reflection: her dark hair (which she normally found so dreary and boring) today lent her a particular chic and grace; her skinniness assumed something which almost deserved to be called ethereal. Finally, she discovered in her dark eyes a new, vivid glow which might be due to her conversation with Gabriel and having been called "sweet", rather than her present surroundings.

Rosalind walked behind her father, so slowly that he wanted to disinherit her—as he kept on mumbling to himself. At last, they entered a sparkling, lavender-scented lift. She carried the memory of handsome Gabriel along with her. Something inside of her jumped up and down, cheerily, at the mere thought of him. But she needed to be careful. For all she knew, he might be the terrible murderer she searched for, some mad fan who had wanted his idol to die. Of course, this didn't sound too plausible. She really struggled to imagine that this gorgeous creature could harm anyone. His smile had been too nice for that. And yet—although this felt like a theory she might have studied for her PhD, not something she filled with personal emotions—people were not always what they seemed.

The lift arrived on the fourth floor and Rosalind, trying to follow her father a little more efficiently now (which meant abandoning all thoughts of Drubenheimer and Gabriel), stepped outside. Mr. Waterloo rang the bell.

They heard footsteps approaching. The door swung open.

"Frank!" Berlina exclaimed, her eyelashes fluttering with impressive speed. "And his lovely Rosalind! At last!"

"Better late than never," Mr. Waterloo stated cheerfully, his mood instantly lifted at the sight of her. He kissed her on the cheek. "Since young Rosalind here has switched to the languid Sicilian mode of her deceased grandmother, we unfortunately made very slow progress. But some sort of miracle occurred and we've finally arrived."

Languid Sicilian mode? Rosalind's grandmother, Valeria, had always been on the move, usually following the orders of her bossy husband.

"Oh, how I love Italy and Italian ways of being!" Berlina chanted, winking at her. Then she shot a quick glance at Rosalind's father.

"Well, my ladies," he said, taking his cue. "Let me go and say hello to Mrs. Drubenheimer."

Her father disappeared down a seemingly endless corridor. There was no point in going after him. In stark contrast, Berlina seemed eager to speak to her, as she put on an almost motherly smile.

"My lovely," she cooed. "I'm afraid you didn't like my little joke much yesterday. Your father tells me you took it quite badly."

Rosalind felt too embarrassed to say "yes" and started to vaguely deny it had had the slightest effect on her, when Berlina enthusiastically cut her short: "You'll forgive me, won't you? I just couldn't help it. It was such a brilliant joke."

She giggled, but stopped abruptly to shoot a questioning look at Rosalind.

"You still don't think so, do you? But don't you find it funny, I mean generally, how stories imitate life and life imitates stories? It's just like in our dear Drubenheimer's novel, isn't it? Don't you sometimes just want to sit down and write about all the strange things that happen to you and those around you?"

Although she didn't quite grasp Berlina's intention, Rosalind liked the comment about her beloved novel *Story*. At least the editor understood the beauty of Drubenheimer's works. She answered with a not overly eloquent: "Oh yes."

"Well, I'm sorry if I upset you, really," Berlina merrily went on. "But the good news is that I'm going to make it up to you! You see," she whispered, leaning towards Rosalind. "I have a present for you which I'll give you a little later. And if you want, I can use my gifts to help you! Believe it or not, I have the most exceptional talents!"

"What kind of talents?" Rosalind asked, intrigued.

"All kinds. I started off with reiki, then yoga. Now I'm even skilled at hypnosis and communication with the dead!

Ah, I told you I find death so awful! I'd kill masses if I had to, just to escape it myself. But since killing masses is a little complicated, I've learned to face my fear by speaking to those who have migrated to the other world. So if you want to give Mark a spiritual call—so to speak—and ask him if he was really murdered and by whom, you just have to tell me. I can arrange for that."

Rosalind was amazed. She had never had much to do with the "esoteric" aspects of life, not because they didn't appeal to her, but because they seemed profoundly prohibited for those in love with intellectual pursuits. Although she had recently granted herself the occasional luxury of believing in the meaning of coincidences, putting people into trances or making them speak from the land of the dead were clearly matters of irrationality and wish-fulfilment, to be treated with suspicion.

"That's very kind, thank you. But for the moment, I think I'll rely on more worldly means of research."

"Worldly means of research!" Berlina shrieked, delighted. "What an eloquent young lady you are! Well, you say no, for now. We'll see if you won't change your mind."

On having pronounced these words, the editor started heading towards the living room and Rosalind followed her at a cautious distance.

As soon as she arrived, the room startled Rosalind. It was both intensely beautiful and lifeless. There were no pictures on the wall; no books. A white piano stood, lid open, in the corner. The curtains were half-drawn, the room brightened by several chandeliers. Two large loudspeakers—also white—in a corner emitted dreamy melodies. Chopin perhaps, or Schumann, Rosalind couldn't tell. Her father might have known. Except she couldn't ask him, because he thought she was ignorant even of his passion for music.

Rosalind detected a lingering odour of incense, mixed perfumes of people present and something indefinable which gave it an air of excessive cleanliness. This was obviously Mrs. Drubenheimer's space. The genius must have withdrawn to his studio, needing solitude to expand his body and mind.

It was high time to concentrate on her search and try to make a little progress, somehow. Get to know more people from her idol's life; dig deeper into his mysterious being.

The people around her had by now been reduced to a rather small group. The lady who might be Mrs. Drubenheimer stood in a corner, surrounded by men in dark suits. Her father was one of them. Others were scattered around the room, yet their fidgety movements implied they were about to leave. She tried to make out the woman who had been the victim of furious glances from among the remaining visitors, but she was nowhere to be seen.

Rosalind felt nervous and unsure about what to do. With a renewed tingling in her chest, face and even—it seemed now—her hair, she thought of Gabriel; of being called a sweet stalker. Well, maybe this was what she would be from now on. A sweet stalker of the people who might have caused Drubenheimer's death! She shuddered. The tingling ceased. Life could be full of horrors, and cancer, and hatred, and… Not now! Not these dark thoughts again. She must focus on her search!

But where should she start?

Suddenly, Rosalind sensed the gentle burn of attention of someone staring at her. She turned around and found Berlina standing only a few steps away from her, playing with an elaborate flower arrangement.

"So, are you enjoying the gathering, my darling?" she asked.

"Yes, very much," Rosalind lied. What was the present she had mentioned? Another joke?

"Oh, I'm so glad, my lovely," Berlina said. "I really want my dear Frank's daughter to be my friend. So, given you have cruelly rejected my offer of communicating with the dead, is there any other way I could assist you with your fascinating search?"

So Berlina really appeared eager to make up for her bad joke. Rosalind felt a rush of warmth, an unexpected sense of gratitude. Then her reservations returned. Could she really trust this woman? Evidently not. But she may put her into contact with someone she might be able to trust. A guide into Drubenheimer's intimate life. His wife.

Rosalind hesitated. She had always been uncomfortable asking for favours. Still, for the sake of Drubenheimer, she made herself speak.

"To be honest, there's something you could help me with," she began, awkwardly.

"Oh, but that's wonderful, my gorgeous!" the editor enthused, pulling a white rose from the flower arrangement. She ripped off its stem and put it behind her ear. "Your wish is my command, my darling! I'd love to help you in whichever way I can."

"That's very kind of you! Then could you maybe tell me if this lady," Rosalind carefully indicated the woman in the corner with a slight inclination of her head, "is actually Mark Drubenheimer's widow?"

"Why, yes!" Berlina replied, theatrically. "This beautiful and fragile creature was once our dear author's wife."

As if aware that they were talking about her, the woman shot a glance at them, and Berlina lowered her voice.

"Unfortunately, you've missed her most hated object, Lisa Croydon-Bay. She wasn't allowed to come."

"Not allowed?" Rosalind asked, fascinated by this piece of gossip despite of herself and the fact that one probably shouldn't experience such heightened emotions in the face of mere chitchat. "Why?"

"I don't know any details, my darling," Berlina admitted, her voice filled with the joy of intrigues. "I told you, there were issues of jealousy."

"But did this woman and Mark Drubenheimer actually have an affair?" Rosalind asked, before she could stop herself. In fact, without even trying to stop herself, as her search probably justified such an inquisitive attitude towards other people's lives.

"Well," the editor answered, fiddling around with the rose behind her ear. "I'd say it's highly unlikely. Have you seen Lisa? If there had been a competition of the least attractive woman at the funeral, she would have been a definite nominee. And authors prefer their muses to be pretty. Still, Mrs. Drubenheimer is convinced."

She looked directly at Rosalind as she spoke, her eyes glittering with excitement.

"Well, I'd love to speak to Mrs. Drubenheimer sometime," Rosalind said. "I would really like to ask her a few questions."

"Not at her husband's funeral gathering, my lovely?" Berlina asked, pretending to be shocked.

Rosalind immediately felt guilty.

"Of course not straight away. I mean, as soon as she has recovered a little from her grief and…"

"Don't worry, my darling!" Berlina consoled her, winking cheerfully. "I was only joking again! The truth is that Alicia Drubenheimer loves to talk about herself. I'm sure she'll be ever so pleased to speak to you. Of course, it's quite tragic your father hasn't yet arranged a meeting for you. Mind you, with him and his interesting privacy principles, he might not have known about this woman's existence."

"Well," Rosalind muttered, awkwardly.

"Anyway, why don't I help you with this?" the editor offered. "Let me go and speak to her."

Without losing a second, Berlina walked towards the lady, gracefully pulled her aside and started whispering into her ear. Mrs. Drubenheimer shook her head energetically. It seemed Rosalind would have to find some other way of talking to Drubenheimer's widow; at the very least, she would have to wait until the worst of her mourning process was over. But how long would this take? Weeks? Months? Years?

But, to Berlina's credit, she didn't seem to give up so easily. The editor leaned towards Mrs. Drubenheimer in a gesture of profound complicity and began to talk very rapidly. The widow's mouth—painted in dark red—turned ever so slightly upward and Rosalind could see the lady's eyes light up with a sudden dark pleasure. Finally, the widow nodded at Berlina, whose lips formed an exuberant "thank you." A few seconds later, Berlina was next to Rosalind again.

"My darling, I'm afraid I might be a genius!" she announced, triumphantly. "Alicia Drubenheimer said she'd meet you tomorrow morning. I told you, she loves to talk about herself and Mark. And guess what? I've offered her my services, too. She was just a little more eager than you, I have to say. But never mind. You'll come around yet."

Berlina smiled, exuding light and happiness as though she had never known as much as an insect bite or toothache in her entire life.

"Thank you so much," Rosalind said. She felt strangely excited by the prospect of tomorrow's meeting. This was finally life! The sparkling side of it; like sun-lit water drops falling onto one's face on a summer's day.

"You're ever so welcome, my gorgeous," Berlina replied, taking the flower from her hair and sticking it behind Rosalind's ear. Then she started fumbling in her black handbag and took out a beautiful, deeply red notebook.

"I told you I had a present!" the editor cried out. "It's a diary, for Rosalind's secret and fascinating world. And a small gift to make up for my hilarious Rosebud joke yesterday!"

"No thanks," Rosalind mumbled before she could stop herself and immediately blushed at her rudeness.

"Excuse me, did you say no thanks?" Berlina asked, trying to smile but looking, for the faintest moment, a little disconcerted. "It's something I picked especially for you. You love writers so much, I thought you might love writing, too! About yourself, your world and your search…"

Rosalind guiltily observed the room's spotless, white carpet. After all, Berlina tried very hard to be kind to her. And what if the editor told her father about the refusal? She stretched out her hand to receive the gift.

"Well, thank you," she said. "That's really very kind."

Chapter Seven

Frank Waterloo lay stretched out on the designer sofa of his home-office the morning after the funeral. Rosalind had left to "interview" Mrs. Drubenheimer, for her bizarre "search". An hour ago, the first draft of Sunny McHay's new novel had arrived. Frank had already printed out the whole thing. It had an odd title—*Collective Cruelty*—but this could be fixed in a moment's inspiration; Sunny's, the editor's or his own.

He felt relaxed and excited. His odd mood after the funeral— his mind had insisted on throwing itself masochistically back into the past and toying with countless what-ifs, as if it were a hyperactive Hollywood screenwriter (apparently, they loved spinning a tale based on life's countless unfulfilled possibilities)—had dissipated.

He reached for a bag of chocolate-covered coffee beans and started chewing them, languidly, delighting in the taste of this sweet-bitter, soft-brittle treat in his mouth. Why had he been so worried? He didn't need Drubenheimer to make money. The man's death had—like an emotional time machine—catapulted him back into past insecurities; had disconnected him from who he was. Frank Waterloo, star agent.

He had written a part of Drubenheimer's success story. Helped imprint it onto reality. He had done it before and he would do it again. Bring forth excellence. Fill up his bank account. And Sunny's new novel would already be another step on this road he had built so well.

Frank Waterloo put aside the chocolate and started reading. The first chapters were already fantastic. Sunny's protagonist, Mike, slaughtered people relentlessly. It was his private revenge against people's indifference. Their joyful spending despite global warming, social injustice and world poverty. The story, potentially very heavy, was well told, with a smooth, enticing, dark prose. What had Frank been doing, digging with such exaggerated eagerness through new submissions and the slush pile, like a starving homeless person going through garbage to find some food? Not that these sources were a waste, of course, they were still a considerable source of his standing and fame.

He felt his own status, his importance in the world again, physically, as if it added strength to his muscles or glitter to his blood.

He rested the small pile of printed paper on his stomach and closed his eyes, fantasising about a bidding war. It wasn't a novel that suited Berlina's list. So he could keep his girlfriend safe—he smiled—and watch some of the other big publishing houses battle over it, instead. What would it be? A six, seven figure advance? How many bricks of a luxurious retirement home, perhaps somewhere by the sea?

He opened his eyes again and read on. Matthew continued to kill his fellow humans, leaving complicated messages on their corpses. This seemed a little counter-productive, given that people wouldn't like to be lectured on world peace by a mass-murderer. But the novel remained thrilling, cleverly playing on people's inner darkness. The shadows all humans shared.

Except suddenly it went wrong. Sunny tried to bring in a love-story. The protagonist fell in love with a girl as he attempted to strangle her. Was Sunny mad? Someone else might have pulled it off, but he didn't. Some recent love affair must have corrupted his brain, because the prose became all conventional, romantic and out of control.

Maybe that's why he had been able to deliver so fast! His was the rapture of love, not of creation!

Frank Waterloo put down the manuscript, disappointed, annoyed. The novel still needed lots of work. By the time it was done, he might as well use his percentage to buy a luxurious tomb!

He got up and walked towards his computer. He knew he was overreacting. The work simply would need some more time, go through the usual process of editing, of revisions before it was ready to be sent out. But he had hoped for something that would help him fast, replace Drubenheimer and restore his calm immediately. He didn't want to wait and see what life sent his way.

He opened his emails, typed in Sunny's address and stared at the web page for a few minutes. He took a deep breath and started writing. "Wonderful prose, enticingly dark, evil and clever, masterpiece potential, a little bit of work needed, nothing major, will be in touch soon…"

He had written countless emails—and initially letters—like this during his long and successful career. Yet now he felt oddly uninspired. Was this still about Drubenheimer's death? Did his author's decision to hurl himself out of the window unleash this lack of peace within? Of course, he had cared for the man. He cared for all of his authors, not only because of the money they brought in. The process of working on a novel together and getting it ready for publishers' eyes ended up being very personal at times. Even despite his policy of always keeping a professional distance, he had witnessed Drubenheimer's elation when he had agreed to take him on, his recurrent nervousness that his words would fail to bring him fame and that—bizarrely—his writing wasn't manly enough. He had seen the ecstatic (if always a little restless) and fearful Drubenheimer, watched the man's moods go up and down like the London Eye. Was he, then, grieving for him? Or had the author connected him, once more, to the issue of Death? The universal plotline everyone else worried about?

Quickly, Frank Waterloo finished his email to Sunny and pressed sent, then put his head in his hands. In his present state of mind, at his age, he no longer wanted to throw himself into the literary wilderness, he no longer felt like taking complicated risks. He longed for a sense of certainty and security. Numbers flowing in, telling him that he was OK. That life could be annoying and cruel, yet—ultimately—he was the one in control.

When Rosalind arrived outside Campden Hill Court, Mrs. Drubenheimer was standing on the balcony, smoking a cigarette and looking down. She thought the widow was already waiting and started to wave, but the lady didn't seem to notice her.

Rosalind grasped on tightly to the new diary inside her bag. Trying to control her nervousness, she pressed the gold button and stepped inside to find the same porter sitting at the same desk, still smiling his expressionless smile.

"I'm here to visit Mrs. Drubenheimer," she announced and detected an unexpected cadence of pride in her voice.

Not that the porter cared very much.

"Very well," he grunted and gestured that she should go right past him into the glorious corridor.

This time Rosalind didn't pause to study herself, but—with an increased sense of purpose—walked straight towards and into the lift. On the fourth floor, Rosalind dutifully rang Mrs. Drubenheimer's doorbell.

There was no reaction. Rosalind rang again. Hadn't she seen Mrs. Drubenheimer on the balcony? She felt an uncomfortable stiffness in her neck—a sudden tension of guilt. Had it been a mistake to come the day following her husband's funeral? Perhaps the lady didn't want this meeting after all and now hid away inside?

Rosalind was about to leave when the door was pulled open and Mrs. Drubenheimer appeared in front of her. She stared somewhat confusedly at Rosalind, her eyes swollen and red. Still, what a beautiful woman! Rosalind stood in awe at the way her black hair—tied into a bun—mysteriously reflected the light. The widow was surrounded by an air of impending catastrophe, as though she had once acted the main part in a tragedy and never found her way out again.

Rosalind remained still for a while, forgetting to speak. Luckily, the fragile woman soon addressed her:

"Oh, it's you," she sighed, a tired expression of recognition on her face. She stepped aside to let Rosalind pass into the flat. "The journalist! I haven't kept you waiting, I hope? Please, please, do come on in."

The journalist?

Rosalind listened, perplexed, as polite phrases sprinkled from the lady's mouth as water from a fountain. Her suffering must have made her mix up the words journalist and research student, maybe. Rosalind ignored this, for now.

The flow of Mrs. Drubenheimer's words ceased and she walked, silently, towards the living room. Rosalind followed her, desperately thinking of something to say. She needed to be clever and inspired. Socially skilled and without inhibitions. Able to pull out people's darkest secrets, like a dentist extracting a rotten tooth. But how was she to go about this?

Should she offer her condolences? Somehow this seemed inappropriate; wrong. Everyone had constantly offered their commiserations after her mum had died and she had never really understood what this strange rite was supposed to mean. Well-intentioned and usually kind, it had made her feel all lonely inside.

No condolences, then. Rosalind stared at Mrs. Drubenheimer helplessly. How should she handle this conversation? Why was she so shy?

Thankfully, the lady came to her rescue.

"Not here," she exclaimed, as Rosalind found herself moving towards a leather couch. "The balcony. It's very picturesque. Do you want to start with some photographs?"

She scanned Rosalind, as if looking for something on her body she could take "photographs" with.

Rosalind winced. Picturesque? Photographs? Had Mrs. Drubenheimer not simply mixed up the words "journalist" and "student", after all? Did she really believe she was from the press? What had Berlina told her? How stupid of Rosalind to trust the editor after the Rosebud joke!

"Well," Rosalind whispered, trying to gain time to think. What should she do? "Well," she repeated; and then, again: "Well."

The lady eyed her suspiciously and Rosalind understood that she had no choice. It was too late. Whatever the origin of this error, if she wanted to find out anything at all about Drubenheimer and his murder, she would have to play along. She owed this to him.

So, Rosalind would take a picture. Students took pictures, too. And if worse came to worst, she could always say she had misunderstood and thought Mrs. Drubenheimer was referring to the academic article she was, in fact, writing about her late husband.

Rosalind made herself pull out her mobile phone and announce, as steadily as she could manage (which was not very steady at all): "The balcony would be lovely for pictures. If you don't mind posing before the interview, I would love to get a few shots."

Get a few shots? Was she mad? Was that the right kind of talk? She wasn't sure about either.

The lady seemed more than a little disappointed that she would be photographed by Rosalind's not even very flashy mobile phone. But then a strange dark pleasure flickered again in the woman's eyes and she said, more to herself than to Rosalind:

"I suppose these things take marvellous pictures these days."

Although she felt almost unbearably ridiculous, Rosalind half realised she would now have to make some affirmative comments. Speak about technology and how modern-day journalists—researchers!—tended to rely very heavily on such small yet sophisticated manifestations of it. Yet she couldn't get herself to lie that much. So she just stared at Mrs. Drubenheimer and stammered: "Well, let's begin."

Rosalind followed the lady onto a small concrete space with a view of the street she had left only minutes ago. It smelled of smoke and rotting flowers. The odours belonged to an unemptied ashtray in one corner and a dying bougainvillea in another. A mother and daughter, both blond, tall and lively, passed by underneath, sending up echoes of their chatter and laughter, the high-heeled click-clack of their synchronised steps. Sunrays illuminated Mrs. Drubenheimer's elegant body, as she positioned herself next to the railing and stared dramatically into the distance. Then she turned towards Rosalind again.

"Your name is Rosalind, isn't it?" she asked.

"Yes," she replied, eagerly, because—for a moment at least—she would be allowed to tell the truth: "I'm Rosalind Waterloo."

The widow nodded very slightly then turned once more to observe the horizon.

Feeling close to tears, Rosalind leaned against balcony wall door for support. She took a tentative shot.

This pleased Mrs. Drubenheimer. She quickly arranged her hair and then glanced directly at the camera, her eyes wide with ostentatious suffering and hurt.

"Is the light good enough?" she inquired. "I want the world to see that I'm the true victim of this tragedy, do you hear?"

Slightly disturbed by the lady's need to show off her grief, Rosalind took another picture and then another. Mrs. Drubenheimer was a very beautiful woman, indeed. Rosalind almost enjoyed eternalising her big eyes, delicate facial features and fragile figure on her little, improvised camera. Then she felt guilty about her betrayal again.

Twenty photos on her telephone later, Mrs. Drubenheimer seemed satisfied. To Rosalind's surprise, she didn't ask to see the pictures. She just nodded at Rosalind, as if to say "enough" and then stared at her with frightening force.

Rosalind felt awkward. The time to ask her questions had finally come. She would have to proceed very carefully.

Quite apart from her search, there was something very special about this opportunity. Being able to talk to Mark Drubenheimer's widow! For if the Drubenheimers really had been as deeply in love as he had stated in his famous interview, wasn't this encounter the closest she would ever get to meeting him? And now she even had twenty photos of her.

"Mrs. Drubenheimer," she began, vaguely inspired now by this sentiment. "You know, it's quite hard for me to express how much I admired your husband and his work. And it's such an honour to be able to speak to you, the person he loved more than anything in the world…"

Mrs. Drubenheimer narrowed her eyes and looked at her with an exhausted intensity, as if trying to judge her earnestness. Then she emitted a short and bitter laugh which made Rosalind jump a little, inside.

"You really think he loved me that much, do you?" she asked. "Don't tell me you were the one who conducted the famous interview? The one full of lies?"

Rosalind recoiled. The press reference again. The lady obviously spoke about the one and only interview Mark Drubenheimer had ever given. The one that had, in fact, informed her about the couple's love.

"No," Rosalind assured her, shaking her head emphatically, relieved that this, too, was the actual truth. If only she could sit down somewhere. By now, she felt the balcony wall cold and rough against her back.

"You didn't?"

Rosalind couldn't tell whether this disappointed or appeased Mrs. Drubenheimer. Maybe a bit of both.

"In any case," the lady went on. "It is time to set the records straight, do you hear? Let the world know that I'm a victim. That I am beyond suspicion. Are you ready to listen?"

And with that ominous glimmer in her eyes—like an animal trying to save itself from impending death—Mrs. Drubenheimer embarked on a passionate, only rarely interrupted soliloquy. "Well, if you didn't conduct this interview—the only one he could bear to give—how can I blame you for your ignorance? He did adore me publicly. Yet in private? I think I'll have to tell you a few things about my husband. Will you take notes?"

Notes?

Rosalind signalled her head, as if to imply she would mentally register every single word. But she could have saved herself the effort. The lady simply talked on without taking any notice of her:

"Let me tell you, for instance, that he was a madman. If in the most attractive of ways. But he was completely mad. That's why he married me. Instead of the bitch that lives underneath."

"A madman?" Rosalind asked, feebly. She figured "the bitch" must refer to the friend Berlina had mentioned, Lisa Croydon-Bay.

"A madman, yes," Mrs. Drubenheimer meanwhile went on, untroubled. "Full of faults, I'm telling you. Above all, he was tremendously insecure. You see? If only I had realised this in time! But I didn't. A frustrated artist myself, I was so drawn to him, the allure of the lost poet, the struggling soul…"

The woman sighed with resigned pride, then lit a cigarette and began to inhale, deeply and frantically. The lady's words deeply confused Rosalind. What was she trying to do? Create a scandal? Stage some sort of vendetta against her dead husband? Was this the woman's rage of loss and grief?

Mrs. Drubenheimer signalled the ashtray in the corner. Rosalind reluctantly picked it up and handed it to the widow, once more craving to move inside and sit down.

"He was atrocious, I'm telling you," the widow insisted, tipping her ash into the tray. Her words were spoken so fast, they tumbled on top of each other. "He went on and on about how bullied he had felt as a child, how unaccepted, unloved. How one day he would show them all, prove them all wrong, be someone, matter, count... I'm telling you, all this tiresome talk, the whole time. And I'm sure it was because of this insecurity that he became such a liar."

Mrs. Drubeneheimer gave Rosalind an almost malicious smile.

"When will this be published?" she asked.

Rosalind blushed very deeply. Panic arose in her and she tried with all her remaining strength to push it aside. It was time to defend Mr. Drubenheimer. It was time to fight for whom she loved.

"I don't know when," Rosalind replied. "And I'm not sure I understand why you claim your husband was a liar. Is it possible that he sometimes mixed fact and fiction, because he was a writer and–"

Mrs. Drubenheimer stopped speaking for a moment and eyed Rosalind up and down. Had she begun to realise her error? Had she understood that there would be no article about this?

Rosalind wasn't sure. The lady herself didn't seem too sure. But, luckily for Rosalind, she seemed intent on taking her chances.

Although it sounded theatrical and forced, she broke into some more bitter laughter that ended in a real cough.

"Oh, how terribly naïve you are!" the lady cried out. "I wasn't talking about his fiction, at all. He was only a liar because he wasn't a real writer. I'm aware he wrote two great books, but you might as well know that he only managed to write them because he had me. There's no doubt I was his muse; his mermaid in *Seabound*, his narrative-obsessed beauty in *Story*! Without me, he wouldn't have managed to do anything at all. Really, I should have been the one writing successful novels!"

Rosalind stared at Mrs. Drubenheimer quite defencelessly. What was she to say to all this? But then again, they were just words.

"Still, I'm telling you, I would have been able to put up with his faults, if only he had truly loved me. I was always there for him and supported him, right until the end!" Mrs. Drubenheimer's trembling hand moved towards her face, then—perhaps in order to comfort herself—onto her chest.

"But he didn't support or love me," Mrs. Drubenheimer carried on. "He just used me, and not only as his muse. There was also my money. Mark had the most ridiculous jobs before we married and before I naïvely decided to support him so he could give himself to this 'tremendously painful calling' of his, as he used to call it. I can assure you, it was most painful for me!"

It was, by now, hard for Rosalind to ignore the deep sense of annoyance that had taken hold of her. Why did this woman talk about Drubenheimer like this? Why did she appear to hate him so? Wasn't this, possibly, the fury of a murderess? Was this why she had agreed to speak to her? To make her seem like the victim, to create a public defence? The lady admitted it herself.

So she was using Rosalind! Strangely, this calmed her down. At least, she wouldn't have to feel so guilty for going along with their misunderstanding.

"For years before his death," Mrs. Drubenheimer continued, still not expecting Rosalind to say anything, just drumming chords onto the railing as though it were a piano accompanying her, "Mark didn't spend much time with me. He was always in his studio, and claimed he was writing, but I'm sure he was with her. Do you hear? She lives right opposite the studio, I'm telling you. They arranged it that way. So easy for them to sneak over and..."

The lady clasped her hands to her chest now, in agony.

"But I won't think about that now! Are you still listening? He usually came here for a silent dinner and then disappeared. I followed the sound of his footsteps, and he always went downstairs, to her. He did the same every day, then crawled back at two o'clock in the morning, maybe three. I'd given up confronting him over the years. Whenever I asked, he got angry with me and shouted that, for fuck's sake, he was working. He always said it like that, 'for fuck's sake, for fuck's sake.'"

Mrs. Drubenheimer savoured the last words, as though they contained his very essence.

"He was a coarse man."

Again, Rosalind felt it was her obligation to properly defend her dear and dead Drubenheimer.

"But he was also a fighter," Rosalind interjected, with some passion of her own. "Don't you think he might have just needed space? And then, metaphorically speaking, maybe he disappeared to save you, like his parents, who..."

"Like his parents!" Mrs. Drubenheimer interrupted her, laughing acidly.

"Well," Rosalind bravely made herself speak on, "after all, as far as I know, his parents did send him to England alone so he may survive..."

"Oh," Mrs. Drubenheimer grimaced. "That story."

"What do you mean?" Rosalind asked, alarmed.

"Well, my dear, didn't I tell you Mark was a compulsive liar? Have you not been listening? He invented all of this for his interview. How typical of him! Why, Aurelia and Fritz, his parents, died within a week of each other in their comfortable London home. About eight years ago now."

"What?" Rosalind exclaimed, incredulously. Mrs. Drubenheimer was lying, lying, lying. Still, hadn't she sensed there was something wrong when she hadn't seen their dates of birth and death on the grave? But then…

"Mark invented the entire story of his heroic parents to have a more interesting history. He said this was an important thing for writers to have, these days. And your colleague helped him to spread all this dirt. You see, it's high time for someone, me, to set the record straight. They all emigrated very comfortably, after the war and—as far as I know—were never involved in any resistance movement at all. He even had all dates removed from their grave, didn't you realise? Well, I warned you. My husband was a fake."

Some space inside of Rosalind opened. It wasn't a nice space.

The sun had withdrawn behind a dark cloud. Rosalind picked a withered flower from the plant, then threw it onto the concrete ground. She had to urgently gain some control over this conversation. Really, wasn't she to urgently ask for the lady's… alibi?

"To change the subject slightly," she began, somewhat abruptly, certain she had turned bright red. "What did you and your husband do on your last night together?"

"Our very last night together?" Mrs. Drubenheimer repeated, hysterically. "Our twenty-eighth wedding anniversary? Oh, I see, you want some more drama! Well, we had dinner together, yes, dinner! Or I tried to have dinner with him, at least. I was in a mood of—well, romance and beauty. I felt very inspired. I wanted to have a grand moment with him, do you understand? He was my husband after all. And so I put candles everywhere and ordered his favourite food. The candles were flickering and music was playing. Amy Beach's 'Gaelic Symphony'."

A flicker of some dark, unidentifiable emotion passed across the lady's elegant facial features.

"He didn't say anything strange or unusual. I didn't–. We were just sitting there, eating and staring at each other—and we had nothing to say. Imagine my pain! He just sat there and stared into space. Then he left. And never returned."

Mrs. Drubenheimer emitted a high-pitched sound of suffering or disbelief.

"This was how we spent our last evening," she concluded, her eyes twitching nervously before gaining control over them again. "How typical of our whole life together."

"And what did you do afterwards?" Rosalind asked, very rapidly. "After he had left and–"

Mrs. Drubenheimer shot a quick glance at her. It was the first time, Rosalind felt, the woman actually saw her and it shook her inside.

"Why are you asking me this?" she snapped. "Surely, I have given you enough information, you ungrateful…"

"I'm so sorry," Rosalind interrupted her, terrified. "I really didn't mean to upset you, Mrs. Drubenheimer."

"But you did," the lady coldly responded.

Chapter Eight

Walking down the flight of stairs from Mrs. Drubenheimer's flat, Rosalind suddenly envisaged the lady choosing the same path the night between the 4th and 5th of May, determined to eliminate Mark Drubenheimer—the "fake"—from her life. She could picture her arriving at his studio, wearing a beautiful white nightgown and cradling the rope like a baby in her arms. "One of us has to go," she heard her declare to her husband; and so Drubenheimer, forever superior in his sentiments, sacrificed himself for the happiness of his wife.

Fine, so maybe this hadn't been the way Drubenheimer died. Still, what an odd woman! The way she had simply "switched off" after Rosalind had asked about her alibi and eventually (though again politely) had asked her to leave.

Rosalind reached the third floor. She heard someone hoovering, in the distance. Although it was immaculately clean, the corridor smelled of dust to her, and smoke.

She felt worn out by all this bizarre make-belief—of playing the role of a journalist—and slightly worried about possible consequences. Then again, the lady was deeply confused and in mourning. Perhaps she would never expect an actual article. Also, it may have been fate that she (and not a real journalist) had received all this angry information about her idol. This way, she could protect his reputation from being unjustly destroyed. Rosalind realised only now how strongly she had expected one thing—a speech about Mark Drubenheimer's magnificent nature, his almost superhuman abilities and kindness—and received another.

A liar! A fake! But how?

This was impossible! So maybe he had lied about some things, like his parents. That was bad. Above all a little perplexing, really. Yet who was she to judge him? She had no idea what may have driven him on. Maybe someone had blackmailed him? Couldn't someone—Berlina even—have threatened she would never publish his work unless he changed the story of his parents and their German past? Or perhaps he was simply like Anette, the protagonist of *Story*. Stuck in narrative. Incapable of distinguishing between reality and fiction, sometimes. And also—

Rosalind didn't get very far with this line of thought, because suddenly her eyes were attracted by nothing less than his name. There it was, "Mark Drubenheimer" written in tiny letters on a shiny plaque at the centre of a door to her left.

This must have been his studio. The sacred place where he created his work, the "chamber of horrors" where he had been murdered! How strange that she had ended up here; and at the same time, how logical. Rosalind was amazed at how the subconscious mind worked; how some part of her must have remembered the location of Drubenheimer's studio and led her here, without bothering to consult her conscious self at all.

The door attracted her magnetically. Slowly, yet with determination, she walked towards it, hoping that at her touch it would magically spring open. But the door remained unmagically locked.

She felt more disappointed than she would have liked to admit. Drubenheimer's studio! His hiding place, certainly, from his aggressive wife. Wouldn't it have been wonderful to be able to look around and see where he used to write his revelational sentences?

Well, given that this was impossible, the reasonable thing would be to go home and perhaps look at her article—or something related to her PhD—again. Still, a part of Rosalind rebelled. She didn't want to go home and do any of these things. She wanted to carry on with this search, so fast she wouldn't even be able to think properly. This was her duty towards Mark Drubenheimer. Yet it started to feel, perhaps even more strongly, like a duty towards herself. She might be destroyed if she watched, doing nothing.

What, then, would she do now?

The answer came to her fast. Really, her subconscious had been marvellously efficient in leading her here. For as soon as Rosalind managed to detach her eyes from the studio, she found the name "Lisa Croydon-Bay" engraved on the door right opposite.

Her heart started beating faster. Of course! Hadn't Mrs. Drubenheimer mentioned that "the bitch" lived "underneath"? Should she try and talk to her straight away? Just ring the doorbell and say—what? Well, anything. She would simply ignore all hesitations and make herself speak.

Rosalind looked at her watch. It was twelve thirty. A time when on a Wednesday people were usually at work. On the other hand, if this woman had really been one of Drubenheimer's closest friends, wouldn't she have taken a few days' mourning leave?

Not a little astounded at what this search made her do, Rosalind rang the bell.

This time, to her pleasant surprise, the door opened immediately. The woman whom she had compared to a sponge at Drubenheimer's funeral stood right in front of her, looking at least as bewildered as Rosalind felt on rather too many occasions. She perceived traces of suffering behind her awkward, questioning smile.

"How may I help you?" Drubenheimer's friend asked with a voice obviously made hoarse from crying.

"I'm very sorry to disturb you, Ms. Croydon-Bay," Rosalind mumbled, a little too quickly, yet proud she managed to speak at all. "My name's Rosalind Waterloo. You don't know me, but I saw you at the funeral yesterday. You see, I'm doing a PhD on Mark Drubenheimer and I'm a great admirer of his work. I heard you were his best friend, so I took the liberty to come and speak to you and–"

The woman eyed Rosalind suspiciously.

"This isn't a good time," she explained, already motioning to close the door. "I'm sorry."

"I understand," Rosalind heard herself declare. She certainly wouldn't have let herself come in, either. "In fact, I know this is a bad time. I'm sorry. It's just that I've been speaking to several people from Mark Drubenheimer's life, his editor, Berlina Marrowing..."

"Yes," Lisa Croydon-Bay interrupted, impatiently.

"Mrs. Drubenheimer, his wife," Rosalind went on, politeness telling her to be quiet, yet the spirit of her search, if there was such a thing, urging her to speak on.

The woman took a deep breath and stepped forward to say something. Rosalind needed to act fast. In a flash of inspiration, she remembered the woman staring at her father during the funeral.

"You see," Rosalind added, in a tone that sounded embarrassingly sly to her. "My father was his agent."

To her great surprise, this highly improvised strategy worked almost instantly—and a lot more potently than she had expected it to.

Ms. Croydon-Bay's eyes widened significantly.

"Excuse me, what did you say your name was?" she asked, after she had spent a few moments staring at Rosalind, as though she were a divine apparition.

"Rosalind Waterloo," she answered dutifully, half waiting for one of the usual jokes about Napoleon.

"And you're Frank Waterloo's daughter?"

"Yes," Rosalind nodded, grateful that her father proved useful to her search, after all.

"Please, call me Lisa. Why don't we go inside?"

Having expected to finally have a door slammed into her face, Rosalind now found herself entering this stranger's world—which also turned out to be a rather strange world. She could hardly believe the amount of mess and even shabbiness that defined it.

At first, the sight of Ms. Croydon-Bay's—Lisa's—corridor left her so dumbfounded she couldn't focus on a single component of it. There were piles of things everywhere, mostly indistinguishable in a dark softened only by a few rays of light falling in through a small window further ahead. But, perhaps because the window was open, it smelled of fresh—if a little dusty—air.

They walked past a kitchen crammed with piles of plates, half-eaten vegetables that looked mouldy, plastic containers, dirty cups entangled with magazines, pens and paper. They passed a door with an enormous, green "Toilet" sign.

When they reached the window, Rosalind's eyes were drawn

to a most fascinating object right beneath it; lying on a pile of books was a shiny key with a holder displaying the words "Studio Mark".

Was this a sign? The answer to her previous temptation? Couldn't she just say she needed to use the toilet and quickly— as Lisa left her alone—borrow it? This would be technically illegal, but wasn't it utterly relevant to her search?

Rosalind felt a physical, almost sensual longing to get hold of that key; a sudden lightness in her shoulders, her chest, in her head. As if she were drunk now, on the "plotline" of her search; and the un-reality of it all enabled her to play, take inconceivable actions, without consequences of any sort.

Should she do it?

No, it was impossible. She was still inside of reality, walking on a messy floor next to Drubenheimer's former best friend. It went against all rules of the SCASA and those of several other committees, internal and external, as well. Rosalind pushed her temptation to the back of her mind. They entered the living room.

Music was playing. A violin screeched frantically up and down. Lisa went to a tiny stereo in the corner and switched it off, leaving only a few street noises of free-floating words and cars passing, behind. She rapidly picked up a worn-out jumper from the floor and hurled it over an open notebook and a fountain pen, lying on a desk in the corner. The woman then removed a few layers of paper from a couch that may have once been light-blue and motioned for her guest to sit down.

"Do you want coffee or tea?" Lisa asked, smiling like an anxious teenager.

"Coffee, please," Rosalind answered, a little worried about the circumstances it would be produced in. At the same time, she looked forward to a hot drink which might help her regain some strength after her meeting with Mrs. Drubenheimer.

While Lisa disappeared into the kitchen, she let herself sink into the dirty sofa, already grateful for a moment's relaxation and calm. A few seconds later she guiltily straightened her back again, reminding herself that she needed to remain focused on her mission. Shouldn't she look around?

Obediently, Rosalind let her eyes wander across the room and allowed them to come to rest on their rather predictable destination: the bookshelves on the wall. In comparison to her father's library, the shelves were a lot smaller, as though they were made of tall trees that had once been terribly humiliated. Unlike the rest of the flat, the books had been meticulously organised. There was an expensive-looking encyclopedia, a lot of contemporary English and foreign fiction; some volumes with exotic sounding titles like *The Path Towards Acceptance* and *Everything is Light*. One of the shelves was almost empty, displaying only the photograph of a young and beautiful woman playing the violin and next to it, a novel called *The Sea* and an *Anthology of Romantic Poetry*. Rosalind started. Couldn't this be the same anthology the police had found open on Drubenheimer's floor after his death?

Her instinct told her to get up and look at it right away; and this she probably would have done if Lisa had not returned at this very moment, carrying two empty cups and an enormous thermos bottle which contained at least three pints of coffee.

Still smiling, yet with increased shyness rather than confidence, Lisa sat down next to Rosalind and poured a cup of suspiciously light brown brew for both.

"I still can't believe you're Frank Waterloo's daughter," the woman confessed, emptying her cup immediately to Rosalind's amazement. "It is almost like a sign! You see, I knew your father once many years ago. I'm embarrassed to admit this, but you could say he was one of the most important people in my life."

"Oh, really?" Rosalind asked, intrigued.

"Well, yes," Lisa said, very quietly. "But that's a long and not very interesting story."

Rosalind muttered what she hoped was an encouraging "is it?" but the woman didn't reply.

An uncomfortable silence followed. Rosalind—pretending to be utterly absorbed by her first sip of "coffee"—used this to observe Lisa more closely and to decide if she could have possibly had a passionate affair with her father, at some stage.

Lisa wore an old summer dress with sunflowers, printed in blue, purple and green. It worried her (especially considering her father's rather high standards of beauty) how much she paled behind these colours. Her skin was ashen; her lips almost bloodless; her hair dry and grey. Only her eyes held a lively sparkle that might occasionally light up into a voracious flame. Still, at least judging from her appearance, her father could have been this woman's lonely obsession, at most.

Half-aware of Rosalind's not overly secret surveillance, Lisa poured herself another cup and stirred it with fast, fidgety movements. Then the woman stated, a little awkwardly: "I'm sorry. I don't know why I brought this up. After all, you're here to talk about Mark. So, what's your PhD about?"

"It's about Drubenheimer's treatment of mortality," Rosalind explained, tensely. Somehow she always felt she was lying when talking about her research. "I realised it's an essential underlying theme in both *Story* and *Seabound*."

"That sounds very interesting and rather complex!" Lisa

replied, with a respectful tone that seemed to suppress some underlying eagerness to hear more. "But where is the theme of mortality in *Story*?"

Rosalind's eyes widened. Lisa knew her way around her best friend's writing.

"Well, it isn't there directly," Rosalind stammered. "I'm writing about its absence."

"Its absence?"

"Well, yes. I will argue that Anette—and everyone else around her—uses narrative to escape from her own mortality."

"Oh, I see," Lisa said, looking sincerely intrigued and almost flattered. In contrast to Mrs. Drubenheimer, she seemed to have cared about her Mark; and relished in his achievements, as if they were her own. The woman leaned in, as if about to ask something else. Then she leaned back again and exclaimed: "I'm sure you're working very hard. But anyway, what did you want to speak to me about?"

Although Rosalind had felt highly uncomfortable talking about her PhD, she now would have babbled on about it for hours—with quotations from Drubenheimer's novels and all—rather than having to stir this conversation towards an inquiry into Lisa's alibi (at least, she had become used to the word, by now). Yet given that this was the only method of finding a murderer she knew, it really wasn't a matter she could avoid. She begged her mind for inspiration and courageously opened her mouth to speak.

"What I've come to talk about?" was all that came out, to begin with. Then she suddenly remembered Berlina, with her offer of esoteric methods, including hypnosis and conjuring up of the dead. "Well, this might sound a little strange, but, given that you and Mark Drubenheimer were such close friends, did you have any premonitions about his death? I mean, did you have a sudden intuition of what went on next door? What were you doing at the time?"

Rosalind felt rather pleased with herself. Not that her little speech had been great in any way; but it could have been far worse. Unfortunately, Lisa didn't look all that convinced.

"Oh," Lisa said, a little too emphatically surprised (which was probably her polite way of being taken aback). "I have to admit I don't quite understand how this relates to your thesis. Unless you're also including Drubenheimer's own death story in your work? For originality, is it?" (Rosalind nodded eagerly to imply that her academic quest for originality was precisely what pushed her on.) "I know they ask difficult things of you students. But to answer your original question, I'm afraid I had no 'intuition' at all."

"And were you," Rosalind went on, blushing from feeling so silly, "here, when you didn't have an intuition?"

A deep frown appeared on Lisa's forehead; yet she complied.

"Well, yes, I was home reading, as most evenings. And, as I mentioned, I was completely unaware of what was going on next door."

A flash of anger appeared on the woman's face. Or was it regret? Lisa breathed in deeply, to compose herself. Rosalind took this as a cue to dig a little deeper.

"So how did you eventually find out?" Rosalind asked.

"Mrs. Drubenheimer told me," Lisa sighed. "Mark's wife. She never normally speaks to me, but the morning after his death she woke me up and told me, almost triumphantly, that he had committed suicide."

"That must have been a terrible shock," Rosalind responded, with real empathy. Then she dutifully added, pretending not to already know the answer: "But why doesn't she normally speak to you?"

At this, Lisa hit her left thigh and declared, her voice shaking a little: "She has always been so horribly jealous of me! And for almost—absolutely no reason! Mark and I have always been very good friends, but no more than that. Still, his wife loathes me. She wouldn't even let me come to the funeral gathering at their flat yesterday. She has always been convinced that we had an affair, especially after I moved to Campden Hill Court."

"Oh, really?" Rosalind asked, feigning surprise and rather enjoying this recurrent theme of gossip.

"Yes! Well, I admit that, given the circumstances, it probably wasn't the wisest idea. But Mark and I often worked together, you see. I acted as a kind of proof-reader for him, and it was just a lot easier this way."

"I see," Rosalind said, grateful for Lisa's trust. "But then why was Mrs. Drubenheimer so certain you were lovers?"

"I really don't know. It's particularly bizarre considering Mark had told her the truth about me." Lisa pointed at the woman with the violin in the photograph. "I mean, she even knew Anne, my former partner."

Rosalind shifted ever so slightly in her seat. Did Lisa imply that she wasn't interested in men? Then why had she called her father one of the most important people in her life?

"How strange of Mrs. Drubenheimer," Rosalind sympathised, shaking her head in what, hopefully, conveyed her notorious open-mindedness.

"Not so strange once you realise how unbalanced that woman actually is!" Lisa stated with some passion. She then fell silent again and stared at her cup without touching it.

"I don't know if I should be telling you this," Lisa eventually voiced. "And I'll only do so because you're Frank Waterloo's daughter. You see, Mrs. Drubenheimer's jealousy was so extreme I even worried that she might have murdered Mark! I mean, he never came to say goodbye to me, and the whole of his death—hanging out of his window like that, not thinking about those left behind—struck me as so absurd. I couldn't believe he had actually chosen to die. And when I saw the triumph with traces of guilt in Mrs. Drubenheimer's eyes that morning she came to tell me the news, my first reaction was to think: 'you murdered him.'"

"You think Drubenheimer might have been murdered?" Rosalind asked, fascinated.

Yet Lisa already regretted having voiced her suspicion so openly.

"I considered it for a while," she admitted. "But then things happened that made me realise I was wrong. I probably just didn't want to admit that Mark would have committed suicide without saying goodbye to me or asking for help. But then I'm afraid our friendship had become a bit strained over the past few months. I just wish we hadn't argued so much. Maybe he would have come to me and I could have saved his life."

In order to repress an onset of tears, Lisa raised her coffee to her lips and poured it down her throat.

"I'm very, very sorry," Rosalind said, feeling close to crying herself.

"Yes, so am I. Mark had been depressed for months. I just never took it as seriously as I should have. I thought," the woman's voice became so dry it sounded almost insincere, "it was simply writer's block and he'd get over it soon."

Chapter Nine

Her eyes half-closed to shut out the sunlight, Rosalind hurried towards Kensington High Street. She was intent on buying a classic in the bookshop near the tube station and eager to finally relax. Despite her momentarily limited vision, she couldn't help glancing at the card Lisa had given her a moment ago, on saying goodbye. *Lisa Croydon-Bay*, it read, *Private Lessons in French*.

What a woman! No, what women! Rosalind felt exhausted, as though all liquids—blood, water and now rather too much of that terrible coffee—had been drained out of her.

She walked on, shutting off her senses, busy trying to convince herself that, so far, her search had gone quite well. She had already interviewed three suspects and discovered their respective alibis. Berlina had spent the night with her father, Mrs. Drubenheimer had been sleeping and Lisa reading. Unfortunately, none of these alibis were particularly revealing. Mrs. Drubenheimer's and Lisa's came across as harmless enough, but couldn't be proven in any way. And as to Berlina's, it was its very nature that made it disconcerting rather than comforting.

Which led her on to the second main question—here Rosalind almost collided with an elderly, well-dressed man and apologised, distractedly—namely that of her suspects' motives. Rosalind had to force herself to think about this in a structured manner. So far, Mrs. Drubenheimer seemed the most convincing murderess of the three, given the extent of her jealousy and resentment. On the other hand, Berlina's behaviour also portrayed a tendency towards cruelty. The editor could have had numerous reasons for wanting to kill Mark. What if she murdered him because he didn't produce a third novel? Or because he had rejected her amorous advances? Or because... well, there were infinite possibilities, really.

Only Lisa—despite the fact that she and Drubenheimer had apparently argued a lot before his death, which caused the occasional signs of resentment and guilt—appeared almost definitely innocent. It was nearly impossible to picture this shy and awkward woman harbouring any aggressive tendencies. Still, there was time before she had to reach any conclusions; and there was also, at least, one more suspect to interview: Gabriel. She would call him later on to arrange a meeting with him.

Leaving elegant houses behind her, she imagined meeting him. He would be enchanted by this coincidence and invite her for a cup of coffee. They would get on amazingly well. When they would finally emerge from the coffee shop three hours later, he would gently touch her hair, then pull her towards him and–

This needed to stop! She needed to focus on her search. In her attempt to no longer fantasise about Gabriel, the idea of stealing Lisa's key returned with full force. She envisioned the shiny thing, lying on the pile of books. She sensed again that strange yearning—a physical craving transferred from a handsome man to the object that would grant her access into Drubenheimer's secret world.

But she really couldn't do anything about this.

Or could she?

No! She should buy a classic and get some rest.

Rosalind took the corner and arrived at Kensington High Street, turned even more glamorous by the sunlight. The buildings' façades reflected the moment's luminescence as if it were their personal gift to the street. The man selling newspapers outside the underground station glowed, as did the girl rushing along the pavement in a skirt and high heels. Rosalind stood still for a few seconds, concentrating on the warmth on her face. Then she walked into the bookshop on the other side of the road.

The shop was almost empty. A bored shop-assistant wandered around, neatening an already tidy row of books. The woman at the counter passionately revised the state of her nails.

As during most of her visits to bookshops, Rosalind moved straight to the classics section. She didn't arrive at her beloved works as fast as she had planned to, because she bumped into a table display dedicated to Drubenheimer instead. Covered in blue linen, it consisted of an enormous pile of his novels. A large poster had been suspended from the ceiling, showing the photograph she had seen in the newspaper after his death. The words "In Memoriam" were printed right across his forehead.

Drubenheimer! Rosalind felt an urge to stroke the face on the poster; or rather she liked the idea of wanting to caress it. For really, she caught herself looking at her idol a little critically. How much of all this talk about "fakeness" and writer's block was true? Why had he lied about his parents?

She frowned, but briefly nodded at the picture, as if to reassure him of her lasting conviction that he must have been a victim of some kind. Then she strolled towards the classics section and started to revise the books in front of her. She felt her body relax. How wonderful to be among classics again!

Remembering the priest at Drubenheimer's funeral and how it had seemed he would recite the whole of the Russian classic, Rosalind pulled out a Subtlety edition of *Anna Karenina*. She indulged in the glittering portrait of a woman standing between two men. Nonetheless—as one shouldn't judge a book by its cover—Rosalind compliantly put it back again. As tempting as it was, she would leave the mesmerising Subtlety editions alone for today and give another publishing house a chance.

Her eyes fell on to a cheap edition of Flaubert's *Madame Bovary*. Considering Lisa, "the bitch", was a French teacher, a French classic seemed suitable for the occasion. It was also a novel Rosalind had wanted to browse through again for a long time. Her mother had loved it, too, and always told her dad, in unconvincing teasing, he was lucky she had not imitated the protagonist's path.

When Rosalind stepped out into the street again, she felt herself floating a little. Perhaps it was the tiredness of hours spent doing such unusual things. The reassurance of holding a classic in her hands. She was overcome by an unexpected, perhaps bookshop-induced sense that reality—her world—was not set in stone, but rather a piece of soft and moist clay she, Rosalind, could help shape with her hands.

The sun was gone and the air had turned cold. Within seconds, her intentions to refrain from all further acts of dishonesty suffered a similar fate. They simply disappeared alongside the image of clay in her mind.

She found herself almost running back to Campden Hill Court. She knew it was crazy; she knew it was most likely to end in disaster. And yet, a profound sense of duty and obligation pulled her along. It was superficially wrong and—it was illegal, yes. But it might turn out to be of the most vital significance, possibly resolving her entire search. She would be like Flaubert, struggling to get to the truth. She would be like Drubenheimer's parents, fighting for what was right. Battling for it. Even if Mrs. Drubenheimer had been telling the truth and they had perhaps never formed part of any resistance movement at all.

Rosalind briefly glanced up at Mrs. Drubenheimer's balcony before entering the building. There was no-one to be seen. The porter almost ignored her as she hurried past him once more. She quickly made her way through the luxurious corridor, entered the lift and at last—panting almost with nervousness—arrived outside Lisa Croydon-Bay's flat once more. She waited for a few moments to catch her breath, then rang the bell. She would ask if she could use the toilet and get hold of the key this way.

As on her previous visit not more than an hour ago, Lisa opened the door almost instantly.

"Rosalind!" she exclaimed, looking a little flustered, as though she had been interrupted doing something important. "Did you forget anything?"

Forget anything? What an excellent idea!

"Yes, I did," Rosalind announced, both shocked and impressed at how potently she could proceed like a reality-shaper—or "fake"?—herself. "I'm afraid I can't find my mobile phone. And I wondered if perhaps I left it on your sofa."

"I haven't seen it." Lisa waved her inside. "But then it's not exactly a very tidy sofa. Why don't you come on in and have a look?"

Rosalind followed her through the corridor. The second they came to the living room, the woman once more hurled her grey jumper onto a notebook and pen. A different kind of music was playing now. A slow ringing of bells, high and low, a sound that carried on in a gentle vibrato, multiplying itself in countless tiny echoes. It was uplifting, soothing and musically evoked the message of *Seabound*. Life, in its true essence, is light. To Rosalind's great relief, Lisa left her alone.

Making use of this providential solitude, Rosalind hurried towards the sofa, dropped her mobile phone onto it and—almost hoping Lisa would return to witness her performance—made a great show of searching for it. Yet Lisa did not come back. Judging from the crazy sound of plates being smashed against each other in the kitchen, she had started to work on her mountain of dishes.

Rosalind's heart was beating so fast now, she could hardly breathe. The bells of Lisa's music rang on, but their calmative effect had ceased; they now seemed to be accusing her. Rosalind anxiously took hold of her phone, walked towards Lisa and held it up into the air.

"Oh, good," the woman said, looking up from a greasy pan. "I'm glad you found it."

Rosalind nodded, to demonstrate that she was glad, too. Then, the terrible moment had come.

"Lisa," she began, her voice shivering. "Do you mind if I quickly use your toilet?"

"You don't have to be so shy about it," Lisa replied, so kindly Rosalind felt moved—and guilty. "Go right ahead."

"Thanks," Rosalind croaked. She could barely believe what she was about to do. "Is it on the corridor?" ("Near the key," she almost added, in a life-long habit of honesty, but stopped herself just in time.)

"Yes, let me show you," Lisa offered and walked her to the

toilet door. Rosalind entered, worried that Lisa might wait outside. Yet when, after having diligently sat on the closed toilet seat for two minutes, Rosalind re-emerged on the scene of her imminent crime, the woman was nowhere to be seen. Rosalind was quite alone, with the key—beneath the lastingly open window—shining at her from its barricade of books.

Should she really do this? Her remnants of emotional composure had gone. She felt sweaty, cold and unstable inside.

"Well, I do hope to meet you again sometime," Lisa shouted from another room. The sentence got louder towards the end, which meant—to Rosalind's absolute horror—that she was approaching.

Rosalind felt onset of dizziness; a weakness in her right arm. It was now or never, never or now! In a single gesture, just a few moments before Lisa entered the corridor, Rosalind grabbed the key and let it disappear into her bag.

Rosalind stood outside Lisa's door, breathing deeply to calm herself down. Where had her sudden powers of dissimulation come from? She had even managed to say goodbye to the woman gracefully, thanking her several times and promising she wouldn't disturb her any longer. As soon as Lisa had shut the door behind her, she felt strangely exhilarated by the way an idea, a simple phantom in her mind, could have such repercussions on reality. The clay image, again. But it was more than clay; less material. As if the air itself, guiding humans with each breath into their future, could be changed by her determined actions and thoughts.

Rosalind smiled and, shivering a little inwardly, looked at the door opposite her. The next crazy task or rather, her second transgression into the space and belongings of other beings, lay before her.

Adrenaline rushed through her body once more. With an acute sense of being someone other than Rosalind Waterloo, perhaps a character in a play or an actress in a film, she turned around to check that nobody was watching. Then she sneaked towards the studio door, afraid the tiniest sound might lead to her being caught.

She took out the stolen key from her bag and quickly unlocked the door. An instant later, she had slipped into Drubenheimer's secret world.

It was filled with unsteady darkness. The curtains of the room's only window were drawn but rays of light tried to sneak their way in from behind. With horror, she realised this must have been the window he had been dangling from!

There was an eerie silence, broken only by an indistinct humming sound rising up from the street. Rosalind inhaled. The air was stale and musty. Only abstract associations came to her, such as anger, sadness and fear. Maybe these had been Drubenheimer's last emotions and she could mysteriously smell them now.

She took a closer look at the walls. Given the imagined nature of her genius, it surprised her to discover only one bookshelf. She scanned its contents, half expecting to find a dusty volume entitled *The Ultimate Secrets of Our Existence*. She squinted and stepped a little closer. Magazines had been squeezed in between a few hardcover editions and frail, over-read paperbacks. There were several volumes of poetry and a number of self-help books with titles like *Free the Creative Inside!*, *Stop Making Excuses: Write!*, *Novel Writing for Beginners* and *Love Yourself and the Words Will Flow*.

Had Lisa been right and Drubenheimer had really suffered from writer's block? Overcome by a sudden lack of confidence, had he felt forced to buy all these bizarre guides for beginning, not outstanding, writers?

Poor Drubenheimer! Had he struggled that much?

Leaving the shelf behind, Rosalind moved closer to the desk which, standing in the middle of the room, marked the sacred centre of his creativity. She experienced—or rather liked the idea of experiencing—a kind of religious awe as she sat down on the narrow chair in front of it.

"This is where he wrote *Story*," she told herself three times, in a low voice, to hype the moment. "This is the place where *Seabound* was composed."

She felt next to nothing. Only a strange emptiness, as if nothing of any consequence had been written there. Was she too inept to sense these things? To re-envisage the conception of *Story* and *Seabound*?

Maybe her lack of emotions was also caused by the desk's surprising orderliness. No pens lay on its surface, no scrap papers, not a single sign of interrupted activity. Rosalind scrutinised the chest of drawers beneath the desk. Maybe this was where Drubenheimer had hidden objects that would evoke the magic of his creative process, for her?

She pulled open the top drawer, discovering piled up pens, pencils, a pencil sharpener, a hole puncher and a few sheets of lined paper, unused and empty. At least her author had been truly dedicated to SCASA ideals of tidiness—though artists were usually exempt from this.

The next drawer revealed the same *Anthology of Romantic Poetry* she had seen on Lisa's bookshelf; the one mentioned in the *Guardian*. It had been found on the studio floor. Why had she discovered it inside a drawer? Was this significant?

Rosalind gave the book an inquisitive look as if, as a prime witness, it would not only tell her how it had managed to wander into a drawer, but also what had happened to its beloved reader before his death. The volume remained inert in her hands. Given the circumstances of her search and her multiple crimes today, she decided to take it home for closer inspection.

She didn't steal the book without profoundly blushing, alone in the relative dark. What was happening to her? The floating sensation, again. A dizziness that seemed to spread from the top of her head all the way down to her feet. This time, it felt like a mixture of exhilaration and fear. Rosalind closed the second drawer and moved onto the last. Inside, an unused packet of tissues, a torch and a pair of gloves.

Where did Mark Drubenheimer hide his creativity?

She slid her hand into the drawer once more. Rosalind produced a large plastic folder. It was exceptionally light, yet she sensed the weight of its importance. At last! With solemn steps, imagining how she would remember this moment for the rest of her life, she walked towards the window and turned her discovery around in the hushed light. The label on the side revealed his name, Mark Drubenheimer. Then there was a title. *Accounts of a Muse*. Was this a lost novel? His third?

Rosalind felt unable to breathe. She just stood there, suspending everything else, staring at the object in her hands. Her body so tense it seemed to have turned into stone, she slowly opened the thick plastic in her hand.

There was, of course, nothing inside.

The copies of *Madame Bovary* and the *Anthology of Romantic Poetry* under her arm (she had reverently put the folder back into the drawer) Rosalind opened the door to her father's flat.

As soon as she stepped inside, she heard laughter from the kitchen. Othello and her father must have been back for some time. They appeared to be playing.

Craving a few moments to herself, Rosalind quietly walked into her room. She carefully placed the books on her desk. This space, with its stylish double bed and mirrored wardrobe, seemed strangely impersonal to her, as though it were a hotel. Her parents had re-furnished it when she left for university without consulting her, probably in the attempt to convey status and style to an imagined visitor. There had been something almost as anonymous about Drubenheimer's studio.

She looked out of the window. A growing darkness invaded the sky which made the street appear sinister, threatening. Within a few hours, Rosalind had put an end to her track record of good behaviour and committed several acts of transgression. Still, within these "fair creatures of hours", she had also made a significant discovery: *Accounts of a Muse*.

She let herself fall into her bed. She felt ashamed but mostly—a further reason, for guilt, perhaps—proud. Really, she might have made an amazing breakthrough! The folder raised so many questions! What had it contained? Another novel? What was it about? And why had it disappeared?

Her head sank into the pillow. There was another Drubenheimer novel out there, full of his wisdom and depth! The title evoked the muse statue she had seen at the cemetery during Drubenheimer's funeral. Surely the book would be about some fascinatingly beautiful woman who inspired the works of several timeless artists, making love to them in the backrooms of bohemian cafés...

Rosalind smiled, dreamily at first; then she stiffened. She would have to ask her father about this to find out more. A disproportionate sense of anxiety took hold of her. All of today's emotions and experiences welling up from inside.

She remained still, breathing in deeply until the waves of fear subsided. She would, first of all, call Gabriel to arrange a meeting with him. Afterwards, she would speak to her dad.

Her body duly reacted as if she had been thrown naked into ice-cold, sparkling water. Could she really ring him, just like that? Wouldn't he get the wrong idea and call her "sweet stalker" or simply "stalker" again?

Well she had no choice. Einstein. Reality. So trying to at least act determined, Rosalind reached for her old notebook (now abandoned for her beautiful new diary) and looked inside.

She came across the article she had written in the library a few days ago—only a few days had passed!—and rapidly scanned her own words. They seemed so alien to her now. She couldn't help thinking of Lisa and her claim that she had spent the tragic evening reading, oblivious to her friend dying next door. Maybe it was true. Rosalind had always tried to find a personal connection to Drubenheimer through his words, to dive into the dazzling depths of his soul. Nonetheless, when she had written these lines, she had been utterly unaware that her genius had already been dead at the time.

Rosalind opened the page containing Gabriel's number. Then, her throat tightening with nerves—and to the sound of Othello screaming merrily in the kitchen—she picked up her mobile phone and dialled it.

"Yes?" he answered instantly.

Rosalind started. She hadn't expected to hear his voice so soon.

"Gabriel?"

"That would be me," he said, cheerfully. "Who are you?"

"It's Rosalind," she announced, begging herself to be eloquent. "We met at the funeral and on the tube the other day."

"Ah, the one with the boyfriend and all that. How's everything?"

"Good," she murmured, embarrassed. "I'm just calling because you said we could meet sometime. You know, to talk about Mark Drubenheimer."

"Yes, about Drubenheimer," Gabriel repeated, his over-confident tone disturbing and at the same time pleasing her. "So when do you want to meet up? And where?"

"I know a nice café near Little Venice," she suggested, surprising herself. She used to go there with her mother after their bookshop visits sometimes.

"You mean that place with the smelly canal and lots of boats?"

Rosalind nodded, but realised the ineffectiveness of her movement. She murmured a shy "yes".

"What time do you want to meet?" she made herself speak on. "Maybe for a late breakfast? Or are you working?"

"I don't work mornings," Gabriel said. "And a nice little business breakfast sounds fine."

"Business?" Rosalind inquired, a little taken aback. Did he know she conducted a search?

"The business of getting to know you," Gabriel explained and she could hear the smirk in his voice. "The mysterious student from the Drubenheimer circle."

Rosalind didn't quite know what the last bit meant, nor did she particularly care.

"What time?" she asked him, instead. "Eleven?"

"Eleven, OK. But I only have until about twelve."

Should she suggest ten thirty instead? But wouldn't she come across as too keen? Pleased she had managed to have this conversation in the first place, she simply said goodbye and hung up.

She couldn't help smiling. Staying next to the phone, she raised her arms to the ceiling and breathed in deeply. After just one night's sleep, she would meet her most attractive suspect. And something in his voice had made her believe he wanted to meet her, too.

What an adventurous day! Rosalind started walking towards her room, longing to cuddle up in bed with *Madame Bovary*. While she was at it, she could also have a look at the anthology she had… removed. At the very least, she might discover what kind of reading united Drubenheimer and Lisa, and–

Of course, Drubenheimer and Lisa! She still had to ask her father a few questions about his connection to this woman and the mysterious folder she had unearthed.

She stopped, expecting anxiety to hit her again. But it didn't. She had rightly chosen to call Gabriel beforehand. It had given her strength and she now felt ready to face her dad.

Rosalind turned around and hurried into the kitchen. Her father and Othello were racing two toy cars on the floor. Instead of letting his little son win, Frank Waterloo bumped his Ferrari against the small kitchen table, laughing out loud at his victory. Then he noticed Rosalind and shook his head with mock annoyance.

"Our detective is back," he told Othello, who now listlessly moved his toy Porsche.

"Hello, you two," Rosalind said, in what she hoped was a friendly tone. Yet her father must have realised her slight disapproval, because he pointed out, getting up: "Usually, I let him win."

Rosalind smiled in reply, took a glass from one of the shiny cupboards and filled it with water.

"Dad!" She tried to sound as nonchalant as possible. "I met this woman who knows you today and–"

"Was she pretty?" her father interrupted, turning towards Othello and placing the Ferrari into the boy's outstretched hands.

"Well, so-so," Rosalind replied, immediately ashamed of her words. In the name of female solidarity, she shouldn't have provided this piece of information! "Her name's Lisa Croydon-Bay."

"Lisa Croydon-Bay? What kind of animal or car is that?" Her dad winked at Othello, but the boy had abandoned his cars in favour of a toy monster and was too engrossed in his play to laugh at his father's feeble joke. "To be honest, I have no idea who she is. Then again, I know so many women, it's hard to keep track. Oops, sorry, Rosy! Don't get jealous again!"

"But you must know her!" Rosalind's slightly raised voice derived from a need to defend Lisa and perhaps all of womankind. "She said you were one of the most important people in her life! She was at the funeral, that woman who…"

… she had compared to a sponge.

"The woman who, what?" her father asked, impatiently.

"Never mind," Rosalind mumbled. If her father knew Lisa, he would have recognised her at the funeral. So why was he so significant to her? Had she once met him at a party, perhaps, and been obsessed with him since? But hadn't she implied that she preferred women? None of this made any sense!

Rosalind looked at Othello now joy-riding the monster on the Ferrari.

"Anyway," she carried on, with a tone of resignation, somehow personally offended by her dad not remembering Lisa. "There's something else I wanted to ask you about."

"What a wonderful surprise, oh daughter! You seem to be full of questions!"

Mr. Waterloo's performance of cheerfulness seemed overdone these days. Rosalind breathed in deeply.

"Do you know if Drubenheimer worked on another novel before he died?"

Frank Waterloo's face barely moved at first. He had clearly not deducted the chain of events that lay behind Rosalind's inquiry.

When he finally opened his mouth to speak, he asked: "Is this going to help you find your 'murderer'?" and chuckled. Then, before Rosalind could react, he seemed to sober up again.

"Fine. Yes, he was working on something," he acknowledged. "Writers always write."

"Really?" Rosalind asked, excited. "But why didn't you tell me before?"

She already knew the answer to that.

"Don't worry," her father said. "I might have mentioned, if it had been any good. He never finished it! Never even started it properly."

What about her fantasy about a masterpiece replete with backrooms of bohemian cafés? The unspeakable pleasure of reading one more novel, of receiving one more message of hope from him?

Othello sent both toy monster and vehicle flying into the air. They bumped against one of the chrome cupboards and fell on to the floor.

"Stop it, Othello!" Mr. Waterloo snapped. He then turned back towards Rosalind. "He only mentioned the bare outline and showed me some not very advanced fragments, I'm afraid."

Rosalind gathered her strength.

"It wasn't, by any chance, about a muse?"

"A muse?" Mr. Waterloo seemed genuinely impressed. Rosalind felt a wave of happiness at this unexpected moment of paternal approval.

"You're not bad, after all, Sherlock," he granted. "It was about a muse. It was called *Accounts of a Muse*, or something like that."

"What was it supposed to be about?" Rosalind asked. Maybe all was not lost!

But her father shrugged and lifted Othello from the floor. He cleared his voice to indicate the conversation was almost over.

"I don't know," he said. "I'm afraid the project was ridiculous. Our dear Mark really had gone mad towards the end."

"Isn't this beautiful?" Berlina asked, handing a bottle of expensive whiskey to Frank Waterloo.

They sat on the dark roof-terrace that came with her flat, their bodies sensually positioned opposite each other, on a pile of gold, red, pink and purple cushions and rugs. Or at least Berlina's body was sensually positioned. Frank Waterloo felt uncomfortable. It was almost midnight; and terribly cold.

Berlina didn't seem to notice. Not even when he only grunted in reply.

"Have you seen the sky? Oh, Frank, isn't this a shooting star?"

She moved closer towards him and stared, cheerfully, into his eyes.

He turned away a little.

"It's an airplane," he grumbled.

"It's not an airplane," Berlina protested, even though they both knew that it was. "Come on, darling, make a wish. All the energies are aligned. I can feel it! Come on."

A wish! He wished he had brought a blanket. He wished they had met in a restaurant instead of, at Berlina's insistence, on this freezing roof. He wished he hadn't called her once Rosalind and Othello had gone to bed. He wished he could know what was wrong with him.

He looked around. There were hardly any stars, only clouds. One really needed Berlina's imagination to evoke a shooting star from this depressing scenery. He took a deep sip of the whiskey. It warmed him immediately, and he drank some more.

"Frank! Darling! Angel! Honey! Sweetie! Star agent of mine!" Berlina playfully kicked him in the shins to get his attention. "Don't you have a wish?"

She wore a short, tight red dress. She looked great. He imagined taking it off, later. He had been right to call her, after all.

"What's yours?" he finally asked.

"To live forever," she sang and giggled. "Or, in honour of that mass-murdering novel you mentioned the other day, should I say world peace?"

She stared into his eyes again, almost pleadingly this time.

"For you to tell me what on earth is wrong," she said, finally.

Frank Waterloo stared back at her. Nothing! Everything was fine. His star author was dead, but he was still an extremely successful agent. He had a mildly crazy but fabulous girlfriend. A beautiful home. Except for Rosalind's own, regular onsets of madness, he had two healthy children. Actually, he needed to revise that thought. Rosalind's strange "search" seems to be going surprisingly well—even though she wouldn't find anything important in the end, she was at least functionally unearthing information, like the fact that Drubenheimer had attempted another novel.

He cringed at the memory of the few pages he had seen of that work. Drubenheimer had appeared in his office one morning about two months ago, with a few fragments and Waterloo had to try very hard to conceal his shock. They had been so unsuitable; so untypical of his author. Promising to "work" on them, Drubenheimer had taken them with him, again, so his agent kept no record. Probably a blessing, given their complete lack of quality. But maybe he should have realised then quite how lost the man was?

"Nothing," he replied eventually and downed some more whiskey. This was exactly what he needed. "Absolutely nothing."

"You're not angry I insisted on meeting on my gorgeous roof, are you?" she asked.

She took the bottle from his hands and let her lips glide down the bottle's top and neck before drinking and giving it back. "Have some more," she seemed to say with her smile.

Frank Waterloo received it, gratefully. The drink seemed to work. He started to feel warmer. And calmer. He actually wanted to tell her what was going on with him.

"It's not that," he said. "Although it's bloody freezing. Something has been wrong with me since Drubenheimer died."

Berlina fluttered her eyelids, then stopped. She must have noticed that something more than her usual repertoire of charming movements was called for. She took his left hand and squeezed it.

"Tell me more," she pleaded. She sat up and evidently put herself into "active listening" mode; she smiled, encouragingly.

"Fine," Frank Waterloo agreed. He felt a little drunk already.

Then he told her. About his worry about money and the future. His occasional listlessness. About his mind drifting back into the past, as if he could fix things, with his imagination, alter his stories and their outcome somehow. Drubenheimer. He carefully mentioned his wife.

"I mean, I know good things come out of terrible events," he concluded fast. "Look at you sexy creature who emerged from my tragedy. But still. I suddenly wish things had been different. Oh, I don't know. Enough soul searching for me. Give me more whiskey!"

Berlina handed him the bottle and watched him drink. She let her left hand glide down his stomach muscles admiringly.

"This is awful," she sympathised. "But it is also wonderful!"

"What?" Frank Waterloo looked at her, with interest. Was she also drunk?

"Look, I'm not a therapist, but you know I'm a very sensitive woman. It looks like you are cleansing your chakras, at last! Hoovering and scrubbing your karmic record."

"I'm cleansing and hoovering what?"

"Fine, let me put it in more secular terms. You are on the path to self-connection, it seems. What you need now is to use your pain creatively! Maybe do an expressive writing course, that's a down-to-earth enough method, for people like you!"

Frank Waterloo smiled, despite himself. Chakras, karma, expressive writing and self-connection. No wonder he had been thinking like a self-help author recently, under Berlina's influence.

"Thanks for the advice," he said and kissed her on the cheek. Her delusions about the workings of life and death didn't annoy him. He found them endearing, somehow. "Have you been alright? About Drubenheimer, I mean?"

A dark shadow passed across Berlina's eyes. He waited, patiently, for an answer. He finished the bottle of whiskey. Even though he didn't really understand what she had talked about, he already felt better. Relieved.

"You know what I think. It has been terrible, for me. Shocking, exhausting and so on. But I think I have found a way to deal with it now." Here she smiled at him, again, seductively and Frank Waterloo started looking forward to what was to follow. "But as I said, my darling! Deal creatively with your pain!"

Chapter Ten

Rosalind waited on a chrome chair in the Little Venice café, blinking at a sky so cloudy and dense, it seemed about to come tumbling down. Muffled street sounds mixed with the music of a chirping bird or two. A breeze carried the mossy smell of the canal towards her. Luckily, it mingled with that of the coffee in front of her.

If she had thought that the shortness of their meeting would have motivated Gabriel to arrive on time, she had been deluded. For it got closer and closer to eleven thirty and there was still no sign of him.

Rosalind turned towards the water and its boats, drained of colour and joy by the lack of sunshine. Once—almost a year ago—she had come here with Mat, the only time they had gone to London together. They had been at the table next to the one she was sitting at now, struggling to find a topic to speak about.

Oh Mat! What should she do with him? Would he be furious she hadn't called him yet? But then again, he too owned a phone! Her neck muscles contracted.

And what about Gabriel? Was he simply late? Or would he not show up at all?

Gradually, as her cup became emptier, the clouds gave way to a tender sun, illuminating the few unused tables and chairs around her. Although the minutes kept passing, Rosalind tried not to worry and prepared some questions for their meeting instead.

At last, Gabriel's handsome figure cut through the empty midday street. He arrived at the table, sat down and smiled at her.

Rosalind automatically blushed and smiled back.

"Sorry, have you been waiting long?" he asked, still grinning. He was clearly convinced that his charm would wash away any potential resentment.

"Don't worry," Rosalind replied. She should probably be angry. Regrettably, she felt far too pleased to see him.

She watched in secret awe as he leaned back in his chair and waved the waiter towards him. If he had been slightly tense both in the tube and at the funeral, he now came across as boyish, relaxed and, with his washed-out jeans and T-shirt, quite shockingly unlike Mat who usually favoured more formal clothes.

The waiter came. Gabriel ordered a pint of beer and Rosalind another coffee. She could suggest asking for some food—after all they had agreed to meet for a "business breakfast," as he had called it. But by now, it was probably too late for that.

"Anyway," Gabriel said and winked at her. "I'll make up for the lost time. You'll just have to come to a party tonight."

Rosalind stared at him. There was a passage in *Seabound* where the mermaid declared one should never judge experience, for good things could come out of seemingly bad ones, and vice versa. Didn't this perfectly illustrate Drubenheimer's wisdom? Had an invitation to a party just emerged from his arriving so late?

"What kind of party?" Rosalind asked, unable to hide her excitement.

"Nothing special, really. Just a friend's bash in Angel. You might enjoy it, though. Well, you most probably will, since I'm going to be there too. And we have lots to talk about."

He winked a little strangely at the word "talk" and eagerly

reached for his pint as soon as the waiter had placed it before him. "Give me your notebook and I'll write down the address."

Feeling a strange thrill, Rosalind produced the new diary from her bag and handed it over to him. She studied his muscular arms as he scribbled it down. He was the first to enter the diary Berlina had virtually forced upon her (and which, almost despite herself, she felt very fond of already). This was a good sign!

Gabriel closed the beautiful book, handed it to her and leaned back in his chair, with an air of ultimate relaxation that seemed just a little forced. He took a deep breath, as if he was about to say something. Then he changed his mind and relaxed again, more genuinely this time.

"So, you have a boyfriend?" he finally asked. "What's his name?"

Rosalind took a sip from her coffee, delighted that Gabriel might—just might—be trying to find out how committed she was to another man. And although she never thought she would pronounce this name with true pleasure anymore, she now shyly mumbled: "Mat."

"Mat!" Gabriel cried out, making a show of being unimpressed, as if a man whose name took up only one syllable posed no real challenge for him. "And have you been together for long?"

Too long, Rosalind's mind suggested immediately.

"A while," she retorted, evasively. Then, to make up for the inappropriateness of her mind and to give poor Mat his due, she added, "We met at university. We were living in the same halls of residence, but he wasn't a literature student and he's now working at…"

Rosalind stopped talking. Had she sounded too keen? Too keen about Mat, or too keen about Gabriel? Then again, what was she thinking? Gabriel was a suspect. She didn't have to impress him, just find out more about him. She had to stop acting like some silly, infatuated teenager.

"So, Gabriel, who are you?" she blurted out. "I mean, what do you do?"

His eyes sparkled right at her again.

"I'm a waiter," he said.

"An actor-waiter? Or a writer-waiter?" Rosalind asked, eagerly. He must be an artist of some kind.

Gabriel coughed, very slightly.

"A waiter-waiter," he said, and for the first time he showed the slightest trace of insecurity. "I work in a pub."

"A pub!" Rosalind exclaimed, as though there were few things in this world she loved with more fervour.

"Yes, a pub."

This line of conversation had come to an end. Rosalind's mind started racing, looking for something, anything, that would keep them talking. Luckily, her mind produced an image of the baseball cap he had been wearing the day she saw him on the tube which read: "Fuerte Ventura—Surfing is my life".

"So, and, do you like surfing?" Rosalind inquired, tentatively. Not that this was particularly relevant to her search.

He looked at her, first pleasantly surprised; then, with deep suspicion.

"How do you know?" he asked. "You aren't going to reveal anything else to me?"

"What?" Rosalind asked.

Reveal anything else? What did he mean? Was he on drugs? She stared at his pupils. Instead of showing the contracted size of a user, they widened as her glance met his. Luckily, his suspicion subsided.

"Oh, I see," he said, and sighed, knowingly. "You're just making conversation, aren't you? Trying to chat me up? But how did you know I like surfing?"

Rosalind blushed very deeply.

"I only know because of the baseball cap you wore when I met you on the tube. It said 'Fuerte Ventura—Surfing is my life'," she explained in a somewhat exaggerated matter-of-fact tone. "And I'm not trying to–" she could not get herself to say "chat you up".

"Oh, I see. Yes," Gabriel replied, with re-established pleasure, imitating her tone almost precisely. Then he added, with one of his disturbing winks: "And, yes, PhD, I love surfing. I love it! Bloody expensive habit, though. But it's life as good as it gets."

He was passionate. Rosalind liked that.

She stared at him for a few moments, smiling dreamily. Gabriel smiled back.

Then, a sense of duty shook her back into action. She looked at her watch and—to her shock—discovered it was already ten to twelve. She really needed to get to the point.

"Well, although we've already talked about this," she began, hesitantly. "I couldn't help wondering why you only watched Drubenheimer's funeral from afar and–"

Gabriel's grin only became more challenging and more cheerful.

"I'm sorry, Miss Formal, have I broken some rule?" he asked.

"Well, no," she conceded. If only he could stop looking at her so charmingly! "But I just thought it was interesting and–"

No false explanation occurred to her; and the real one could obviously not be mentioned. So it would be best to confound her appealing listener by the number, not the meaning of her words.

"You see," she started to verbally bombard him, "I also spoke to other people related to Drubenheimer's life, to his best friend, Lisa Croydon-Bay, his editor, Berlina Marrowing, his wife, Alicia…"

Gabriel flinched ever so slightly at the mentioning of these names.

"Drubenheimer," he completed Rosalind speech, taking another sip from his beer.

"You know her?" Rosalind asked, surprised.

"Well, PhD, if she was his wife, I stood a good chance of getting her surname right," Gabriel said and Rosalind frowned, noticing her silliness. "I've probably never met her, but I know that she must be very happy now."

"Happy?"

Rosalind recalled her conversation with that dismal, unbalanced woman yesterday. Instead of being "happy", she had struck her as the embodiment of misery.

"Well, considering all the money she now gets!"

"Money?"

If Rosalind had felt silly before, she now regarded herself as downright stupid. How could she have been investigating a murder case without ever thinking about money, probably the prime cause of unnatural deaths in the world?

She could hear Mat laughing at her internally. Also, all eloquence had abandoned her. She could do no more, it seemed, than repeat Gabriel's words.

"Yes!" Gabriel said, with a smirk. "Drubenheimer must have earned quite a lot from his bestsellers, don't you think? Do you know if he left a will?"

"A will?" Rosalind asked. How could she not have thought about this earlier?

"Yes, a will," Gabriel repeated, a little impatiently. "You must know about this. You're a PhD student, right?" Gabriel hesitated for a second. "You do know about inheritance laws?"

More than a little embarrassed, Rosalind shook her head. "I'm a literature student," she said.

"Well, if there's a will," Gabriel pointed out, "I think the people named in it get everything. If there isn't, the spouse ends up with everything up to two hundred and fifty thousand quid. Not bad for Mrs. Drubenheimer, is it? If there's more, it's supposed to be divided between the children and the spouse."

"Are you a lawyer? As well as a waiter, I mean?" Rosalind asked, disturbed.

"No, everyone knows about this. I got this from the internet."

"Do you mean Mrs. Drubenheimer now gets all the, what are they called, royalties?" Rosalind asked. "I'm sorry, I don't know anything about these things. It's just not what I'm usually interested in."

She needed to talk to someone about this. Unfortunately—despite the Rosebud joke and journalist confusion—she still preferred to ask Berlina rather than questioning her father again.

"What? You're not usually interested in money?" Gabriel asked. "Well, I suppose you don't have to be interested in money, do you? It seems to be quite naturally interested in you."

The sun vanished, once more, behind shapeless clouds.

"I'm sorry I said that, PhD," Gabriel said. "It's not your fault. It's just money has always been rather tight in my... family. But, yes, I think Mrs. Drubenheimer gets all his royalties. Unless he did leave a will? Did he?"

"I don't know," Rosalind repeated, a little offended by his tone, but reassured by his immediate apology.

"And was his 'estate'," he pronounced the word strangely, as if it was the first time he used it in his life, "worth more than two hundred and fifty thousand quid?"

Rosalind stared back at him.

"You don't know, do you?" Gabriel asked.

"It doesn't really matter," Rosalind remarked, a little more defensively than she would have liked. "Because Drubenheimer had no children at all."

Gabriel pushed forward his lower lip.

"You know that for a fact?" he challenged her.

"Yes, I do," declared, remembering Drubenheimer's only interview, then cringing at the notion that much of its information had apparently been invented.

She sighed, nervously. Gabriel observed her for a moment, biting his full, sensuous lips. Once more, he breathed in, as if he was going to say something else, but he didn't. At last he just smiled strangely and said:

"Well, we'll have time to talk all about this," here he winked again, "tonight."

Rosalind didn't reply and tried very hard (and very unsuccessfully) not to have her stomach react blissfully to Gabriel's winks. Wasn't this interest in money very suspicious? Why did he care? If only he weren't so ridiculously attractive! She couldn't think clearly while she was near him. Then again, he was right. She would be able to find out more about this at the party. For the moment, she could simply do her pre-established duty and question him about his alibi.

The things this search made her do!

"You know," she began, awkwardly, deciding to exploit yesterday's inspiration. "I spoke to Drubenheimer's best friend yesterday and we talked about what we were feeling and doing the night he died. I asked if she'd had any premonitions, but she said she didn't at all. Nor did I! That's horrible, don't you think? That we're not connected enough to feel such things? Did you sense anything when Drubenheimer died? Where were you at the time? And what were you doing?"

What a speech! Rosalind was almost breathless by the end of it. How would he react? Would he get angry too, like Mrs. Drubenheimer? Or imply he had been busy having sex, like Berlina? She felt a stab of jealousy, and cursed her overactive imagination, while Gabriel looked bored by her questions.

"You aren't the supernatural type, are you?" he asked, a little warily. "The kind who goes to Stonehenge for blessings?"

"No," Rosalind said, vehemently shaking her head. "No, not at all. Why?"

"Oh good," Gabriel replied, his mood lightening up again. "Not that I would have minded that much. You'd probably look quite sweet chanting Hare Krishna. Anyway, that should answer your question. I don't do premonitions. I had no idea!"

Rosalind didn't quite understand how Stonehenge may relate to Hare Krishna, but she beamed inside at having been called "sweet" again, this time even without any reference to stalkers. Yet did he mean she would be sweet only if she chanted, or that she was sweet anyway? But enough! She needed to stay focused on her mission and, so far, his answer had not been particularly revealing. She would have to try again.

"What were you doing at the time?" she insisted, almost voicelessly.

"Working."

"At your pub?"

"No, as a call boy. Of course at 'my' pub. I only found out about his death when I read about it in the paper."

Rosalind nodded. She knew she should probably ask where the pub was and go there to verify his alibi. Still, she decided not to. It seemed enough for now that his alibi was actually verifiable.

"Why are you asking me all this?" Gabriel asked, a little suspiciously, again.

"Just making conversation," Rosalind replied, feeling just the tiniest bit proud of herself. For the first time, she began to feel like a detective, not one from the few crime novels she had read, but rather like one of those capable lady detectives occasionally seen on TV. Like Anette, she created her own story, now.

"And did you also read the poem in the newspaper?" she asked, keenly. "Drubenheimer's wonderful goodbye poem?"

"Yes."

"Isn't it amazing?" Rosalind insisted, convinced that he must be shy about his literary love.

"Thrilling," Gabriel replied and by now the sarcasm in his voice was difficult to deny.

"So you prefer his novels?" Rosalind asked, puzzled. "Which one is your favourite?"

Gabriel moved about in his seat and, to her disappointment, dropped a few coins onto the table for the waiter; their time was up.

"I don't know, I really have to go now, PhD," he said, smiling again. He got up and Rosalind accidentally had a good look at his very well-formed body. He noticed and added, before he turned to leave: "I haven't finished either. I found them quite dull, to be honest. Except for the mermaid sex scenes, of course."

The sun had just come out again. A foreign looking couple sat down on a table next to her, holding hands and shooting amorous glances at each other. An excited, sensual energy emanated from them. Rosalind shut her eyes to enjoy the sun's warmth on her face. Despite of some awkward moments and his strange interest in Drubenheimer's finances, she had enjoyed her meeting with Gabriel and couldn't wait to see him again at the party tonight. Naturally, she would have to be careful. For all she knew, he might be a terrible killer, the very person who had hurled Drubenheimer out of the window, tied to a robe. His relationship to the genius was clearly a little weird and she would have to find out more about that later on. Oh, handsome, handsome Gabriel!

So, what should she do now? Call Berlina and ask her about Drubenheimer's royalties and will? Did she have to do this straight away? Rosalind took a sip from her almost empty cup and eyed her new diary still lying on the table in front of her. No, her talk to Berlina could wait. She smiled and ordered another drink. It was time to write about herself, her world and her search, the way the editor had encouraged her to do.

By the time she had finished, almost two hours had passed. Rosalind felt wonderful, as though writing had relieved her of an inner weight she only really noticed now it was gone. Words had come easily to her. She had written about her morning in the university library; the news of Drubenheimer's death; Mat; her trip to London, her search. But strangely, her mind had then wandered off to her mother's death; her desolation. Her father. The wet-nurse. The tension that followed. She had splashed a lot of anger onto the page. Not her father's. Her own. A suffocating throat-rage that must have been hiding inside of her, waiting to get out. How good she felt!

It struck her as decadent that one could spend hours in such disconnected bliss. The experience made her think of a phenomenon she had once read about, this sense of completely losing track of time... Yes, it was called "Flow". Well, what a pleasant state to be in and–

How obvious one's subconscious could be. Flow Publishing! She had to ring Berlina and ask her about Drubenheimer's money. Had she not better ask her father, after all? She would probably have to put up with some silly joke again. And yet, after so much writing about him, she wanted to give herself and her father a rest, at least for a little while. The editor, then. Rosalind waved the waiter towards her and settled the bill.

She got the number online and dialled it on her mobile. The friendly receptionist whom she had caught reading a Subtlety edition of *Don Quixote* greeted her. Rosalind felt like chatting to the girl, but aware that this would be a little inappropriate, she merely asked for Berlina, whose voice finally resonated after brief exchange with her assistant.

"If you're an agent, press one. If you're a boyfriend, press two. If you're an author, hang up and stop procrastinating," she chirped, merrily.

"Berlina?" Rosalind asked a little bewildered by her greeting and the fact she didn't fit into any of the categories.

"Rosalind!" the editor screamed feigning surprise, then added, as if she had just read her thoughts: "I'll have to invent another option for you. Agents' daughters, press four. I could also put you in the boyfriends' daughters section, of course. How have you been? Have you found your murderer? Why haven't you called me? You never even told me how your little talk with Alicia Drubenheimer went!"

Rosalind's mind became flooded with embarrassing memories of having to take photographs of the posing lady on her mobile phone.

"Quite well," she lied. She wanted to ask Berlina if she had deliberately caused this misunderstanding, but she didn't dare.

"How wonderful, my gorgeous," Berlina said, then lowered her voice and added with acted seriousness: "Is she wondering when your piece will be published?"

She broke into giggles. Rosalind didn't reply. So it had been Berlina's fault. Why did she even call this woman? Her throat started closing in anger. Strangely—perhaps because of all the writing she had just done—she didn't feel the need to push it away. She called her for Drubenheimer's sake. Because of his death and—she suddenly noticed—the added importance of proving to the world that he had not been a fake.

"Oh, you aren't angry about this, are you?" Berlina asked. "You do realise this was the only way she would accept speaking to you? It was only when I told her you were a journalist that she was willing to have this talk. You should thank me, my lovely, you know."

"Thank you," Rosalind pronounced, grudgingly—only to be able to ask her next question. Still, the oppression in her chest lifted a little. "Did Drubenheimer leave a will?" she burst out.

"Did you just ask me if Drubenheimer left a will?" Berlina asked and added, with theatrical pity, "Doesn't your father tell you anything? Maybe you should consider family therapy, you know! Or use one of my methods. We can have a spirit session about this, my gorgeous, you just say the word! Remember I have the most extraordinary gifts. In any case, did our dear Mark leave a will? The answer is no. Isn't that sad?"

"Well, not for Mrs. Drubenheimer," Rosalind emphasised, remembering Gabriel's words. "Because she gets all of his estate up to two hundred and fifty thousand pounds."

If she had looked stupid in front of Gabriel, she now felt terribly proud of having become so informed, thanks to him.

"Oh, somebody has been on the internet," Berlina said, laughing, her tone more maternal than dismissive this time. "You're a very thorough investigator. Let me take note of that. And guess what? I suppose Alicia Drubenheimer does get his royalties now. As far as any of us know, Mark didn't leave any children. But, given your particular 'research interests' at the moment, I hope you don't mean to imply that our poor Alicia would have murdered him for that?" Berlina giggled again. Before Rosalind could say anything else, she declared, "My darling, she comes from a very rich family. I'm sure she would never kill anyone for money. Other, of course, than herself."

Rosalind felt overwhelmed. She had spent the past hour lying in the bathtub of the St. John's Wood flat, desperately waiting for the warm water to have its soothing effect on her. It didn't work.

Sentences of past conversations flew rapidly and in no apparent order across her mind. Pictures of Berlina, Lisa, Mrs. Drubenheimer, Gabriel. The mentioning of money and a will had made her feel completely out of her depth.

She sank into the tub until a thick, transparent layer of liquid covered her head. Something else bothered her—something about Mrs. Drubenheimer's words, the whole idea that Mark Drubenheimer was a fake. She hoped that the lady would be proven wrong, eventually. Yet she wasn't sure how she could contribute to that.

An image of her mother came to her, with unusual clarity. She stood in their kitchen, her black hair tied into a complicated plait, wearing a dark, elegant maternity dress, Othello pressing against the expensive fabric from inside the womb. It was a memory of the last time Rosalind had seen her.

How strange! She had asked everybody about premonitions over these past few days. But somehow the search had almost made her forget about her mother, for a while. They had drunk their last coffee—an important ritual for an Italian mother despite her pregnancy—together that afternoon, before Rosalind had to leave for university again. Had she felt anything different at all? Had she known her mother would soon be—forever—gone?

No. There had been nothing sublime in their emotions; their conversation. In fact, Rosalind had been in a rush to get back. About a month later—they had spoken on the phone once or twice, but barely beyond the interchange of "hello" and "how are you"—she had received her father's call. "Rosy, I'm afraid something terrible happened." And that was that.

Tears would have started rolling down her cheeks, if she hadn't been covered by so much water, already. Now they mixed with the bathwater, imperceptibly. She had felt so helpless then, and was starting to feel so disoriented, again, now. Maybe it was time to give up on her search and go home.

Rosalind's head shot out of the water. No, no, no! Going home meant going back to the library and going back to Mat and going to the cinema with Mat and having him call her Rosalinda during his moments of passion and… it was simply impossible.

Her tears had been frightened away. She looked at herself in the mirror on the ceiling, and through the vapour she could make out the contours of her skinny body. Oh, what was she to do then? Regarding just about anything?

Very slowly, Rosalind got out of the bath and wrapped herself in a towel. Although the image of her mother remained at the back of her mind, her head felt a little clearer. At least clear enough to decide on the following course of action:

a) She would go to the party.

b) If worse came to worst, she could always ask Berlina for her esoteric help if she didn't know how else to continue her search.

Impressed with this sudden, rather uncharacteristically structured approach to her future, Rosalind slipped into a pair of jeans and black top she had prepared for the evening. She put on some make-up: red lipstick and black eyeshadow, she didn't own much more. She would stay in London. She would find Drubenheimer's murderer. She owed this to him.

Rosalind, separated from the world by a cab's dirty window, was intent on the putting point a) of her plan (going to the party) into action. Glancing at the darkening city outside, she could see no moon or starlight, only the twinkling colour show of advertisements, announcing products and plays. Night wanderers sprinkled the streets. She could hear their laughter; their drunken singing; she could feel their "electric joy".

Or was it her own? The Gabriel buzz in her body. A tension in her forehead she experienced only when reading novels full of suspense. Something pleasurable that drove her on. Anticipation. Infatu-. Guilt! She had a boyfriend, after all.

The cab entered Angel. A few moments later, she already stood outside a miniature sized house, ringing the bell, feeling a mixture of terror and delight.

The tiny door opened and a girl in a cut T-shirt that barely covered her chest appeared. Rosalind squinted at the garland of flowers loosely attached to her hair.

"Who the hell are you?" the girl snapped.

"I'm Rosalind," she introduced herself, bravely, although intimidated both by the young woman's decoration and tone.

"Did I invite you?"

Rosalind was tempted to say "no" and leave, very fast. But having made it thus far, she might as well ignore all hesitations and utter the one phrase that might take care of the rest.

"You see," she replied, looking up from the floor for only a few tentative seconds. "Gabriel said I should come."

She had to admit, it felt rather delicious to put it that way, "Gabriel said… ", as if they were old acquaintances, former lovers even, and she had been invited to join him and catch up on old times. In addition, it worked, for the girl's stare, though alcohol-glazed, became a little friendlier.

"Why didn't you dress according to the theme?" she inquired.

"There's a theme?" Rosalind asked, genuinely puzzled. Were parties with themes the thing to do these days?

"Obviously," the girl blurted out, proudly pointing at what remained of her T-shirt and stepping aside to let Rosalind in. "It's prehistory. Cave men and cave women. Hunters and gatherers. I suppose you must be Gabriel's new girl."

She pronounced the last sentence with the complacency of a woman who had already tasted all the forbidden fruits of life. They arrived in a darkened living room and the girl vanished among the dancing crowd.

About thirty half-naked people shook their painted limbs to the rhythm of drums. Some of the men carried spears and jumped around in a circle; some women had brought little baskets which they tried to balance on their heads while moving their hips. Rosalind flinched a little at the overwhelming—not strictly pre-historical—smell of wine and beer. She couldn't help feeling absolutely delighted at the fact she had been called "Gabriel's new girl".

In an attempt not to be trampled down by the heaving bodies, she walked towards the nearest wall, displaying improvised cow designs. Was this a new fashion she knew nothing about? Was it all wrong, socially speaking, to read classics all the time rather than to throw theme parties and paint cow designs onto one's walls? And, quite apart from all that, where among these samples of homo erectus would she possibly find Gabriel?

She felt a touch on her shoulder and turned around. He stood right behind her, wearing a short skirt made out of rushes, and beaming. He wore a painted bull on his forehead and the affectionate glare in his eyes made it clear that he—like the girl at the door—had already consumed a few pints.

"Rosalind!" he shouted and put a hand around her waist, at which she instantly blushed. He acted as if they had known each other for a long time. She liked that.

"Hello, Gabriel," she almost whispered, trying to hide quite how happy she was by toning down the volume of her voice.

"Do you want some beer?" he asked, unfortunately removing his hand from her waist.

Rosalind nodded and watched with some—not unpleasant— confusion as Gabriel shook his rushes and entered the still heaving crowd. Within minutes, he was back again, holding two bottles. Inside of each, a lemon danced sensually.

"Let's sit down, my sweet stalker," Gabriel suggested.

She ignored the resurgence of the stalker motive because of the recent addition of "my" to the "sweet". They walked together to a corner of the room and sat down next to each other on the floor.

What should she say? Really, she had to ask him more questions relevant to her search, because this was why she was here, very close to him in a space so crammed and crowded she didn't even dare to inhale.

Gabriel touched her on the forehead, right between her brows, interrupting her slightly unfocused reflections.

"Stop thinking all the time, academic! Do you want me to paint something on to your face? A dinosaur or a cave? Imagine a cave painting of a cave!" he babbled, laughing.

Rosalind blushed again, but struggled to ignore it.

"That would be meta cave painting," she commented.

"Yes," Gabriel replied, not understanding a word but lowering his finger and now pushing his beer bottle against hers. "Cheers."

"Cheers!"

Rosalind allowed herself to observe him for three seconds. The alcohol had softened his features and slightly curled up his lips. He looked less attractive, more vulnerable than in the café. She scrutinised her own feelings for a hint of rejection; but, really, she found only tenderness inspired by this change. He seemed more open and childlike when he was drunk.

"So," he said, slapping her upper thigh. "How's everything? Have you found out about the will?"

"Fine," she answered. She couldn't help feeling taken aback. "I did ask about it, actually."

"Really?" He leaned more closely towards her, his eyes sparkling, and smiled. "And?"

"There's no will," Rosalind pointed out, calmly. "And you were right. Mrs. Drubenheimer gets everything."

He slightly pushed forward his (lovely) lower lip.

"That's not fair," he complained.

Rosalind tore her stare from his mouth and took a deep breath, preparing herself to fully embrace her internal search-mode again. She downed her beer, to gather some strength.

"It seems quite fair to me," she said, even though this didn't sound very convincing, even to herself. She remembered again the harsh words Mrs. Drubenheimer had employed about her husband. "After all, he had no children."

"If you say so," Gabriel retorted, still in a somewhat child-like, sulky manner. He glanced nervously at Rosalind's empty bottle and gulped down the remains of his, too. Then he got up and announced: "Let me grab some more beer."

Watching him walk away, Rosalind knew that her mind should be racing. Above all, she should ask herself why Gabriel cared so much about Drubenheimer's money. But her thinking had slowed down through the beer and her helpless attraction to the caveman who was already moving unsteadily back towards her again.

He let himself sink down by her side. He stared at his drink, his forehead furrowed. He took a few sips and glared at his beer some more.

"Would you trust someone who told you strange things, simply like that?" he suddenly asked.

"Are you taking about me?" Rosalind inquired, worried.

"No, no, no," Gabriel cried out, laughing and looking at her almost tenderly. "You say strange things, too. But in a nicer way. And then you know the whole Drubenheimer crowd. You must know something!"

What was he talking about?

Rosalind looked at him, a little lost. She shot a glance at

the people dancing nearby, wildly and seemingly ecstatic. She suddenly wished she were one of them.

Gabriel downed his beer, breathing agitatedly—which Rosalind found pleasantly disturbing.

"So can I trust you?" he finally asked.

"Yes," Rosalind assured him. "Of course you can trust me."

Adrenaline shot through her body. He wouldn't confess to murder, would he?

"You see, I should get some of his estate," he said, evidently more familiar with the word "estate" by now. He paused, staring intently at her. "Given that I'm Mark Drubenheimer's son."

Rosalind's eyes rested on Gabriel's face where, for a moment, she perceived no distinct features but only colours and an overall shape. Then she recovered from her onset of myopia and laughed. Drubenheimer's son?

"That's very funny," she said out loud.

"I don't find it all that funny," Gabriel replied, almost soberly, now.

Rosalind's hand hugged her beer bottle tightly.

"You can't be serious," she almost begged, Mrs. Drubenheimer's words about her husband being a fake again echoing in her mind. "I know for a fact that Drubenheimer had no children."

"You know for a fact, do you?" Gabriel asked, with a slight tone of annoyance directed at the entire subject rather than at her. "That's because Mr. Great Author apparently did just about everything to make people think that. But believe it or not, about a week ago this strange woman appeared at the pub where I work and asked if she could have a word with me. I'd never seen her before but she knew my name and everything. It was like in that song, 'Killing me Softly'. And she told me there was a secret I might want to hear more about."

"But this is…" Rosalind began. She didn't know what to say.

"Well yes," Gabriel went on. "I know it's mad. She told me my parents weren't my real parents and that I'm the son of 'famous and rather dubious writer'—as she put it—Mark Drubenheimer. I asked her to leave the pub, but she just talked on and on, told me that I grew up in the Midlands…"

"Which is true?" Rosalind asked, very quietly. The entire pre-historical crowd had disappeared.

"Which is true," Gabriel confirmed, almost as silently. "And apparently we moved there to hide the whole thing. She said my mum was Drubenheimer's sister and that she had taken me on as a favour to her brother, and so on."

"My god, Gabriel!" Rosalind exclaimed, shaking her head. No wonder she had found him so attractive! But could this really be true? What did this mean? "What did your mother, or aunt say?"

"My mother's dead," Gabriel pronounced, heavily. "So she didn't say anything. But I spoke to my dad, who lives in Coventry. My poor, exhausted old man! He became all evasive at first but since then we've had several phone calls and it turns out that yes, they took me away when I was a few days old. Apparently, he had been meaning to tell me all along and the right moment just never presented itself."

"And so who's your real mother?" Rosalind asked, more shaken than intrigued.

Gabriel started rummaging around in his jeans pocket. Then he once again leaned very closely towards her and held out a small business card which she immediately recognised.

Lisa Croydon-Bay, it read. *Private Lessons in French.*

Chapter Eleven

Wearing only a pair of designer boxers, Frank Waterloo walked into his kitchen to prepare himself some breakfast. The window had been left open and cool morning air streamed in, like a tentative caress.

He opened several chrome cupboards reflecting the sunlight to take out coffee, cereals, a spoon. He watched as the machine spat out the caffeine he needed. He put the cereals into a bowl, produced some milk from the fridge and generously poured it in.

One of his neighbours' children practiced out of tune scales on the violin. A man walked past the window, talking to himself or into a phone. Rosalind and Othello were fast asleep. Apparently, she had gone to a party yesterday; he had heard her get home late. Good! Maybe she was, at last, living a little.

He felt sad he knew so little about her days. Although they were father and daughter, they seemed to exist in separate worlds, each lost in their private struggles, concerns. He had basically been absent from the world since the night on the roof. He should have gone easy on that whiskey. After making love to Berlina, he had actually thrown up in her bathroom, twice, like a teenager who couldn't hold his drink. He had been so hungover yesterday, he hadn't even been able to do any work. Out of character, he had slept and slept. Attended Othello, then slept some more.

Frank Waterloo gulped down his coffee, then poured himself a large glass of water. He opened another cupboard, took out an Alka-Seltzer, threw it into the water and watched it dissolve. His body still resented the excess of alcohol, it seemed. Still, overall, he felt a lot better; more enthusiastic and energised. Some of Berlina's words had stayed with him. Especially the idea that he should use his "pain"—as she had called it—"creatively". She was right! He was Frank Waterloo, after all! All he needed was to think outside of the box and find a solution to his key concern.

There was a noise. He heard Othello hopping across the corridor. He couldn't face the boy yet.

Frank Waterloo quickly sat down at the small kitchen table and started to eat his cereals. Othello passed by the kitchen and moved towards Rosalind's room, then back again, singing "Twinkle, twinkle, monster puke" and giggling.

Frank Waterloo momentarily shut his eyes with relief. Hopefully, he would wake Rosalind first and she would look after him.

What then should he do? How could he follow the advice of his gorgeous muse?

Muse. Wait. Muse. This reminded him of something.

That was it!

This was simply brilliant! He was simply brilliant!

Othello jumped noisily into the kitchen. Frank Waterloo ignored him. He reached for a napkin and a pen on the table.

Accounts of a Muse, he scribbled, enthusiastically. *Make ghostwriter produce a last Drubenheimer novel.*

"Daaaad!" Othello screamed, cheerfully. "Watch me, Dad!"

He attempted something like a somersault, then fell onto the floor.

"Excellent, Othello!" he finally reacted. He was in control, again. "Your rap moves are getting increasingly professional."

He gave the little boy an exuberant hug. He wasn't sure this new project was entirely legal. He didn't really care. Luckily, Mark had no off-spring. All he had to do was check with Mrs. Drubenheimer, ask her to be discreet and find the right ghost-writer for the job. Soon, the world would be his oyster—which he, with someone else's pen, would open—once more!

Late morning light made its way through the blinds, projecting lines of shadows onto Rosalind's body. Someone played the violin nearby, disharmoniously and she had the indistinct feeling that this sound had accompanied her for a long time, during her sleep. She turned around in bed and, without opening her eyes, pulled the duvet over her head.

Although she remained physically still, her mind instantly jumped back to last night's revelation. Gabriel was Drubenheimer's son. What was more, he was the child of Drubenheimer and Lisa "the bitch" Croydon-Bay. Lisa had complained about Mrs. Drubenheimer's jealousy, had emphasised that she and Mark had always been "very good friends, but no more than that". Ha! And now it turned out they even had a child together. How callously Lisa had lied to her! It served her right that Rosalind had stolen that key.

Although Rosalind found this difficult to admit, Drubenheimer himself also had dramatically manipulated the truth. What about the statement in his interview? All this talk about having no children because he couldn't possibly share the passion he had for his wife?

By now, it had become rather hot under the duvet and Rosalind's reddened head emerged gasping from underneath.

Had Mark Drubenheimer really been a fake, then, a liar? And was she and her search in some way responsible for uncovering all this?

No! Yes. No.

Well, evidently, a little.

Rosalind felt like crying at this realisation. A pang of self-doubt spread across her shoulders, her face, her chest. Her body could perform the dance of Rosalind's lack of belief in herself almost perfectly; a complex choreography of muscle weakness and tension.

Then again, shouldn't she give herself a little more credit? She had discovered *Accounts of a Muse*—if not the actual manuscript, at least its existence! She had learned the truth about Gabriel. It seemed unlikely now, but maybe her search would still end up vindicating Drubenheimer, proving his immense human worth. She needed to carry on with her investigation. What if, for instance, Mrs. Drubenheimer had called her husband a fake because of Gabriel and this was why she had murdered him?

Rosalind climbed out of bed and slipped into her dressing gown. Were her father and Othello around to see her, sleeping in so late, running about in her dressing gown? But she had vaguely registered Othello singing something to the melody of Twinkle, twinkle, little star. Then she had heard them leaving.

She looked at her watch. It was past eleven o'clock. This must have been more than two hours ago! Soon, she would have to call Lisa and arrange another meeting with her, to discuss what she had discovered. The mere idea terrified her. What if Lisa had meanwhile noticed her "crime" of stealing that key and had simply not called the police due to the supposed importance of

Rosalind's father in her life? Well, she would have to call her anyway. But for the moment, she would simply read a classic and relax.

The library emanated a beautiful late morning atmosphere, as if the sunlight falling into room had become music. It was a melody the ear couldn't quite distinguish, yet the body could perceive in the form of a gentle gratitude and joy.

Rosalind had come here on the first day of her search and gone through *Mrs. Dalloway*. She had considered re-reading *The Betrothed* by Manzoni but discarded it, then. Maybe the moment to browse through it had come? She had neither looked at *Madame Bovary*, nor at the *Anthology of Romantic Poetry* from Drubenheimer's studio yet. She associated both with her search and wanted some rest. So Manzoni it would be.

She pulled out the Subtlety edition, walked to her father's chair and sat down, entranced by the book's beautiful cover. It showed the silhouette of a young couple holding hands. Behind them laid a glorious Mediterranean landscape and, almost invisible, merging with the clouds and the hills, a woman with abundant blonde hair seemed to be winking at the reader. Even though Rosalind didn't quite understand what this picture was meant to portray, she found it comforting and appealing. She opened the book at a random page and began to read:

The moment of first awaking after a misfortune, while still in perplexity, is a bitter one. The mind scarcely restored to consciousness, returns to the habitual idea of former tranquillity: but the thought of the new state of things soon presents itself with rude abruptness; and our misfortune is most trying in this moment of contrast.

Rosalind could relate to this. Wasn't this the kind of stupor she had experienced after her mother's and Drubenheimer's death? Waking up to the knowledge of a broken world?

Her stomach tightened. How lonely she had felt. How she had longed for someone to catch her once her mother was gone. Soon, there was Mat and she had to thank him for that. But he had caught her imperfectly. She would have really needed—her father. The only one who could have understood. He had lost his mother too, although to a different country, not another dimension—if there was such a thing. He had lost his wife. They had lost their Eleonora with her dark hair and her very long, Italian eyelashes, her cool personality, her elegant body. Rosalind had dreamed of her dad holding her; drying her tears. Telling her how strong she was; how much—this might have been pushing things—he loved her. Except he had been busy kissing the wet-nurse, instead.

Had he longed to be caught, imperfectly, too? Had she really been too immature to comprehend this and to ungrudgingly take care of herself?

She bit into her upper lip and started scratching it with her teeth. The novel didn't sufficiently distract her. She forced herself to return to Manzoni and read:

Renzo set off with the light step of a man of twenty, who was on that day to espouse her whom he loved. He had in early youth been deprived of his parents, and carried on the trade of silk-weaver, hereditary, so to say, in his family.

Did the classics deliberately try to make fun of her? Was it possible that she now came across a man who—just like Gabriel—"had in early youth been deprived of his parents"?

What next? Had his father been a writer and his mother a so-called "bitch"? Was Lisa a bitch? Rosalind had liked her in so many ways, found her more approachable, more real than Mrs. Drubenheimer and Berlina and–

Was there no remedy against a restless mind? She would give the book another chance to have nothing whatsoever to do with her search and her life. Maybe she should look for a female protagonist. Most of them, especially if they were grand heroines, were bound to be quite unlike her.

She came across a passage with a few women and scanned it quickly. Unluckily, instead of presenting some marvellous opportunity for identifying away from herself, the female protagonist, Renzo's fiancée Lucia, seemed even more "immature" than Frank Waterloo considered her to be, and overly catholic into the bargain. Lucia was feeble and almost completely eclipsed by her mother Agnese:

Though no longer young, Agnese was a woman of lasting beauty and charm. They said she had special talents and gifts. People often wondered, on seeing her walk through the streets, if the young husband-to-be would not have preferred the overflowing hair, the sparkling eyes of the mother to the rustic attractions of the girl, who now— the very moment before the wedding—seemed to have doubts herself but barely dared to voice them.

"Now I will tell you all," said Lucia, as she dried her eyes with her apron.

"Speak, speak!—Speak, speak!" at once cried both mother and lover.

"Most Holy Virgin!" exclaimed Lucia. "Who could have believed it would have come to this!"

Rosalind rolled her eyes to the ceiling. "Most Holy Virgin", she repeated and dropped the book on the floor. No, this wouldn't do as a diversion strategy. This definitely wouldn't do.

She got up very, very slowly. Then she walked to the phone and even more slowly dialled Lisa's number to organise a meeting with her. Maybe her father's recent idea of this languid Sicilian mode hadn't been so bad after all.

A little more than an hour later, Rosalind stood by the Thames, waiting for Lisa who had agreed to meet her straight away. In fact, the woman had been so kind to her on the phone that Rosalind safely concluded she hadn't noticed the absence of her keys. Also, Lisa's reaction had made it difficult to imagine her guilty of anything other than too much concern.

Afternoon heat radiated from her neck through her entire body; a tang of algae hung in the air and reminded her of Mediterranean beaches she had visited as a child.

Rosalind turned away from the river. Next to her were the usual rows of second-hand book stalls, outside the National Film Theatre. A young couple leaned over an ancient hardcover book, holding it into the sun to gain a better view. Both smiled. Then, without the slightest intention of buying it, they put the volume back and—the girl chasing the boy—ran away.

How lovely! A couple who was interested in books, in reading! Neither Mat nor Gabriel seemed likely to ever be converted into ardent bookworms. She had been very mistaken there with regard to Gabriel. Still, wasn't it worth more that he had Drubenheimer's genes? And, apart from being mysteriously handsome, hadn't he touched her waist, stared into her eyes and thought her worthy of such personal and secret confessions? Also, differently from Mat, who didn't love anything other than his job (and her, of course, thrice!), Gabriel adored surfing. Maybe he would teach her, one day. She could picture them in Italy both half naked, gliding up and down waves in the sunlight.

Rosalind resolutely strode towards one of the stands and picked up the book the couple had been looking at. To her surprise, it was a very old edition of *Crime and Punishment*, the novel she had flicked through in honour of her mother, the day Drubenheimer had died. She was about to open it and read again the first page, when Lisa came running towards her.

"Rosalind," Drubenheimer's friend uttered when she reached her, out of breath. "I'm so sorry I'm late." She glanced at the object in Rosalind's hands. "What book is it?"

"*Crime and Punishment.*"

"Oh, I do love that novel!" Lisa said enthusiastically. "I think it's one of the best books ever written!"

"It's wonderful," Rosalind agreed and added, feeling a little bit like a lady detective in a film again (because she was sure lady detectives said such things, every so often), "Why don't we walk?"

She pointed at the path along the Thames that would lead them towards the Tate Modern and the Globe Theatre.

"Alright." Lisa smiled warmly. "I like strolling along the river."

They started moving slowly, the rhythms of their steps synchronised.

"So, how are you?" Rosalind asked, more than a little awkwardly. How could she possibly introduce the topic of Gabriel?

"Fine," Lisa replied. "A bit stressed, to be honest, because I'm moving out. I suppose that's why I could meet you so quickly, though. I was dying to get a break from it all!"

"You're moving out?" Rosalind repeated, mainly to keep the conversation going.

"Yes, it's about time, really," Lisa explained. "Campden Hill Court is great, but it's just so expensive."

Rosalind nodded and observed Lisa a little more closely. A sunray brightened her face, making her look prettier, livelier and a little more suspicious than usual. Gabriel was right; Rosalind hadn't paid enough attention to money. How could she not have realised that a big flat in Kensington would be far beyond a private French teacher's budget? Had she inherited some money? Or was she secretly involved in some criminal activities that might be related to Drubenheimer's death?

Rosalind's face must have taken on such a tense expression, that Lisa asked, disconcerted:

"Are you OK, Rosalind? You seem a bit worried. Why don't you tell me what you really wanted to talk about?"

Rosalind should be grateful, really, that Lisa had given her a cue to bring up the difficult topic. Yet her heart started thumping in terror and she had to tell herself four times to ignore all hesitations, before she managed to say, "I wanted to talk to you about a discovery I made yesterday."

"Really? What discovery?" Lisa asked.

"Well," Rosalind said. "I found out Mark Drubenheimer had a secret son. And I was told that you were his mother!"

The woman stopped. "I'm sorry?"

Lisa narrowed her eyes and stared at her in what Rosalind interpreted as a sign of complete miscomprehension and surprise. Rosalind felt immediately taken aback. Not so much with Lisa, as with herself and Gabriel. What if it wasn't true? What if Gabriel had lied to make himself more interesting? Or because he was a crazy fan and murderer after all, who had picked up Lisa's card at the funeral and used it to invent the whole story? Wasn't it possible—plausible even—that Rosalind had fallen for it because she wanted so much to believe that some part of Drubenheimer was alive?

"Maybe this is all wrong," Rosalind murmured. "Please forget all about it."

But in the meantime, something inside of Lisa had changed. Her eyes rested on Rosalind with a mixture of gratefulness and fear. The tension in her face revealed that her thoughts were racing, as if some obsessive question pulsated behind her forehead and cheeks. She looked very pale; she took a breath as though she was about so say something, yet clearly failed to speak.

"Oh, I can't," Drubenheimer's friend finally managed to whisper.

Then, before a rather startled Rosalind, Lisa turned around and staggered towards a stretch of lawn behind them. She let herself fall onto the ground and, without any further preliminaries, burst into tears.

Every so often, Lisa made an obvious effort to calm down; but it was too early and she just kept crying on and on. Whatever flowed out of her must have been held back for years.

Upset by what she had unleashed, Rosalind hurried after her as soon as she had recovered from the initial shock. She sat down next to Lisa on the lawn and hesitantly put an arm around her shoulder.

"It's alright," Rosalind comforted her, pressing a handkerchief into her palm, as yet unable to reflect on what all those tears might mean. "You're going to be fine."

"Oh, Rosalind," Lisa eventually announced, still sobbing so much she could hardly understand a word. "You found out the truth."

"You and Drubenheimer really had a son together?" Rosalind asked, very carefully removing her arm.

Lisa nodded and started crying again. Then she stopped.

"Yes, we did. Do," she conceded, with a steadier voice now, as though she had already started achieving some sort of catharsis.

"But didn't you say that Drubenheimer and you had only been friends?"

"And that's also true," Lisa declared, to Rosalind's utter confusion. "Very, very good friends. Which is probably why I shouldn't be telling you this. But then, I have been hiding all of this for so long, I cannot put up with it anymore."

She looked at Rosalind in an almost childlike manner, as if asking her for reassurance; as if begging her for permission to reveal everything and heal some old pain.

Rosalind smiled, awkwardly and—she hoped—encouragingly.

Lisa fell silent for a moment, in an attempt to focus and order her mind. Then she took a deep breath, relief streaming from her eyes.

"I mean, when we conceived Gabriel, Mark and Alicia were already married," Lisa confessed. "And yet—oh, it's such a long story. Do you have time? Do you want to hear it? We hardly know each other, but I trust you somehow. I have this strange feeling that the time has come, perhaps now that Mark is dead, to speak about everything. Wait, I have a million questions! Who told you? How did you find out?"

"Through Gabriel," Rosalind admitted and could tell from the peculiar warmth in her face that she blushed again. "Your son. I met him the other day and... well, it's a very long story, too. He claimed that someone came to his pub shortly before Drubenheimer died and told him the truth."

"I know his name," Lisa exclaimed, guiltily. "Whenever I

got the chance—or rather, every so often—I tried to find out something about him. But who told him?"

"I don't know," Rosalind said. "Gabriel said that it was some woman and–"

"A woman? Wait, you met Gabriel!" Lisa inadvertently slapped her left thigh, the way she had done once during their first meeting. "This is just so, so confusing."

She stared up at Rosalind in almost unbearable bewilderment, as if a wave had crashed on top of her and she was struggling for air and for light.

With an effort to compose herself and to remain calm, Lisa went on, "Maybe Mark wanted to let Gabriel know before he died? And hired some woman to break the news? It could have been anyone, I'm sure he desperately wanted to clear his conscience. So how did you meet Gabriel?"

"I also met him because of my PhD," Rosalind revealed and couldn't help adding proudly, "We get on rather well."

Lisa nodded and seemed to understand.

"Oh, this is just madness. But then again," the woman said, in a confidential tone, about to embark on a lengthy speech. "Ever since you came to my flat the other day and told me you're Frank Waterloo's daughter, I knew you had come into my life for a reason. I believe in things like this, you know? Life seems awful sometimes, but then—all of a sudden—you realise some beauty can emerge even from your former pain. Anyway, let me try to explain. I'm just afraid I'm going to start crying again. Well, as you probably know, Mark and I met at university, doing the same degree. During our first year we barely talked. Still, I remember how, at the start of our second year, we had to prepare a presentation together, on Romantic poetry. The irony of it! So we went for a drink and started talking about how we both wanted to write. It was a dream, or rather, a craving we both shared."

"I didn't know you also wrote," Rosalind interrupted, unable to stop herself.

"Sometimes," Lisa mentioned, quickly. Then she went on: "That day our friendship, our deep connection, began. There is—and I don't know if you write fiction and have ever experienced this—but there is among people who write or simply want to write a strange spiritual link. Perhaps two people who share a love for tennis feel the same way. I doubt it, though. I think it's that, when you choose to write, you also choose to sacrifice. You see, on the one hand, writers can plunge themselves into multiple worlds in their mind, invent them, create them, live inside of them. But that's only their minds, Rosalind, while their bodies are glued to a chair, their eyes to a screen and their fingers aching. So when two people meet in this limbo of creativity, I think they somehow feel that their halves will add up and they might end up as one!"

Lisa paused and looked directly at Rosalind who—strangely moved—blinked back at her. A magpie walked past near them, performing a throaty bird song. Lisa was about to salute when a second bird emerged from behind a tree.

"I'm sorry," Lisa said again, and this time, her humility didn't seem entirely real. "You may ask yourself why I'm talking about all of this when you're really here to learn more about Gabriel. He wouldn't exist without our desire to write. After university was over, Mark and I were both determined to make the necessary sacrifices. We both plunged ourselves into the writing process. Your father has probably told you about this already. How I wrote a manuscript I loved, about a woman living inside the ocean. I'm not saying it was a stunning novel, but it had something; if nothing else, much of my life-blood in it. Anyway, your father rejected it. And I couldn't deal with this rejection which—to be honest—was more than a little dismissive in tone. So, I'm afraid I gave up."

"What?" Rosalind asked, incredulously. "You gave up writing because my father didn't accept your manuscript?"

"In a way," Lisa responded, embarrassed. "I mean, it was obviously my fault for taking it so badly. But still, it was at a moment when all I needed was a little encouragement and–"

The woman fell quiet and closed her eyes. The magpies seemed to look at her. Then one of them gently, almost sensually, lifted his wings and flew away. The other followed.

Lisa seemed ashamed of what she had just told her. Rosalind put on the warmest possible expression, to show that she understood (which she did, in a peculiarly visceral manner).

"So that's why my father was so important to you," Rosalind almost whispered. "And all along I thought you had an affair with him."

"What?" Lisa interjected and, to Rosalind's pleasure, even smiled. "Now, that's a horrible thought!" She appeared to shudder slightly, then recovered. "I didn't mean that, Rosalind, sorry." Rosalind remained stoic. Lisa went on. "It's only—but let me get on with the main story."

The woman reached for a strand of hair and chewed on it for a few seconds, as if drawing strength from its dry ends. In an uncharacteristic moment of impatience, Rosalind felt like pulling the hair out of the French teacher's mouth to hear more.

"You see," Lisa eventually continued. "Mark didn't have too much luck with his work either. In fact, his situation might have been even more precarious. Because… " she suddenly paused. "Maybe it's time to go home."

Rosalind looked at her in shock. "Time to go home"?—mid-sentence and worse, mid-revelation?

Rosalind tried one of her awkward yet encouraging smiles again. Lisa smiled back, as if appreciating the effort, yet still waiting for her guest to say something.

"Do you really want to go home?" Rosalind asked, trying to keep the desperation from her voice. "Wouldn't you feel better if you told me?"

She felt very sly at suggesting that it would be beneficial for Lisa to unburden herself, when, clearly, it was to the dramatic advantage of her search.

"Fine," Lisa mumbled and closed her eyes. She spoke as if in prayer: "I suppose it's high time I learn to say this out loud."

Rosalind had never heard the word "loud" said so quietly. Lisa stared at Rosalind, her eyes begging her not to react. "So, Mark didn't seem able to construct even the simplest of plots. He wrote interesting poems and had an impressive talent for stringing words together in an unusual way." Her eyes widened with regret. "But the problem was he didn't want to write poetry. He was dying—he died—to write fiction. According to him that was the only writing that counts in this world."

Now, this comment was a little strange. Rosalind glanced disapprovingly at the suddenly sun-less sky. How dare Lisa claim that Drubenheimer couldn't construct plots or write fiction? What about *Story* and *Seabound*? And how could she talk about his talent for poetry, if the only poem he had ever written—as far as Rosalind knew—was the one just before his death? Shouldn't Lisa praise his amazing gift for novel writing? Didn't she speak out of jealousy, because she had failed?

"Oh-oh," Rosalind uttered, sounding a little like Santa Claus in a clumsy school play, this being as much acoustic disapproval towards Lisa as she could muster.

But, luckily, Lisa understood. For she added, to Rosalind's relief, "Of course, he improved massively. And yet, back then, he had no idea he would. He was simply desperate. And so was I."

Lisa didn't dwell on the details of this miraculous change as much as Rosalind would have liked her to; still, she was overall appeased and eager to hear the continuation of what would somehow turn out to be Gabriel's story.

"You see," Lisa indeed went on, increasingly relieved and relaxed, "back then—and this is a gift I have lost—writing plots came naturally to me. I invented different stories all the time, but still felt deeply discouraged. Mark, on the other hand, wrote and wrote, but mostly bizarre fragments and observations. He had piles of notes but nothing that could be collected into a publishable work like a novel. I had a novel no-one wanted and was too frightened to work on any of my other ideas. So we met up one night as we so often did, both feeling completely frustrated. Like ultimate failures, incapable of life, that's what we both said. And then we weren't even drunk when we had the idea. To have a child. To somehow, genetically, combine our two talents—my ability to construct stories, his fluidity and courage—hoping that a real writer would come out of it. So that very same night, Mark and I slept together. And by some ridiculous irony of fate, I fell pregnant straight away."

"Are you trying to tell me," Rosalind asked, puzzled, "that Gabriel was a kind of literary experiment?"

"In a way," Lisa conceded. "I know it must sound completely absurd. And unethical, because the Drubenheimers were already married and I was pregnant right beneath Alicia's eyes.

Well, almost. I did live on the other side of London, then, and yet—oh, I don't know. I realised I would never be a real mother and we gave Gabriel to Mark's sister. She was so eager to have a child and couldn't have one herself."

Rosalind nodded, already too exhausted to pass judgment on what she had heard. Gabriel! How convinced she had been from the start that he must be an artist of some kind.

"So do you think it worked?" she asked, accompanied by a vision of him being a world famous writer, one day.

"I don't know," Lisa replied, by now almost cheerfully. "It was him at the funeral, then, was it? Well, judging from the glimpse I caught of him, he seems to be an attractive young man. But from what I know about him, I suppose he's not exactly Shakespeare."

Chapter Twelve

The office was soothingly quiet. His assistant had left and Frank Waterloo had finished most of the day's urgent work. His eyes wandered across three new manuscripts he had just looked through and found wanting. Two love triangles—one in Iceland, the other in Tobago (the settings were great, he just didn't find the stories convincing) and one tale, interesting, but boringly told, about a man from an isolated farm in Texas who gave up everything to move to London and become a rock-star. There had been the usual sequence of submissions, and queries. Nothing new under the sun!

Only a few days ago, this would have bothered, even—given his recent fragility—depressed him. But his idea about a "last Drubenheimer novel" had provided some necessary motivation. It was everything he needed. Even if—god forbid—the quality of the work turned out to be limited, people would buy it eagerly. Thinking about quality, it might be best not to use the fragments Drubenheimer had showed him from *Accounts of a Muse*. Their awfulness went some way to explain why the man, terrified that he had lost his gift, had jumped out of the window. It might be better to have a ghost-writer produce something from scratch.

Frank Waterloo felt inspired. A lovely feeling, like butterflies flying around in his head. Was this what authors experienced when they embarked on a new work?

He hadn't told Berlina yet, but together they would create the most fascinating hype. He could perhaps cash in on a story of Drubenheimer being so immersed in his art that he couldn't find his way out of it again. Carry on with the idea of the suffering genius the *Guardian* had created after his death. Great! The unpublished novel to be written could focus on an artist about to commit suicide. And so, trapped in his imagination, in the imposing cycle of life imitating art or art life, Drubenheimer had to kill himself as well.

Should there be elements referring to Drubenheimer's own life? But it seemed too boring for that. Undying love for his wife; faithfulness; no plot-twists in the author's personal history. As far as he knew, it was all a straight line.

Well, he could see what the ghost-writer came up with! Unfortunately, Frank Waterloo had only been able to produce a list of three potential candidates. Two professional ghost-writers he had met at parties, and one aspiring author; very productive and fast. Still, they would fight over who could get the job.

Now, it was time for the part he dreaded the most. Calling Mrs. Drubenheimer. Asking for her permission.

He took his mobile phone this time and scrolled through his contacts. He didn't have her details and would have to dial Mark Drubenheimer's home number.

He had only seen her a few times, at Mark Drubenheimer's book launches, the odd party and his funeral. Hadn't Mark mentioned she had dreamed of becoming a concert pianist? Apparently, her father had prohibited it, old style, and she had become an eccentric housewife instead. A rich housewife, as she had inherited a lot of money.

Frank Waterloo closed his eyes to focus and gather his energy. Then he dialled the number.

"What?" Mrs. Drubenheimer snapped into the receiver.

Frank Waterloo straightened himself in his chair.

"Hello, Mrs. Drubenheimer?" He searched his memory for her first name. Lewis Carroll shot into his mind. Alice, then? No: "Alicia. How are you? This is Frank Waterloo. I just wanted to offer my condolences, one more time. And see how you are getting on."

"Thank you. I'm fine," she replied courtly. "How can I help?"

"Alicia," he said. "I'm really sorry about your loss. But listen, I have a very interesting proposal for you."

"What proposal?"

"I'm afraid I'll have to ask you to be extremely discreet about this, even if—for some reason—you don't like what you'll hear. Is this fine with you?" He tried to make his voice sound as charming as possible.

"I'm always discreet," Mrs. Drubenheimer screeched, alarmed. "Have you found out about something? Regarding my husband's death?"

"What? No,"—he was hardly Rosalind! What had she told this poor woman? He preferred not to know. "It's about a book. Another book by your husband. But written by somebody else. A ghost-writer."

His instincts told him to be direct. Not to mention money. He conjured up her image at the funeral. Aging, but beautiful. Tragic, somehow. Like a grand actress who had never had the chance to play an important part. He would make her feel significant!

"I know, Alicia, that all of his books have a strong link to you. That you have always been his inspiration, his muse. But in this novel I thought we could explicitly bring in elements of your life story. I understand you are an accomplished pianist?"

He expected many questions as an answer to his proposal. Why a new novel? Why a ghost-writer? Was this ethical? What was in it for her?

But Mrs. Drubenheimer just giggled, almost like a little girl. Was she drunk?

"I am. Or rather, I would have been. I was a kind of child prodigy," she declared and now her voice took on an almost surprising dignity. "I performed Beethoven, Bach, Liszt, Mozart, Schumann at a very early age. I even composed a few pieces of my own. But my father said I couldn't become a professional. It was too un-lady like! So he silenced me. My fate was like that of Amy Beach!"

"Like Amy Beach," Frank Waterloo repeated. "Who's she?"

"A composer," Mrs. Drubenheimer retorted, shrilly. "Don't you know her? She's one of America's finest. Her parents— and husband—limited her, too. After she became a widow, she finally flourished as a performer."

"I understand," Frank Waterloo lied. He doubted Mrs. Drubenheimer would flourish as anything other than an alcoholic, perhaps. "See, all these elements could be mentioned, and more. We could even play one of your pieces at the launch. What do you think?"

Had he gone too far? Would he actually do any of these things? Frank Waterloo didn't know. He needed her to agree. A repeated noise of fast inhalations followed by slow exhalations reached him. Sobs. Was Mrs. Drubenheimer crying?

"Mrs. Drubenheimer?" Frank Waterloo asked, surprising himself with the gentleness in the voice. "Are you OK?"

"I'm fine," she said, her voice trembling. "I need to go now. Go ahead, agent. Ghost-write away."

Frank Waterloo hung up the phone. How simple Mrs.

Drubenheimer had made things for him. How blindly she had consented. And comparing herself to this composer, Amy Beach! He might look her up, one day.

He nervously tapped his feet on the floor to an unknown piece of music performed in his mind. He reached for his list of potential ghost-writers. Philip had already looked up the numbers for him. He typed in the first one. Mr. Moron. What a name!

He let it ring seven times. No-one answered.

Someone had turned on screechy Latin music near the café downstairs. A car honked. Frank Waterloo got up and angrily shut the window. Then he sat down again.

He dialled the next number. A woman immediately picked up the phone.

"Yes?" she asked with an irritatingly nasal sound.

"Hello there!" Frank Waterloo's voice immediately sprang into jovial mode. "Could I speak to Mike Wilkinson, please?"

"About what?"

"A writing project," he pointed out. "Allow me to introduce myself, my name is-"

"Mike doesn't write anymore," the woman interrupted.

Then Frank Waterloo heard a shuffle and, rather abruptly, a male voice appeared.

"Hello?" it asked, shyly.

"Hello, Mike? Is that you? This is Frank Waterloo, the literary agent."

"Hello, yes, how may I help?"

"Tell him you don't write anymore," the woman kept on repeating in the background, like a mantra, until it almost turned into a scream.

Frank Waterloo grinned and ignored it.

"Well, there's this project and I need a very talented, experienced writer to take it on."

"You promised you would get a real job," the woman screeched.

Frank Waterloo heard some whispering. Then a silence.

"Is it ghost-writing?" Mike's feeble voice reappeared, although he now sounded further away. She must have put him on speaker.

"It's funny you should ask," Frank Waterloo replied. "As it happens, it is."

"Then he is not interested, thank you," the female voice said, strangely polite this time and one of the two hung up the phone.

Frank Waterloo stared at the dark red painting on his wall. A few tea stains, on his floor. He was annoyed.

He had no experience speaking to ghost-writers and he hated to admit that it showed. He wasn't sure how to handle them. He would have to be more careful during his next call.

Slowly he dialled the next number. Nobody picked up. He rang again and this time there was an answer.

"Mr. Haywood speaking?" the hesitant voice of someone who may have debated picking up the call of an unknown number and decided against it the first time around.

"Yes, hello, Peter? This is Frank Waterloo. The literary agent."

"Oh, Frank! How are you? What a pleasure to hear from you. Sorry about that author of yours. And so young," Peter replied, like Frank Waterloo's mirror figure. Equally eloquent and self-assured.

"Yes, it's terrible news. We're all really upset here," Frank Waterloo said mechanically. How he should approach the subject at hand?

"So, how may I help?" Peter asked.

Frank Waterloo breathed in deeply.

"There is this project," he began. "A very special project. Difficult, but not impossible. A project that has your name on it, Pete."

"That sounds very interesting, indeed. Tell me more. A ghost-writing project, I take it?"

"Yes," Frank Waterloo granted, cautiously. "I was just wondering if you're busy at the moment. Or if this might be something that take your fancy."

"What genre?"

"Literary. Drubenheimer-like in fact. I can't say too much yet, but it needs to be imaginative, quirky and on the light side. About 70,000 words. Some self-help phrases, but so well concealed that none of the cleverer readers notice. I have some ideas for the plot already!"

A suicidal writer. A would-be composer as a wife. It would all work!

"Oh, jolly good," Peter said, with a slightly sarcastic undertone. "I still have a number of questions. The main one being: will you pay me fifty thousand pounds? Because this will be the minimum I'll be asking for."

Fifty thousand pounds? For a little ghost-writing? Was this man mad? And he had sounded like the only sane one, so far.

Frank Waterloo laughed out loud.

"Are you practicing for the project already? Very funny. Obviously, times are difficult, so, I am afraid, not. But I'm sure we can work something out."

"I'm not joking," Peter snapped. "I am tired of grub street ripping the piss. I need fifty thousand quid."

"Well, so do I," Frank Waterloo countered, still grinning—

although he no longer felt cheerful at all. "Nice talking to you, Peter. I would have liked to work with you."

He hung up. So what now? How he craved for a break! Quickly, he called Moron's number again.

He was luckier this time; Moron answered the phone. Frank Waterloo explained. The man listened, attentively.

"Blimey, Waterloo," he cried out, once he had finished. "You're fulfilling my dream!"

Frank Waterloo smiled. At last!

"I'm glad to hear," he said.

The man laughed, a little wildly.

"Me too!" he hollered. "I'm glad you need me! You were one of the agents who rejected my last novel, *Filmstar*. A masterpiece."

Filmstar? Frank Waterloo couldn't even remember it. It must have never passed the slush-pile.

Then, with a sudden flash, he did recall it. A novel about a woman trying to be like Marilyn Monroe. A good novel. But he had been tired the day he read it. The writing had failed to thrill and awaken him—so he had rejected it.

A standard letter. *So sorry, we didn't fall in love*, or something like that. Well, tough luck. It was a competitive business.

"Oh, yes, I remember. A very good piece of writing. Lovely prose. Not suitable for our list, though. Sorry!"

"Lovely prose? It took me ten years to write."

This was a lie. Moron was known in the business, because he simply never gave up. And sent in about two new manuscripts to agents a year.

"Ten years?" Frank Waterloo asked. Usually, when he took on a new author, they cried with joy. Told him they loved him. Insisted he had made their life's biggest dream come true. Without any sarcasm in their voice.

"That's way too slow for this project, I'm afraid," Frank Waterloo said. He wasn't that needy.

"I wasn't going to accept it, anyway," Moron grumbled, but he knew that he had lost.

Frank Waterloo hung up his transparent phone and breathed in three times, slowly. For a few seconds, the sense of triumph over the ridiculous author lingered. Then it was replaced by a question. What should he do now? Find more ghost-writers? Pay a fortune? Beg?

There was only one solution.

He would write the novel himself.

How hard could it be?

Wherever its precise origin, several literature degrees had notably strengthened the moral presence and influence inside Rosalind's mind of the Secret Committee Against Superficial Affairs (SCASA). It wasn't that it had a clear goal, other than being against everything vaguely classifiable as "superficial", such as buying things, personal beautification, gossip and the like. Adopting a set of limitations and naming them had somehow helped Rosalind to structure her life, and given her a sense of safety and security. As a result, she had—for several years now—been virtually prohibited from shopping; especially shopping for clothes, which Rosalind's committee considered an ultimate representation of superficiality.

But, as soon as she had said goodbye to Lisa outside the Globe Theatre, Rosalind had taken a tube to Oxford Circus and started to wildly—at the very least for her standards—empty all shops she found open and affordable.

Rosalind's recklessness might still have counted as caution for others. And yet, she experienced something akin to a guilty yet joyful vertigo as she piled up jumpers, shirts and trousers that were not too expensive or on sale. In a crowning moment of her liberty from these requirements, she even bought a purple dress which she wanted to wear for the rest of the evening. It made her look a little fuller and more feminine.

She wasn't sure where the connection lay between this sudden buying frenzy and her recent conversation with Lisa Croydon-Bay. It felt like an act of reclaiming something, of indirectly (and very gently) hitting on the head someone who had kept her unnecessarily imprisoned by high ideals. What exactly was superficiality, anyway? Was it really about doing one's nails and caring about one's clothes? Wasn't this, equating superficiality with what many women tended to do, in a way, a subtle way of looking down on them? Perhaps superficiality was more about leading one's life on a surface-level, as a show to others, not as a gift to oneself.

Lisa's revelation about Gabriel's origin had stayed with Rosalind on her way into and out of every shop. She felt both shocked and strangely delighted by what she had heard. Also, she had the distinct and growing sense that there was more to come. But how could anything top this? Drubenheimer having a secret son, engineered to be a great writer? Was this in any way related to his death and her search?

She left Selfridges behind and headed towards Marble Arch. Buses passed; elegant cars; Londoners mingled with tourists. As she had felt on the tube on arrival, representatives of the entire planet seemed to be here. Many of them looked in the grip of some intense emotion; cheerfulness, excitement, anger or fear. She had once read that this was the route taken by prisoners from New Gate on their way to execution. People used to watch, exhilarated and eager, moved by impending death. Later, they could purchase from the hangman the ropes that had sent the prisoners to their end.

Rosalind shuddered. Yes, she had discovered many things— yet was she really any closer to finding Drubenheimer's hangman or hangwoman? Had she gathered enough information to solve the entire puzzle in her own mind?

In the middle of Oxford Street, Rosalind tried to think very hard, oblivious now to its colourful disarray and noise. She went through all her conversations again, let her suspects parade in front of her inward gaze. But this only confused her further. This was terrible! That one couldn't plan on having a clear mind when one most needed it! How could she possibly find out the truth?

She kept on walking. What would a real detective do in her case? Once again, she almost bumped into someone—an old lady with several dried flowers in her hair, talking cheerfully to herself.

Should she, just maybe, resort to point b) of yesterday's plan and ask Berlina for her unworldly assistance now? Didn't even the police and government agents consult psychics for difficult investigations, occasionally, even though this was usually well hidden from the public?

Numerous principles attacked esotericism; and yet, if she had already broken one major rule today, she might as well break another, less serious one. There was also the issue of trusting Berlina, again. She wasn't sure if asking her for help once more was an act of masochism or heroism.

Really, at this point of her search, what did she have to lose? Nothing, she told herself, with the same mock Italian accent her father had used during their telephone conversation the day she had decided to come to London. Nothing, except for her dignity.

Twilight washed over the streets, intensifying the gaudy decorations of little cafés and shops. Men sat in restaurants, smoking Shisha pipes. On her way down Edgware Road, Rosalind passed several veiled women, their eyes smiling at her.

She smiled back. This had been easier than she had thought. Berlina—who had still been in her office—had seemed ecstatic about her "new friend" ringing her again. When Rosalind mentioned she had an interest in Berlina's methods, especially a communication with the dead, the editor's auditory display of delight had become almost obscene. Berlina had emphasised that she lived "almost uncannily near" on Edgware Road and that Rosalind should come that same evening, after she had finished going through some manuscripts and attending to some more "spiritual business". She had recommended that, in the meantime, Rosalind scribbled something into her diary, which apparently cleared the mind for psychic experiments. She had been able to picture the precise nature of Mat's derisive smile if she ever happened to tell him about it.

Once arrived in a small café, Rosalind had filled pages and pages of her beautiful red notebook which she always carried around. Berlina had been right. Although she wasn't sure about her increased openness for psychic experiments, she felt better after writing. Maybe she should keep this up. Again, she had noted down the experiences of the search, her unexpected discoveries; but also found herself writing about her mother, her father, Othello. Her desire for peace.

A sports car cut through her calm, blasting pop tunes. Accompanied by a heavy rhythm, a thin female voice sang higher and higher in spirals, like smoke rising into the sky.

Rosalind reached the number Berlina had indicated, a freshly renovated building, painted in white with small, flowerless windows. She had expected Berlina's home to be far more plush and luxurious.

Rosalind rang the bell. Her diary writing had intensified her emotions. If a little while ago she had been anxious and confused, she was now full of excitement. She felt glad she would try Berlina's methods at last. Who knew what they might bring?

The door sprang open and Rosalind climbed up a narrow staircase to Berlina's flat. She knocked and immediately heard a distant but cheerful, "It's open!"

She walked inside and passed a dark corridor, wondering what would happen. Were they really going to call Drubenheimer from a different world? Was there such a thing? Was her mother there too? And would any of this help her resolve her search?

She arrived in a living room cluttered with copper tables, lamps, elaborate carpets and cushions, in a sparkling rainbow of colours. Candles were lit everywhere and incense sticks made the air thick and alluringly heavy. Every object seemed abducted from an unfamiliar world, yet assembled with a more familiar sense of beauty.

"We're in here," Berlina shouted and Rosalind followed the voice until she reached a door in a corner of the living room.

Rosalind quickly put down her shopping bags and knocked, yet no-one answered this time. She could make out the sounds of heavy breathing and quiet chanting inside. Her stomach tightened. She pushed down the handle and opened the door.

Rosalind blushed straight away. Sitting right in front of her—in what turned out to be a small room with a grey carpet and no furniture except for a small mattress—were two elderly ladies, stark naked. Their legs crossed, she could see the dark shadow of their vaginas and their flabby bellies on top of which their breasts hung, prostrated. They both moved their lips and emitted low and half-musical sounds. Berlina was in the middle of them, fully clothed.

Rosalind stared at them, panic rising inside of her. What on earth were they doing? Why were they naked? Yes, she really craved for her search to move on, but there was no way she would ever, ever undress in front of Berlina! She should have known better than to come here. She needed to leave!

"Nice dress!" Berlina interrupted Rosalind's thoughts, winking and clapping her hands like a patient primary school teacher. "And welcome to the world of spirits."

Both ladies opened their eyes. Rosalind watched disturbed as the two women blinked at her sleepily and with remote embarrassment. Berlina rewarded them with a charming smile which was, apparently, also the sign that they were allowed to get up and get dressed.

"We're finished, my lovelies," the editor announced, with her usual sing-song voice. "Say goodbye to your husbands, will you?"

When and how could Rosalind disappear?

One of the ladies—a pretty woman with big red hair— sprung up quickly and hurried towards a pile of clothes in the corner. The other took her time and walked with determined slowness which might also pass as "languid Sicilian mode" in the eyes of some beholders.

Only now did Berlina avert her glance and pretend that the ladies had some claim to privacy.

"I'll wait for you next door," she said, generously. "That's it for today."

She nodded at Rosalind, indicating that she should follow her. Leaving the two ladies alone to prepare themselves for the material world, they walked next to each other into the living room.

"So, what do you think?" Berlina asked, triumphantly. "They come here to talk with their dead husbands. And have a bit of spiritual hanky-panky, as well!"

She indicated a pile of cushions surrounding a table and observed Rosalind, with a proud and almost maternal smile.

"There's no way I'm going to undress," Rosalind burst out. "I'm afraid I'll have to leave."

"Undress?" the editor interrupted her, grinning. "No, of course, not."

"Are you sure?"

"Oh, absolutely positive, my darling," Berlina announced and Rosalind felt relieved until she added, signalling the bags: "You can keep that for your boyfriend. Have you bought all this to impress your man?"

Rosalind felt heat and cold rush to her face, simultaneously. What should she answer now? Silence seemed the most diplomatic option so she just smiled, wordlessly and a little falsely.

Berlina flashed her eyes and clapped her hands again, this time in delight.

"There's someone else, isn't there? I mean, someone else you'd like to impress, aren't I right?" Was it so obvious she liked someone else? Did she like someone new—called Gabriel—in that way? "Isn't it like magic, my sensitivity? Anyway, have you brought your diary? Is your psyche clear?"

Rosalind nodded, slightly shocked.

"Oh, good," Berlina praised her, warmly. "I'm glad you're using my special present. And don't worry, I won't ask you any more questions about, well-" she indicated the bags and winked at Rosalind. "Just tell me, would you like some coffee, tea or mint tea?"

"Mint tea, please," Rosalind replied, suddenly realising what a long day it had been, what with all the classic reading, her talk with Lisa, the shopping frenzy and now her evening visit to Berlina's flat. It looked like she would stay. She walked towards the cushions and sat down.

"Your wish is my command, my darling," Rosalind heard the woman chant with her endless enthusiasm, before she disappeared into the entrails of the flat.

Meanwhile, the door opened and the two ladies walked out, both perfectly composed and with a moving look of domesticity.

"Thank you so much for everything," the one who had demonstrated her lack of inhibitions said, nodding politely at Rosalind, but addressing—by raising her voice—the absent Berlina.

"That's alright, my bella," Berlina shouted from the kitchen. Then she remembered. "Oh, Rosalind! Your mum was Italian, wasn't she? An extremely vivacious lady, I'm sure?"

"Oh, was she?" asked the same woman, the other remaining obstinately quiet.

"Yes, she was," Berlina answered for Rosalind, cheerfully entering with a small tray. "She must have been a very glamorous woman. I'm always horribly jealous of her. You see," she turned with a glance of conspiracy to both ladies, "this is Rosalind. Frank's daughter."

The languid woman's lips formed an "ah" of understanding.

"We've got to go now, Geraldine," the quiet woman finally spoke.

"You're right, Lizzy. Goodbye, Berlina. Goodbye, Rosalind. Very nice to meet you. And good luck!"

"Nice to meet you too," Rosalind said, thinking how nice it was to hear her mother spoken about like this.

At last, Berlina put the tray on the table and sat down.

"I made you think about your mother," she acknowledged. "I'm sorry."

She poured fresh mint tea into two elaborately decorated cups.

"You shouldn't be sad," Berlina commanded, rather than advised. "Rather tell me, what do you think of my flat? Isn't it wonderful? A lot of the things are from my ex-husband. He was from North Africa. I mean, not really. He was English and all that, but he lived there for a while."

"Oh, really?" Rosalind asked, a little distractedly. When would they start their communication with the dead?

"He's a writer," Berlina added, beaming at her guest and seemingly untroubled by her slightly impaired attention. "What a coincidence! I was quite hooked on writers when I was younger, like you. You just think they help you seize every moment in life—live every day as if it were your last and things like that—and that they hold eternity in their hands." She playfully pronounced "eternity" with an American accent. "Well, having said that, my ex-husband certainly wasn't around to stay. Not as a writer—and certainly not in my life."

Berlina threw back her blonde hair and opened her already big eyes widely, then narrowed them again.

"You left him?" Rosalind asked, unfortunately thinking of Mat the very moment she had said the sentence out loud.

"Yes, my darling," Berlina replied, pushing her fragile looking tea cup against Rosalind's, as if to say "cheers". "Of course I did, as soon as I realised he was no good. I don't expect you've ever heard of Henry Blazer? Well, why would you have?

Why would anyone? He was a promise without content. And how can a woman like me—an editor with a vocation—stay with a man like that? A writer who cannot write well is like a man who cannot make love, don't you think?"

"I wouldn't know," Rosalind mumbled, embarrassed.

Berlina pulled a face at her and laughed.

"Enough, enough!" she told herself off. "You've come here for my methods, and here I am, talking on and on about my own life. If only it weren't so fascinating! You brought your diary, didn't you?"

"Yes." Rosalind sensed with renewed excitement that they were about to begin. "Do I need it?"

"I think you might want to take some notes, probably."

"Just a moment," Rosalind muttered and rapidly emptied her cup. She went to fetch her book and declared, surprised by the sudden gravity in her voice: "I'm ready whenever you are."

"Perfect," Berlina said, taking Rosalind by her hand and leading her back into the small room next door. "Then let's go and bother the dead."

Rosalind carefully placed her diary on the floor in front of her. Berlina handed her a cushion to sit on, then produced candles, a few sheets of paper and a fountain pen from a small wooden box in the corner. She quickly distributed the candles around the room and lit them, until they created dancing shadows on the floor and the wall. Then she switched on some music, or rather some—noise. A persistent, low humming that started buzzing in Rosalind's head and went all the way down to her feet.

"This is the Om of the earth," Berlina explained, probably catching Rosalind's puzzled expression. "It's the planet's rhythm, its sound, its breath! Marvellous, isn't it?"

She sat down opposite Rosalind, cross-legged like the two naked ladies, the smile of a Buddhist monk on her face. For once, this lively and exuberant woman looked tranquil and almost solemn.

"Are you ready?" she asked in a calm and low voice.

"Yes," Rosalind replied, even though she wasn't.

Somehow, the editor noticed.

"Look," she said, with an unfamiliar gentleness. "I know this might be new to you. But if you want this to work, you'll have to trust me, my darling, even if just for a little while, OK? Be a good literature student! Suspend disbelief."

"I'll try," Rosalind promised, more sincerely this time.

"Wonderful! Now, is this going to be about your search or about something else? I mean, do you want to ask Mark Drubenheimer who murdered him—unless you found the murderer already—or do you also want to contact someone else? Your mother, maybe?"

Without any warning, tears shot into Rosalind's eyes.

"My mother?" she whispered. "I could contact my mother?"

Berlina smiled at her, her expression gaining warmth in the flickering semi-darkness.

How Rosalind would love to do just this! It would be like a profound, unspoken dream coming true. But it was also nonsense. There was no way Berlina could perform such metaphysical feats, cross the biggest wall of all... Then again, hadn't she promised Berlina she would try to suspend disbelief, just for a little while?

"Please, let's try!" Rosalind heard herself say, with an almost childlike eagerness that surprised her.

"No problem, my darling," Berlina reassured her. "And afterwards, we'll try to contact Drubenheimer, too."

Rosalind attempted a nod. She felt very strange.

"So shall we begin?" Berlina asked. "Look straight into my eyes and repeat after me."

Rosalind watched confused as Berlina made a dramatic gesture with her right hand and, accompanied by the continuing buzz of the music, began to sing with a resonant voice: "Om."

"Om," Rosalind joined in, very slowly.

"Om," Berlina chanted a second time and whispered: "What was your mother's name, again?"

"Eleonora," Rosalind replied. "Eleonora Waterloo."

Berlina nodded gracefully, then took a deep breath and started reciting an invocation.

Do not disturb the peace of the dead unless you crave them
Leave them to sleep and grow and be
Up in their distant dimension
Give them freedom as they grant freedom to you.

Berlina raised her hands to the ceiling, invoking a presence from an imagined sky. Her body flickered rhythmically in the candle light, giving her the air of a high priestess fulfilling her task.

And yet we need you, Eleonora,
Come to us first, your daughter
Needs to speak to you!

Rosalind started shaking a little. Was this really happening? Would her mother appear? Would they be able to speak and finally say goodbye? Or would there be a sudden, horrible repetition of something like the Rosebud joke? The air buzzed with tension; ghost-less London air left for a moment without human interference.

"Eleonora," Berlina continued to chant. "Eleonora."

Speak to us. Speak yourself onto this paper!

In what almost seemed like a trance, Berlina handed her the pen and pointed at her diary. Rosalind experienced a sudden sensation of terror. Did she have to write something down?

"I can't," Rosalind admitted, desperately. "I can't."

She felt mortified, but instantly calmed by Berlina's lack of reaction, as though her behaviour were entirely normal, perhaps even expected.

The editor just smiled again, reached for a piece of paper and asked, in an even lower voice:

"What would you like to know?"

Everything! Too much, so much! And yet, Rosalind only pronounced, her voice trembling: "Anything my mother wants to tell me."

Berlina closed her eyelids in acknowledgement, then leant over the paper, breathing deeply and loudly until her fingers—in a terrifying miracle—started to move.

Rosalind couldn't watch any longer. She felt exhausted. She shut her eyes. When she opened them again, a few seconds later, Berlina held out a piece of paper to her.

Rosalind, it read. *My dearest. Let me go!*

Rosalind cried and cried in the darkness, only half-aware of Berlina sitting next to her, holding her hand. She remembered the message in *Seabound*. That there was no death. That beyond everyone's losses and sufferings, there was light. As sadness kept flowing out of her, she felt the sudden truth of this. A glimmer began to fill the void left by the desperation gently draining from her, through her tears. Was she healing, somehow? Was she coming back to life?

"Darling, do you want to stop this?" Berlina asked, after what seemed like a very long time; as if her voice were coming from a great distance. "Would you like to lie down?"

"No!" Rosalind heard herself cry out with unexpected determination. "No, really, no!"

She already felt better. Just like Lisa this afternoon, her mother's words had allowed her to shed tears about a long hidden pain, somehow lessening its inner force. She felt suddenly determined to take her mother's advice straight away, combine it with the editor's words during their meeting in her office and, from now on, seize every moment in life.

Rosalind sniffed, slightly.

"Drubenheimer?" she asked, impressed by her own courage. "Are you here, too?"

Berlina winked at her and said: "I do admire you! Just let me get him ready."

She repeated some of her dramatic invocations, then asked: "So what exactly would you like to know?"

Cleansed by her tears, Rosalind entered a different world. She was sure of it. Not, perhaps, the land of the dead, but more the space of Rosalind than ever.

"Who murdered him?" Rosalind asked, firmly. "Who murdered you, Mark?"

This time, she was ready to do the writing herself. Rosalind felt her shoulders relax. Some energy escaped from its hiding place and, like a wave rapidly approaching, exploded over her limbs, making them tingle. The light intensified. Rosalind opened her diary and closed her eyes as the pen began to wander across the page.

Rosalind stepped out into the night. She was still sleepy. After the session, Berlina had asked if she wanted to rest and Rosalind had accepted gratefully, worn out by her recent emotions and a madly eventful day. She had fallen asleep on a low mattress inside the room where they had conducted the session, until she had woken up less than five minutes ago, bashfully said goodbye to Berlina and hurried out into the night. Berlina had even been so nice as to offer that she could leave her shopping bags so that she didn't have to carry them around at this hour and that she would return them to her dad, the next day.

Silence covered Edgware Road, interrupted only by the rhythmic footsteps of a man walking past. For an instant, Rosalind wanted to stop him, so desperate was she to talk to someone, to share what had happened to her. She felt at once reassured and utterly confused.

Although she had believed everything while it had taken place, her refreshed mind and the cool night air made her wonder if she had truly contacted her mother and Drubenheimer. Wasn't it possible that, rather than establishing a communication with the dead, Berlina had put her in touch with her subconscious?

A pleasant quiver ran through her body, as if some invisible creature were massaging her head, sending down waves of gentle delight. Somehow, it didn't matter where her mother's message had come from. She would always remember the editor calling out "Eleonora" and her mother's simple but powerful order to let her go. It gave her a sense of closure; of a new awakening.

And then there was the issue of Mark Drubenheimer. Had he truly appeared to provide her with an answer? Had the force which moved her hand been her own? The result had been a name, the possible solution to her quest: Alicia.

Rosalind experienced a strange absence of emotion regarding this revelation. Instead of anger, perhaps even hatred, relief, there was simply the calm knowledge that she needed to talk to the lady as soon as possible, that she couldn't simply rely on her own inner voice or a ghost. Still, a quick look at her watch told her it was one o'clock in the morning and she wouldn't be able to do anything until daybreak.

What then should she do now? Go home, go to sleep? No, she was far too restless for that. Really, she desperately longed to talk to someone; and she had almost reached Church Street by the time she acknowledged to herself that the person she wanted to speak to was Gabriel.

With the same uncharacteristic daring that had made her steal the anthology and Lisa's key, Rosalind took out her phone and dialled his number. Despite her attack of courage, nervousness began invading her so intensely, she wasn't sure she would be able to speak at all.

She needn't have worried. When Gabriel picked up the phone, words seemed to come tumbling out of her all by themselves, although perhaps not the ones she might have chosen on careful consideration.

"I know who murdered your father," she announced. "At least, I think so."

"Who on earth is speaking?" Gabriel asked, sleepily.

She had woken him up.

"It's me, Rosalind," she confessed, blushing.

What was she doing? Why did she call him at this hour? Why hadn't she called, for instance, Mat?

It would be best to hang up. A moment later, she realised

she should have, ideally, done so before mentioning her name. Now there was no way back.

"I'm sorry," she said, trying to sound as casual as possible. "Did I wake you? I thought you might have just returned from work."

"I never get home this late," Gabriel grumbled. "What time is it, anyway?"

"Just before midnight," Rosalind lied.

"Don't lie," Gabriel replied.

"Well, it might be a little later. I'm sorry. You know, this might be a bit forward, but could I possibly come over? It isn't what you think. I just really need to talk. A lot of it is actually about you!" she added quickly, remembering her afternoon talk with Lisa.

"Fine, that's an interesting topic, at least," Gabriel commented, by now awake enough to give his voice a teasing tone. "Come on over. It's obviously the sweet stalker in action again."

As soon as Rosalind arrived at the place he had indicated—a block of council flats near Waterloo Station—she felt a familiar urge to escape. What if he completely misinterpreted her visit and thought she was desperate to be close to him?

She made herself ring the bell. There was a slight grunt and a buzzing sound. She opened the door and stepped inside the building's humid and dusty air.

A lingering stench of cold ash and sweat filled the house. Regrettably, the dim light radiating from the staircase didn't allow her to estimate the full poetic shabbiness of the place.

Despite the hour, two different types of music were playing. Rap and some Latino genre she couldn't place. Behind a closed door a woman shouted at someone; her husband perhaps. She received no reply.

Rosalind hurried up the four flights of stairs without stopping to breathe. By the time she rang the bell of a door that announced Gabriel's name on a rusty plate, she was shaking. A fly circled around a bare bulb coughing out its last glimmers of light.

Gabriel opened the door wearing nothing but a pair of black boxer shorts, content to present himself in this condition of half-nudity. Rosalind looked at his bare chest, swallowed and forced her eyes to return to his face.

"Good early morning hours, PhD!" He kissed her on the cheek, then ruffled his hair for special effects and stepped aside. "Why don't you come in? Do you want tea? Or vodka?"

"Vodka, thanks," Rosalind replied, in the voice of a hopefully sexy lady detective as she walked past him, inside.

Gabriel nodded, a little sleep-dazed still, and moved towards a corner of the room where bottles had been lined up on the floor.

In honour of its name, the small bedsit didn't contain much apart from a very large bed and, piled up around it, magazines displaying surfboards, muscles and half-naked women.

Rosalind searched for a chair but found none; she had no other option than to sit down on the edge of the bed, on top of its ruffled sheets. They smelled nice, of a body that sleeping had breathed out its dreams there. This caused a fierce tenderness in her which had for months—or always?—been absent from her relationship with Mat.

"You probably think I'm a bit mad for turning up at this hour," she began, tentatively, as she watched the beautiful genetic experiment busying himself with the drinks.

He slowly walked towards her with two glasses and a wide grin on his face.

"Don't worry, PhD," he said, with playful generosity. "I understand you needed to see me. I know I'm irresistible."

"No, but it's not that," she lied for the second time tonight. "I just wanted to tell you so many things."

"For instance, that you're in love with me?" he asked. "Or that I'm going to be disgustingly rich, spending the rest of my life surfing in Australia?"

"No, no, no," Rosalind stammered, turning far redder than her new diary.

"No to both? No money and no love?"

Rosalind didn't answer. Which of the two did he care about? She felt far too emotional to think clearly about this, now.

Gabriel looked at her, as if wondering what to do next.

"So what on earth were you on about on the phone?" he asked. "You mentioned something about my father?"

She hadn't told him about her encounter with Lisa, yet! Well, this would have to wait. She was too eager to share tonight's event.

"Yes," Rosalind said. "Something very strange happened to me this evening, Gabriel. I know it's all crazy, that's why I need to speak about it so badly. I went to Berlina—your father's editor—and we performed a ritual. She isn't the most trustworthy of women and it may have all been some big joke or magic trick, but I just felt so touched."

Tears filled her eyes.

"Oh, Gabriel," she went on, vaguely surprised at her trust, at how comfortable (if constantly embarrassed) she felt in his presence. "As I said, it may have all been a joke, but the effect was so real. I kind of spoke to my mother who died several years ago and it really, really moved me! And then we contacted your father and I found out who might have murdered him! Well, maybe it was only a projection, a way of getting in touch with my own knowledge, my subconscious, but… "

"Wow," Gabriel cried out, smiling a little sadly. "Could we contact my mother, too? Not my real mother, the one who raised me?" He looked at Rosalind appreciatively but seemed to notice she was still waiting for a reaction. "Anyway, but why would you want to know about my father? I thought we both knew who his murderer was all along."

"What?"

"Well, PhD, let's think. It was suicide. So the killer must have been…"

"But it wasn't!" Rosalind blurted out with such vehemence, she almost spilled her drink it the process. "It wasn't suicide at all. I wish I had told you before, about my intuition, my search. Anyway, this is why I came to London in the first place. Because I knew Mark Drubenheimer had been murdered and I decided to come and find out by whom. To be honest, for some time I even worried it might have been you."

"Thanks," Gabriel said. "That's kind."

She looked at him. Why had she told him all this? The model behaviour of a composed lady detective had all but disappeared.

"It was all in his poem, his goodbye poem. But it's a long story, a very long story. And tonight I was told that, supposedly, if I am to believe in any of this, Mrs. Drubenheimer, his wife, murdered him and I just don't know if it's the truth. It's Hamlet's predicament, really. You know, the question is always, can you trust a ghost? Especially if you yourself might be the ghost, I mean." Listening to her own words,

Rosalind got increasingly self-conscious. She must sound like a complete madwoman to him.

"So Mrs. Drubenheimer murdered him? And he told you from the beyond, did he? Do I need to worry about you?" Gabriel asked, with a renewed, if slightly forced, grin. "Will you go around chanting Hare Krishna after all?"

Rosalind suddenly felt very silly.

"You know, the police and even government agents do consult psychics to resolve very difficult cases," she explained, trying to save her dignity.

"They do?" Gabriel said. "Well, let's go back and ask about me then, shall we? Ask the ghost about his doubtful parenting methods!"

Rosalind took a large sip to gather her courage then announced rather dramatically: "Well, there is more."

"What now?" Gabriel asked, a little wearily but trying to retain a teasing tone.

"I spoke to your mother today, Lisa Croydon-Bay, and she confirmed everything you heard. And, well, I don't know about the money, but I'm sure we will find out."

We will find out?

"Wow," Gabriel said. His eyes opened wide as he tried to take in the full implications of this. "You'll see, I'll get something! My dad will be so happy!"

"Your dad?" Rosalind asked. "Is that what you want the money for? Your—the man who raised you?"

It was Gabriel's turn to blush now. Only very slightly, of course.

"Whatever."

"Your dad?" Rosalind insisted, enchanted.

"Well, yes," Gabriel mumbled, Rosalind-style. Then he

added, more emotionally: "He is and always will be my dad, no matter what this mad author may have been up to. And the money is for him. Fine, us, whatever. I want to surprise him and myself, of course, with a nice holiday. I'll go surfing. He can relax. I figured he's exhausted raising a child—even a gorgeous one—that's not even his."

"That's really nice of you, Gabriel," Rosalind said, tenderness rushing all over and into her, once more.

Gabriel made a face at her that implied he would personally strangle her if she ever brought up the issue of his niceness again.

"Oh, and you're also a genetic experiment," Rosalind burst out, more to hide her feelings and change the direction of the conversation than to actually inform him of this.

Gabriel's took a slow sip from his vodka and seemed to swallow down both his drink and his confusion. His glance became absent for a moment and he frowned as if talking something over in his mind.

"Whatever you say, my crazy stalker," he claimed, eventually, shuffling a little closer, his mood and intention changed.

"No, but really, Gabriel." She could hear his breath now. "Lisa Croydon-Bay and your father tried to mix both their talents to turn you into a writer."

He turned his face fully towards her. He no longer appeared to be listening. His smile grew wider still, and more charming.

"I don't really care," he said. "As I told you, my dad is my dad. If we can have a nice, long holiday sponsored by my… sperm donor, so be it. People say all kinds of things when they're trying to have sex."

Rosalind blushed very deeply.

"Do you not mind being a genetic experiment?" she asked, a little nonsensically.

"I don't mind at this particular moment," Gabriel clarified cheerfully.

Despite herself, Rosalind smiled at this.

He pulled her towards him and gently touched her lips with one finger. Rosalind's body went into frenzy.

"Anyway," Gabriel whispered. "Has anyone ever told you that you have very nice lips? Do you think I'm allowed to kiss them?"

Rosalind closed her eyes, delighted.

Then they shot open again.

"Gabriel," she whispered, as he moved even closer. He stopped. "Gabriel, you're not just using me to get to Drubenheimer's money, are you?"

Gabriel grinned, but gently.

"Well, PhD, I actually am about to use you," he said, teasingly. "Though I wasn't thinking about money. Sex and romance was what I had in mind."

And then, at last, he kissed her.

Chapter Thirteen

Frank Waterloo opened his office window, shooting a brief glance at the lively café underneath. A group of Latino-looking tourists sprang up from their coffee shop chairs, oozing over-eagerness to immerse themselves in London's excitement. They clearly ached to find enormous, chaotic, loud—if admittedly inspiring—London wonderful. How much mental editing would they have to do? Frank Waterloo chuckled. He loved his hometown; the feeling that he somehow lived at the centre of things, right inside of the universe's many cores. He just didn't think that these tourists would find what they probably sought. A distraction, from their lives, from their thoughts and old pain in the mid of the city's dirty-clean, sparkling-grey, over-filled and lonely streets. Its half-light, half-dark microcosm of the human condition. Frank Waterloo watched the tourists—three men and two women—walk away, laughing, then closed his eyes. Humid air—it had just stopped raining—came streaming in the room and he inhaled it deeply and gratefully. It felt tropical, almost; refreshing. Invigorating, for the task that lay ahead.

He opened his eyes again and sat down at his desk. He looked, once more, at the empty Word document on his computer screen. So this was it, then. He was going to write.

He grinned with an attempt at smugness, made without

conviction. If all truth be told, he had never had much respect for writers. Most of them—and that included Drubenheimer—seemed strangely child-like to him. They were in the business of avoiding reality. He, as an agent of his calibre, had always been in the business of facing it.

Now he would have to write, just like them. And to imitate Drubenheimer's voice. He felt motivated; but also tired. Should he call Rosalind to check on her? She had not spent the night at home. Berlina told him she had come to her flat for some crazy spiritual activity and that she had left late. Well, maybe she had seen that man from the funeral again. He reminded himself that he wasn't a worried father. He was far too busy for that.

He grabbed the piece of paper lying on his desk. It contained a few ideas he had picked out from his kitchen's cold morning air during breakfast. How odd creativity was. How random. But he was in a rush and felt like accepting all the words and images his mind had shot forth. He had already invented a working title: *The Drowned Poet's Piano*. It was vaguely reminiscent of a work by an Italian author his wife had adored and he was rather proud of it.

So. To work. First, the opening. The list read: protagonist Oreon Mahoo on the coast, crying, deploring his entire life. A sad beginning. No sunshine. A rainy coast. A threatening coast, but poetic and beautiful.

Would some place in Wales be appropriate for this?

No.

France. Brittany. That was more exotic. Excellent. What was Oreon Mahoo like? What was his basic character? A poet. An imitator of Romantic poetry. No! A contemporary poet. Or better yet, a musician-poet, how else would the piano come in? Of course! He would be a present-day Schumann who composed and wrote. Did Schumann write? Who cared? Oreon Mahoo did.

Perfect. With that new parallel established, Frank wouldn't have to invent too much. He would simply look up more details about Schumann's life and take it from there.

He smiled. This was going quite well. Maybe he should have started writing earlier; done the entire job himself from the beginning. Become one of the rare agent-writers who were brilliant at both tasks.

He remembered the anecdote of Schumann's ghost appearing in a séance and asking for one of his locked away works to be performed again. That, already, was good story material, but he didn't know much else about the man. Quickly, he typed "Robert Schumann" into his search engine. It turned out the artist composed a lot, drank too much, alternately encouraged and inhibited his wife's, Clara Schumann, own impressive musical creativity (a musical heritage of its own, apparently), attempted to kill himself, then died in a sanatorium, accompanied by visions of angels and demons. Drubenheimer; Schumann. Two mad geniuses with composing wives. A match made in ghost-writer heaven!

Frank Waterloo could already picture the cover. He was sure that Berlina would come up with something wonderful, irresistibly attractive, as she always did. Should he let her in on his plan? He decided to be discreet. *This is my baby!* He sniggered at himself, consciously imitating author speech.

He closed the site on Schumann again. There it was, the empty document, waiting for him. The famous blank page.

Cold air streamed over... No! *Ominous waves kept crashing...* Surely he could do better than that? *Oreon Mahoo thought he could make out a siren's song?* No, this was too much like *Seabound.*

Frank Waterloo sighed. He tried to imagine the coast he would have to describe, to feel the wind, smell the sea, do all this sensual stuff he knew writers had to do. But he couldn't see it, couldn't feel it. He only felt something akin to nausea.

It wasn't that his mind went blank. He shut his eyes and images kept rushing in, not of France, not of a coast, but of England and a hospital room and his wife suddenly dead.

Neither of them had wanted another child. Who would want to start over with sleepless nights and dirty nappies after all these years? But Eleonora had had a car accident when she went to Sicily to meet up with some relatives. When Frank had mentioned this to Berlina, with her spiritual inclinations, she explained it was a "first warning". A sign that she needed to change her life, unless she wanted her soul to be "called back" and her body to disappear.

Eleonora had "only" broken a few ribs, but she had suffered from deep shock and apparently this had messed up with her hormones. So, even though she took the pill, when they had very careful, post-accident sex, she fell pregnant.

Frank Waterloo opened his eyes; rubbed them, then stared at the blank page. Nauseous. Confused.

She had insisted on having the child and had even seemed somewhat happier than usual. When Othello was born, Frank Waterloo had felt vaguely proud and content himself and then...

...the bleeding had started. In the 21st century. In a beautiful, expensive private clinic, with a near-famous doctor attending, his wife had *died.*

He remembered her lying lifelessly on the bed—he had just gone out to get himself a coffee after Othello was born and the complications had started while he was out—surrounded by blood and blood.

For Christ's sake!

He hit the table with his right fist, savouring the pain in his hand that started to cover the ache in his mind.

Rosalind strode through a glorious spring morning. Everything seemed light and wonderful. It was as if Gabriel's body had imprinted itself onto hers, his smell, his touch, his enchanting presence.

He had fallen asleep after making love to her and Rosalind had waited for the first light of dawn to watch his features, the way sleep softened them, making him look even more beautiful, more real. She had thought of *Romeo and Juliet*, lying next to each other after a night of passion. Then, for fear that the power between them would fade (at least on his side) with the night's last traces of darkness, she had quickly left before he had woken up.

She sighed out loud and smiled. A magic she had—like Anette, in *Story*—known only from precious books, had now escaped the prison of covers and come to invite her in. Somehow, even if perhaps only briefly, Gabriel had made her feel what she most needed to feel: special. A valuable human being, with the right to fill some space in this world with the colours, scents and thoughts of her Rosalind-ness.

She entered the vastness of Waterloo station and winked at the reflection of herself in the mirror of a photo machine. She was so special, even this enormous train station was named after her!

Her first impulse was to hop on a train to Paris and spend a day or two walking past its cafés, filling unfamiliar spaces with last night's memories, hurling every sensuous detail into the Seine and watching it circle and flow. Of course, she knew she would have to push her dreams aside for a while. There were other things she needed to do and celebrating her night with Gabriel—with Gabriel!—would have to wait.

The thought dampened her spirits a little, but it was her duty towards Drubenheimer to bring her search to a conclusion and a duty towards Mat, to—well, bring their story to a conclusion, too.

She took out her mobile phone, yet quickly put it away again. Instead, Rosalind bought a tube ticket from the machine, took the escalator down and headed for the first telephone booth she could find. Maybe it would be easier to call him from underground, with several layers of London life sheltering her from above.

For at least two minutes, she stared at the telephone, amazed at what she was about to do. Then, she dialled the number, hoping that his mobile phone had perhaps been stolen or lost.

He picked up almost immediately, as if he had been waiting with the phone in his hand for days.

"Hello?"

"Hello, Mat."

"Rosy, is that you? A miracle!" Mat exclaimed, with an aggressive edge to his voice.

"Well, you could've called me too," Rosalind wanted to say, but realised this might not be the right tone for the occasion.

"I'm sorry," she murmured, instead.

"So, have you found your murderer?" Mat asked, and she could see him smirk.

"No," Rosalind admitted, then added recalling last night's

revelation. "Well, maybe."

"Now that comes as a surprise," Mat said dryly. "Anyway, my hysterical girlfriend, how's the city?"

The hand Rosalind used to hold the phone started shaking ever so slightly. The city! What a silly expression this was! As if London, with Big Ben's eternal erection, were England's only city, in fact the only city in the world!

"You know what," she suddenly heard herself say, delicious daring overcoming her body. "I think I want to break up."

"You think you want to or you want to?" was the slightly unexpected reply.

"I think I want to," Rosalind explained then blushed, noticing her repeated error. "I mean I fear I want to. I have to, somehow."

"Oh whatever, whatever, whatever! So you're doing this again," Mat complained, in a whiney tone. When was the last time she had broken up with him? "Running away from everything, running away from life! But fine, if you want to throw it all away, so many years together, an entire future, feel free! I had lots of plans, you know. I was even going to ask you to marry me in a year or two. Have children together. Move abroad for some time. But never mind, never mind. You just go and run away from life."

Rosalind felt strangely unmoved. When had he prepared this entire speech?

"You know," she finally whispered, when he had finished. "I feel I'm running towards it, rather."

"What?"

"I feel like I'm running towards life, actually," Rosalind repeated, more loudly this time. "But I am really, really sorry. And I hope…"

"That we can be friends?"

"Yes."

"No way. I knew this was coming. Goodbye, Rosalind," Mat said icily. "Have a nice life."

Did words have such power, Rosalind asked herself as she was walking towards the Northern Line, that they could slice the connection between two people in an instant, like the cutting of an umbilical cord? Reality—her life—really was like a piece of clay, after all. A soft, sensual, sometimes stubborn material she could shape with her thoughts! At least now that she was no longer too shy to let them take the shape of actions.

The night with Gabriel and the act of pushing Mat out of her life seemed to have cancelled each other, leaving a buzzing void. She would be sad about their separation, eventually. At least she hoped so. For one couldn't just break up with someone and feel relieved! Yes, she would probably find it hard that Mat was no longer part of her Saturdays, her flat, her bed.

A sudden tiredness washed over her. She knew she needed to go speak to Mrs. Drubenheimer, but she also craved for a moment to simply sit down and be. What about the benches on the platform? But there was something depressing about the dreariness of her environment. She settled for one of the station's many coffee shops instead.

Once arrived, she ordered an espresso and sat down on a silver chair, overlooking the coming and going of people around her. This was life. A crazy, cheerful, callous, colourful chaos. And she, Rosalind Waterloo and her overjoyed dizziness of having slept very little and made love very often, were both a part of it.

Once more, an internal picture of her mother came to her.

This time, she stood in the entrance to the flat. Her hair had been loosened and framed her beautiful face. She was no longer pregnant, and now wore a wide, pink and blue dress. Her skin was lighter than usual; it almost glowed. She smiled, somehow looking at Rosalind, although she was only inside of her mind. Then she left, shutting the door behind her.

Rosalind really hoped that yesterday's contact—whether truthful or not—had marked a new beginning, a fresh start. Maybe she would be happier, both with a world inside and outside of stories and books. And become less hysterical.

Rosalind took a sip of her hot and pleasantly bitter coffee, oblivious to world around her. The word "hysterical" kept pulsating in her mind. Mat had used it during their phone call. Her father had called her this, too, when she had surprised him with the wet nurse. Since then she had taken it for granted that she was, indeed, unstable. That something was wrong with her, deep down inside.

She had felt too emotional; too out of control. But was she?

For years she had accepted the distance between her and her father as an uncomfortable consequence of what had ultimately been her inappropriate behaviour. Yet had her actions really been unjustified? Wasn't it at the very least understandable that a girl who had just lost her mother was very fragile, especially on finding her father grieving in such a seemingly cold way? She hadn't so much felt an oedipal jealousy, as an insult against her mother. With her mother gone, she had experienced the urge to act on her behalf. She had wanted her father to honour her—not kiss other women as soon as she had gone. And, she had so longed to lean on him… Maybe she hadn't been able to get to the core of the issue yet; maybe she never would. But something inside of her had opened.

Luckily, now was not the right time to do so. And feeling strengthened by her reflections, Rosalind finished her drink, got up and walked towards the tube station, again.

The train arrived and Rosalind got on without looking back. She got off at Embankment and took the Circle Line. She reached the grand entrance of Campden Hill Court and walked straight in and past the porter's empty seat into the corridor. She glanced at herself in one of the beautiful mirrors and noticed that the glimmer in her eyes had intensified. Was this simply the effect of the corridor again? Or had this change in her looks been worked by some process inside of her soul?

With a playful wink at herself, Rosalind turned away and took the lift to Mrs. Drubenheimer's floor. A sense of unease started to creep into her mind. Was she sure this meeting was necessary? Would she really confront the lady with something she had heard as part of a séance? And what should she do if Mrs. Drubenheimer still believed her to be a reporter? But there was always room for optimism! Maybe Mrs. Drubenheimer had forgotten all about this confusion, by now?

With renewed courage, Rosalind stopped at the lady's door and rang the bell. Once, then twice. There was no answer. Determined, she knocked again. Nothing still. When the door at last sprang open, it seemed she had run into Ophelia, rehearsing her own end.

Mrs. Drubenheimer looked wild. Her fingers tightly clutching a piece of paper, she stared at Rosalind with black eyes surrounded by dark stains of make-up. Tears had spread them all over her face, with the evident help of rubbing and scratching. Her hair stood on end, giving her a look of dramatic insanity which made her more beautiful than ever.

"Hello?" Mrs. Drubenheimer shrieked, pulling at her dress which had slipped off one shoulder, revealing a patch of smooth but ageing skin. "Who let you in?"

Even though a part of her couldn't fight the impression that the lady was pleased to see her, Rosalind's previous hesitations turned into a full-blown attack of guilt. Who was she to turn up at the home of this woman—who was still possibly innocent—and disturb her with her own problems and needs?

"I'm so sorry, Mrs. Drubenheimer. The porter wasn't here and I–" Rosalind stammered.

At this point of her awkward speech, the widow already seemed to have composed herself a little.

"It's alright, you're the woman from the press, aren't you?" Mrs. Drubenheimer inquired, with slightly exaggerated dignity. "I suppose you've come to bring me the article. I've been wondering why it hasn't been published yet. I never asked you which newspaper it was for. But I am far too discreet. And I'm not used to all this attention my husband's death seems to have unleashed."

Rosalind looked at the lady in shock. Not such a good idea to be optimistic, then. Mrs. Drubenheimer had not forgotten at all.

The widow let the piece of paper she had been holding disappear into her cleavage. Meanwhile, Rosalind's mind started roaming in all directions. She felt a little desperate. What should she do? Tell the widow the truth? No, she would never trust her, then. Rosalind would confess it all, eventually. For the moment, some half-truth would have to do.

Rosalind remembered the lady's abuse of her idol to strengthen her resolve and said, nervously: "Mrs. Drubenheimer. I'm afraid the article hasn't been published yet. I'll need more information."

The widow stared at her, doubt flashing over her face. Then she clutched at the paper in her cleavage again and nodded at Rosalind with childlike determination.

"You want information? I'll give you information. Come on in."

Mrs. Drubenheimer started walking towards the living room, gesturing for Rosalind to follow her.

On entering the living room's spatial composition in white, Rosalind's nose was instantly unsettled by a smell of alcohol, "sadness" and smoke. The causes of each seemed obvious enough: cigarette butts spilled over several ashtrays; wine glasses stood everywhere filled to different heights, as though Mrs. Drubenheimer had been planning to play them as an instrument. Finally, to account for the somewhat abstract stench of sadness, Mrs. Drubenheimer herself had by now thrown herself onto the couch and started mumbling: "my life is pure misery" with exaggerated calm, before her limbs started to tremble.

"Take note of my tragedy! Your name is Rosalind, isn't it? Write all of this into your piece, so the whole world may see what my husband has done. It will all be written elsewhere too, you'll see."

The lady grasped at her throat, pretending she was about to throw up. Rosalind looked at the woman, horrified and at the same time full of compassion. How would she ever be able to confront her with what she might have found out?

A little awkwardly, Rosalind made herself sit down by Mrs. Drubenheimer's side. "Please calm down, Mrs. Drubenheimer," she whispered. "Please, please calm down."

To her surprise, the lady glanced at her slyly, as if pleased that her display of suffering had achieved its desired effect.

"So what else did you want to know?" Mrs. Drubenheimer asked.

Rosalind wrinkled up her face for a second.

"Have you murdered your husband?" she pronounced, in her mind. In reality, all she mentioned was: "There are a few details that need clarification."

"Details?" Mrs. Drubenheimer shrieked, as if offended by this. She touched the paper hidden in her cleavage again. "I have a detail for you."

"Remember I told you my husband was a fake?" she said. "Well, what I disclosed to you last time wasn't the worst of it yet. The worst I found out today. I'm glad you came back, you know? Very glad. Hear this, it will make the headlines."

"What happened?" Rosalind asked, intrigued, unable to guess what the woman may be talking about.

"I received a letter," Mrs. Drubenheimer stated, dramatically. "Indeed, it must have arrived many days ago, as it was dated the 4th of May. But I had been too weak to open my mail and only today—oh, the dreadful irony of it—I felt a fresh surge of energy after a phone call I received. I thought I'd organise everything, start anew."

"And what did the letter say?"

"Not much," Mrs. Drubenheimer whispered and now the tears in her eyes seemed more real. "That the fake had a son. A hidden child, with the bitch. Now I know what Mark hinted at that night; 'People might soon tell you some lies about me and Lisa. Please don't believe them' and so on. Lies! What lies! I sensed it all along!"

So the widow, too, had found out. Possibly through the same mysterious source as Gabriel, maybe even through Mark Drubenheimer himself. She felt like asking what exactly Mark had hinted at, but knew that this wasn't the right moment to do so.

"I couldn't have any children," the lady whispered, in demonstrative pain. "Everything is my fault."

Mrs. Drubenheimer got up and hurried past Rosalind unsteadily, grabbing a bottle of wine. Then she sat down again and started gulping it down.

Rosalind watched. The woman was in utter pain, that much was clear. If only she knew that Gabriel was not a child of passion, but a literary experiment! Would that help? Should she tell her? She couldn't. Mrs. Drubenheimer was still her prime suspect. She appeared plagued by almost unbearable guilt. Maybe this was why she had been trying to convince the world that Mr. Drubenheimer had been some awful, inhuman creature? Maybe she had actually received the letter on the 4th of May and murdered her husband out of rage?

Rosalind felt like downing a bottle of wine herself. What was she to do now? Comfort a woman in need? Or question her about a possible act of horrendous, unthinkable violence? Well, maybe there was a way of combining the two.

"Mrs. Drubenheimer," she said, very quietly, gently touching the lady's arm. "I need to ask you something, very strictly off the record. Please don't get angry with me."

Mrs. Drubenheimer stared at her, confused, alarmed. At least Rosalind had managed to get her attention this time.

"What is it?" the widow asked, suspiciously.

"Well," Rosalind mumbled, and drank one of the half-empty glasses of wine herself, for courage. "I'll be completely honest with you. I had a very strange experience yesterday. Berlina Marrowing, your husband's editor, organised a spiritual session, a kind of 'calling of the dead'. If you'll forgive us, we even contacted your husband and asked him a few questions. And he said—not that I take any of this very seriously—but he said–"

"That I murdered him?" Mrs. Drubenheimer interrupted, completing Rosalind's near stuttering with deadly calm.

The lady inhaled very deeply and narrowed her eyes.

"You're not a journalist at all, are you?" she asked. "You're from the police."

Rosalind began to tremble. She was uncertain—deeply uncertain—what precisely was going on. She just knew that the moment to confess the truth had arrived. Much earlier than she had hoped or expected it to.

"I'm a student," she said, almost whispering. "I'm not from the police. And I didn't mean to–"

She stopped speaking. Perhaps she didn't have to apologise.

"Well, whoever you are," Mrs. Drubenheimer shrieked. "I suppose I'm really tired of all this make-belief. I thought this moment would kill me, but it actually feels rather nice. My life is such a disaster! Music was everything—it became nothing. Love was everything—it became nothing, too. I gather I have nothing left to lose. So, fine. I did it. I murdered him. Or rather, I might have. I'm not even sure I did. I was so drunk that night. So disappointed after our meal. I took a lot of pills."

"What do you mean, you're not sure?" Rosalind burst out. "How can you not be sure if you murdered someone? You must have some flashbacks, memories, proofs of some kind!"

The lady smiled dismissively at Rosalind and helped herself to more wine.

"Oh, do I?" she snapped. "Do I really? A student, are you? And you've never been properly drunk? Well, I have no flashbacks of anything. Other than being angry with him. And saying some rather cruel words, which I didn't mean. The ridiculous fake! And so I thought that I might have…"

"What words?" Rosalind asked gently, confused.

Mrs. Drubenheimer hesitated for a few seconds, then exclaimed, "Remember it was our anniversary dinner? As I said, he was extremely worried that people would soon tell me something about him and Lisa that I shouldn't believe. He almost started crying, the weakling. Apparently, his writing was not going well, and his soul was aching, and if I believed these lies it would kill him."

"And?"

"Well, I lost my mind. My composure. Years of stored up anger, frustration and pain. So I told him I would believe the earth was flat, if he promised that my doing so would finish him off. I said—"

The lady looked utterly horrified.

"I said that he should do the world a favour, tie a rope around his neck and jump out of the window. Relieve me—us—of the torture of his ridiculous existence."

Rosalind's face mirrored Mrs. Drubenheimer's shock. Her eyes had widened so much, their dryness ached.

"And then? You went and did all this to him—and murdered him?"

Mrs. Drubenheimer stared at Rosalind like a doubtful child; as if she—the student, the expert—might have an answer to this.

"Then," the widow said, "I took those pills. And I thought I might have murdered him."

Mrs. Drubenheimer remained almost motionless for a few moments. Eventually, she began to look around herself, taking in the chaos of her living room, with a disoriented but vaguely thankful expression on her face, as if waking up from a bad dream.

"Coming to think about it," the lady suddenly commented, becoming more animated, "and having said all of this out loud, it starts to seem rather unlikely, don't you think? That I hurled him out of the window, all by myself?"

Rosalind glared at the woman, more thoroughly bewildered than ever. She didn't know what to think, or say. She had never met anyone who had confessed to a murder and some very harsh words preceding it; then claimed that she didn't really remember doing it; then reflected that she might not have done it, all within the space of two minutes.

"In any case," the lady now snapped. "It's really none of your business. You're a liar yourself and a fake." Mrs. Drubenheimer jumped up and pointed a shaking finger at Rosalind. "Count yourself lucky I won't call the police to let them know!"

At last, the lady pulled up the part of her dress that had slipped off her shoulder, smoothed down her hair and wiped some of the dark make-up smudges from her face with her palm.

"From the press!" she cried out, looking at Rosalind challengingly and almost cheerfully. "And my husband's ghost accused me? Ha!"

The lady breathed in slowly and out again, perhaps savouring a newly found peace.

"I might have been a little insensitive, but I certainly didn't murder anyone!" Mrs. Drubenheimer hissed. "The bastard was obviously lying again. Slandering his wife from his grave!"

Chapter Fourteen

On opening the door to the flat in St. John's Wood, Rosalind half-expected Othello to throw a toy monster at her or her father to inquire—with a smirk—where she had spent the night. Yet the flat was quiet and there seemed to be no-one around.

Glad to have a little time to herself, Rosalind took a quick shower, then walked into her room, took off most of her clothes and sank down onto her bed.

It was so warm, she didn't need a duvet. She just stretched out her body in a rather atypical gesture, crossing her arms behind her head. She felt a little calmer. She started thinking about her life and what no longer formed part of it. Like Mat. What would university be like without him? Would she be lonely? And more importantly, would she see Gabriel again? As she formed the question in her mind, a ray of light came through the window and fell right onto her face. She took this as a good sign.

Her meeting with Mrs. Drubenheimer had been awful and more than anything else, she felt immensely relieved that she had escaped. There was still the question of Mrs. Drubenheimer's implication in her husband's death. Rosalind had to acknowledge that the whole thing was just crazy. She had been told about the lady's guilt twice now: once by a ghost and then by the woman herself who had immediately taken her confession back again.

Really, it no longer seemed likely that Mrs. Drubenheimer had murdered her husband. She had seen the woman's fragility. Following the widow's own counterargument, it struck her as impossible now that she had gathered the strength for hurling him out of a window. How could she not have seen this before? Probably because she somehow needed to believe in Mrs. Drubenheimer's guilt. Did this mean that Berlina's séance had been some trick the editor had played on her, once more?

Then again, what about the lady's cruel, callous words that Drubenheimer should throw himself out of the window with a rope tied around his neck and this was precisely what happened to him that night? And why had he mentioned that someone might soon tell her some lies about Lisa and him? Who? Did that person also send the letter?

Rosalind turned around in her bed, lifted her bent knees towards her stomach and embraced them. Wasn't it rather plausible that Mark Drubenheimer had sent it himself? To have it all out in the open before he "ceased to be"? But why did he say that people were going to tell Mrs. Drubenheimer lies? This just didn't make any sense! Had he gone mad? Did he perhaps—Rosalind barely dared to even think it—commit suicide after all?

No, no, no, no, no! She vehemently shook her head. She couldn't give up on him now by believing this! It wasn't that she was morally against suicide; she hadn't even deeply considered the matter. But it seemed wrong that Drubenheimer, whose writing was so very full of hope, of light, of strength would have given in to his suffering in this way.

Rosalind hugged her knees more tightly, feeling sadness

approaching again. She would call Gabriel. Or take a bath. Or better yet: read another classic.

She remembered the copy of *Madame Bovary* she had bought the other day and had hardly paid any attention to so far. Wouldn't now be the perfect time to go through it again? Deal only with fictional characters for a while and let everything else drift from her?

She smiled a little forcefully, got up, fetched the novel from her desk and crawled back into bed. She couldn't help thinking how the cover (displaying a lady with a large hat) didn't appeal to her nearly as much as those of all the Subtlety Classics she had come across.

As Rosalind's eyes started wandering across the print, her smile instantly became more authentic. Every word she read aloud in her mind made her more peaceful. How she loved her classics!

Here he was, little Charles Bovary—Madame Bovary's future husband—on page three, entering his new school. She had forgotten the book had such an unusual beginning. She had expected to encounter the work's famous heroine straight away. But it didn't matter; she had forgotten a lot about classics lately.

Eagerly reading on, Rosalind came across Charles Bovary's adulthood, his first marriage and, finally, the meeting with Emma, his second wife. A woman so bored, a need for adventure drove her to commit the most destructive acts. Even though Rosalind had planned to let everything drift away from her, it was difficult not to connect her to Mrs. Drubenheimer. How sorry she felt for the lady, after all!

Rosalind rapidly scanned the following pages, hoping for something—some word or phrase—to particularly attract her attention. Within a few minutes, Flaubert complied. Her eyes collided with a reflection on language, so magical it made her entire body tingle:

Human speech is like a cracked tin kettle, on which we hammer out tunes to make bears dance when we long to move the stars.

How very, very beautiful! Rosalind imagined Mark Drubenheimer sitting in his dark studio, beating wild rhythms onto a kettle with a kitchen spoon, trying to gain inspiration for *Accounts of a Muse*.

Was it the prerogative of those who translated their soul into words and hurled it, bravely, into the world—to become most fully alive? Was it through words that authors could exert a most strange and inexplicable power, relate to people, deeply move them the way classics moved her and had moved her mother, always somehow commenting on her life? What was this magic great writers were able to work? So really, for Flaubert, language was not a cracked tin kettle, but a musical instrument. Writers like him and Drubenheimer played it bewitchingly, making the entire universe blush because it felt caught and found out.

Before she could stop herself, Rosalind felt her tears rising. No, Drubenheimer couldn't have possibly killed himself! She could never have misinterpreted his poem to such an extent. She couldn't have misunderstood his prose, her beloved *Story* and *Seabound*! So what if he had lied about some rather important things. Really, he had a certain right to do so, if he was one of the chosen people to "move the stars" with his words.

Naturally, that was a very Romantic way of defining writers;

this whole idea of the writer genius who had a right to harm others and themselves in order to produce grandiose works of art. As far as she knew, the Romantic poets had helped to create it and–

The *Anthology of Romantic Poetry*. The volume she had removed from Drubenheimer's studio the other day. Wasn't it high time to look at it too?

She got up once again and—not without a certain reminiscent wonder at the attack of momentary madness that had led her to it—carried it into her bed. As she lay down again and opened the thick and heavy book, a slight shiver ran down her spine.

Rosalind wasn't used to poetry. Her passion was almost exclusively dedicated to fiction; poems bewildered her, a little: Wordsworth celebrating nature and himself; Coleridge the imagination and himself; Byron freedom and himself, Shelley celebrating Keats and himself.

It wasn't until she reached Keats that Rosalind began to be moved by what she took in. There were several poems she liked with attractive titles. There was something appealing about *La Belle Dame Sans Merci* which once again reminded her of Mrs. Drubenheimer ("Full beautiful—a faery's child… her eyes were wild"). She was also drawn to, and embarrassed by, *O Blush Not So!* which she couldn't but associate with herself and spending a night with Gabriel ("There's a blush for want, and a blush for shan't, And a blush for having done it"). Rosalind read them out loud to herself. Did Drubenheimer perhaps do the same just before he died, calming himself and fighting his fears of some terrible murderer with these words?

Still, no poem had ever had quite the effect on Rosalind as

the one she now discovered, on turning the page. For in front of her was:

When I Have Fears that I May Cease to Be

When I have fears that I may cease to be
Before my pen has glean'd my teeming brain,
Before high-piled books in charact'ry
Hold like rich garners the full ripen'd grain;…
When I behold upon the night's starr'd face
Huge cloudy symbols of a high romance,
And think that I may never live to trace
Their shadow with the magic hand of chance;
And when I feel, fair creature of an hour,
That I shall never look upon thee more,
Never have relish in the faery power
Of unreflecting love;—then on the shore
Of the wide world I stand alone, and think
Till love and fame to nothingness do sink.

Rosalind shut the book in a daze. It wasn't true. It simply wasn't true. She didn't understand. How could she not have noticed this before? Why didn't she, at the very least, pay more attention to the fact that Drubenheimer's goodbye poem was so very clearly not contemporary? Why had no-one else realised this? Shame and panic overcame her. Hadn't her father claimed that the poem had made him doubt Drubenheimer's authenticity as a writer? Hadn't Lisa been telling her how she had made friends with Drubenheimer preparing a presentation on Romantic poetry? Was this why everyone had spoken about "inter-textuality"?

No! Could she blame her own shock, the sense of denial Mat had been so insistent about? Rosalind quickly went on the internet again and retrieved an electronic version of the *Guardian* article where she had first read the poem. She had jumped a few lines when she had first, eagerly, read the text. Now she felt mortified to find out that it did mention, even if briefly, that the goodbye poem was actually by Keats. How unbearably stupid of her! Everyone must have known that Drubenheimer's wonderful goodbye poem was not by Drubenheimer at all.

Frank Waterloo entered his home office and switched on the computer. After his first writing attempt in the morning, he had no longer been able to concentrate. Memories had attacked him, relentlessly. His wife; her death. His pain!

How irritating this was!

He had gone out to meet Berlina for lunch in Chinatown and had strolled through Soho afterwards, trying to calm himself down. Eventually, he had decided to work from home.

He sat down at his desk and stared ahead of him, without taking anything in. He would get this writing project done, somehow. He had always managed to keep what seemed like a million balls in the air. He was proud of this. In fact, he could easily write a book about this, too. *How to stop whining and get everything done.*

His eyes wandered towards the afternoon light falling in through his window. It projected shadows onto the wall were the sofa was placed; a few parts of his desk, his computer, his body.

He remembered speaking to Mrs. Drubenheimer. Her

strange behaviour, her sobbing. Her songs, her music. Right, music! He started googling Schumann again. He needed to research his protagonist!

It turned out the composer had done a good deal of strange things during his lifetime. Like ruining his own finger, and career as a pianist, in an attempt to improve his playing technique. How lucky he had been born a genius! If one did things like that, and died without composing immortal music or writing mind-blowing novels, everyone just recalled one's trauma as silliness. Then moved on.

What would Drubenheimer be, without his novels? A man in a delayed midlife crisis who tied a rope around his neck and jumped out of the window, rather than face his fears. Then again, outstanding writers were allowed to kill themselves; it made a good, serious ending to their life's gripping tale.

Well, he would write his own fascinating story now, without a need to grow emotional in the process. Frank Waterloo closed his eyes to focus his energies, then opened them again, determined. It was time to set the scene. He would now have to tie in all the senses, draw in the reader, set out the conflict immediately. He had detailed knowledge of all these mechanisms, had explained them to some of his authors, many times. Then again, as an agent, he had never been one to play by the rules. He had his own way of doing things and found it ridiculous the way so many people in his industry—in any industry, really—struggled for years to learn the manner everyone else handled things. Society was a copy-cat business, and this was exactly why he liked Romantics like Schumann so much. They may ruin their fingers to improve their piano technique; but they didn't just imitate other people, they were original, and famous for being different. This was how he had always conceived of his "agenting". His writing would be just the same.

So, break the rules.

He opened a blank Word document. He thought of Sunny McHay's novel with his murdering protagonist and the one by the woman called Gold with her female-poet in India. He felt inspired by them, after all. Darkness and India! No more Wales, no more Brittany. Frank Waterloo now pictured an Indian street. A cow crossing. There were cars everywhere. Early morning light. In Benares—or was it called Varanasi?—the holy city of death. Brilliant!

Scratch the streets and the cow, he would describe the river. There it was: the river Ganges, and the sun rising, illuminating small boats. It was early morning and people were bathing already. Someone was setting up a funeral pyre to burn a woman. A man would burn his wife. He was glad she had died in this city, because it was holy and she would have broken the cycle of, what was it called? Samosa? No, that was food. Samsara? He would look that up, later. The endless cycle of life, death, life. Anyway, all was quiet and mystical and then, suddenly, the silence was ripped apart by a scream. It was an English man, arrived three days earlier, a… poet pianist, who had just injured his finger.

He was good at this! All he needed to do now was write it all down.

He put his fingers on the keyboard; his mind returned to the woman on the funeral pyre. It was made up of small wooden sticks; the corpse was laid out on it already. There were no flames yet, in Frank Waterloo's imagination; only smoke enveloping it, thickening, almost disappearing it from view.

Frank Waterloo had been to India once, with Eleonora,

about seven years ago. They had seen the holy river, taken a boat, let some candles float, watched people bathe, bodies burn. Afterwards, they had visited Rajastan together, seen countless castles, slept in expensive hotels. Eleonora had been happier than he had ever seen her. Despite the country's problems, India was her paradise. She had been fascinated by the depth and diversity of culture, the food, the colours, the life force. She had complained that industrialisation had almost ended up ruining Britain's magic—she had just translated a book about this.

Frank Waterloo himself had not been able to love the country as much as he had hoped he would. Worse, he felt this had been his companion's fault more than India's. He could no longer work up any enthusiasm for his wife.

He felt a kind of shivering at the thought of this; not physical; more like a trembling of his mind, accompanied by a sensation of weakness, of cold. How he regretted not loving her then, or rather not loving her the way he thought he should. For some reason, he had all but worshipped the fact she was always so measured, so cool. Always holding her body upright; keeping her feelings to herself. Her childhood as a migrant child had not been easy and it had made her tough, in a beautiful, elegant manner.

So when, in India, she had suddenly became so emotional, so excited by small things like saris and the country's multitudes of gods ("that's what we need," she had said, "not one god, one truth, but many!"), he had become restless with her; annoyed. He hadn't been able to understand his reaction. Why did her sudden enthusiasm irritate him?

Why hadn't he been able to embrace it, join in?

He felt close to tears now, even though he would never cry. If only he had been taught to love properly. If only he knew what loving really, really meant. He saw this skill in other people, even in Rosalind. What was wrong with him? Or was he too harsh on himself? Had he loved her, in India? Had he loved her enough during the past years of their life, together? No, because daily life hardly allowed one, didn't allow him, to love with the intensity people did in some of the novels he represented. Not like Anette and Gwen in *Story*, Frederic and his mermaid in *Seabound*, or—even—like Sunny McHay's ill-conceived mass-murdering hero. Loving required such a fragile mixture of distance and closeness. He had hoped for this trip to India to bring him both. It hadn't worked. Did this matter, now?

Perhaps it had only been the tiredness of the journey. But Eleonore had begun to remind him of his mother, too lively and cheerful. His mother had been so warm in her expression it had probably been exhausting to be with her.

He remembered this, viscerally. Her warmth. She left home, for Morocco of all places, when he was eight years old. She had asked him to come along, but he had refused, always taking his father's side. Somehow, to her friends, she had managed to look like a victim, leaving her husband and child, just like that. Because her husband, Frank's dad, had been so cold. Because he had been unfaithful, at times.

She had died in Casablanca, over twenty years ago, catching some ordinary stomach bug that turned out to be deadly, for her.

Frank Waterloo loathed thinking about his mother. He felt an ancient fury rising inside of him; a desire to ruin something, smash his computer, throw a cup outside of his window; scream. He never normally felt anything as strongly.

Was this what writing would do to him? Bring back hurtful memories? Make him tremble over one single journey, as if it gently contained his entire life? They said writing was healing. What if the opposite was the case? What if, as he had imagined with Drubenheimer, it really drove one mad?

Chapter Fifteen

The porter didn't even try to stop Rosalind when she went past him with a worried face and fast, yet uncertain, steps. The only trustworthy person who might be able to tell her something about this was Lisa.

She crossed the corridor and entered the lift without looking up. She was still carrying the anthology like an unwanted foundling in her arm.

Tears started welling up inside of her, but Rosalind courageously gulped them down. Before she gave into her emotions, she at least wanted to know what exactly she cried about. Maybe there was an explanation. Maybe Mark Drubenheimer had taken the poem deliberately, trying to make an artistic statement. He might have intended to express that the fear of being murdered robs even the most gifted writers of their originality, for instance.

Yet what about the conclusions she had drawn from the poem? Hadn't it been the very cause of her search, hadn't its words enlightened her on the true nature of Mark Drubenheimer's death? Oh, what should she think?

The lift doors opened and closed several times, with Rosalind absentmindedly pressing the lift button. At last she got out and stared at Lisa's door, noticing voices coming from inside.

She rang the bell and barely had to wait before the door was pulled open and out came none other than Gabriel.

"My God, you do deserve to be called sweet stalker," he said. "How did you know I was here?"

"I had no idea," Rosalind whispered, even though trying to speak with a full, confident voice. Her stomach felt warm and she wished she could do something against the sudden smile on her face. For a moment, she forgot all about Drubenheimer's poem. "What are you doing here?"

Gabriel smiled back. She hadn't seen him since she had left him—naked, in his bed!

"Well, I wanted to meet my biological mum," he told her. "Obviously. And, guess what, PhD, Lisa will help me with the money issue, so it looks like I might go surfing, soon."

Neither of them spoke for a few seconds. What should Rosalind do or say now? She didn't know the rules that governed post possible-one-night-stand behaviour. Was it all over between them? Or would she see him again?

Then he winked.

"Can I still use you, though, for other things?" he asked, with his wonderfully malicious sparkle.

Rosalind's body contracted with excitement. Her smile turned into a beam. She wasn't all that good at flirty speech, so she remained quiet. What was the answer to that question, anyway? *Use me? Please?*

She nodded, at last and caught Gabriel's eyes. His pupils dilated so much his irises seemed to turn black. Rosalind's knees softened and, embarrassed at the strength of her reaction, she worried she might fall.

He moved towards her, grinning, then kissed her on the mouth. So did this mean she—

Lisa appeared and duly blushed.

Gabriel stepped away ever so slightly, still grinning. Rosalind shook her head to make herself return to reality.

"Hello, Lisa," she mumbled. Unfortunately, she remembered the poem again. "I came to visit you."

People like Berlina, or her father would have made some joke about interrupting a kiss between two people they had probably never connected romantically in their mind. But Lisa looked too shaken and confused to say anything witty.

"That's nice," she replied, stiffly. "As I just mentioned to Gabriel, you're both lucky to still find me here. I think I told you, I'm moving out in a few days."

The three of them stayed in a silence awkward for anyone other than Gabriel, who seemed to enjoy himself in the presence of these two women, suddenly connected to his life.

At last, he noticed the tension and announced: "Well, I'll be off."

Rosalind felt almost incapable of dealing with her two favourite "suspects" in the same place. Still, she didn't want Gabriel to leave. At least not without knowing if she would see him again.

Luckily, Lisa intervened.

"There's no rush," she emphasised, smiling shyly. "Why don't you come along inside. You two seem to be quite good friends."

Lisa attempted a grin and Rosalind blushed happily.

"Fine," Gabriel replied. "But only for a few more minutes. The pub is waiting for me."

"What a funny sentence," Lisa said and even Rosalind, who was quite ready to worship everything brought forth by Gabriel's mouth by now—including but not limited to words—couldn't quite see where the funny part was.

"Everyone else says that when they're going for a drink," Lisa commented. "But it's work for you."

"Yes, ha, ha," Gabriel looked at his mother, rather enchanted at her being so gratuitously enchanted with him.

"Yes, well," Rosalind added, dramatically. "The meaning of words always depends so very much on their context, doesn't it? And on our state of mind, our own needs, the moment of interpreting them."

Suddenly, Rosalind all but burst into tears. She might as well have announced another tragic death, rather than a mild, half-academic platitude. The whole weight of the discovered poem had returned to her.

Lisa turned towards her and asked, alarmed: "Is everything alright?

"Yes," Rosalind almost shouted, still standing in the doorframe. "I mean, no. Not really."

The time to speak about everything had come; and "everything" included the confession of her two crimes of madness. For how else could Rosalind explain the details of her most recent finding? Somehow, Gabriel's presence seemed to give her strength.

"Please don't be mad at me, Lisa, please! I took your key to Drubenheimer's studio. And there I also borrowed the *Anthology of Romantic Poetry*. As I read it I noticed—oh, it's horrible!—that his goodbye poem I so loved is actually by John Keats."

Gabriel looked at Rosalind, surprised but clearly not put off by what probably struck him as a minor transgression. Rosalind hoped that Lisa, too, would smile once again stiffly and tell her that everything was alright. That she was somehow even grateful someone had stolen her key and the anthology. She would make some sort of joke about it and they would both laugh it off.

Unluckily, Lisa didn't appear amused at all. Her eyes became tiny slots that shot forth rays of disapproval.

"You stole my keys?" the woman inquired with an unsteady voice, stepping towards Rosalind, then taking a few steps back again, remembering herself. "And you took the anthology?"

"Yes," Rosalind murmured. She felt mortified. "I'm really so sorry about the keys! But please understand that I only took them because—Lisa, it's such a long story. Please don't be angry with me."

"This is about your murder case, PhD, isn't it?" Gabriel came to her help.

"What murder case?" Lisa asked.

Rosalind glanced at Gabriel. He looked at her, bemused and nodded, encouragingly.

"I had an intuition that Mark Drubenheimer was actually murdered," Rosalind admitted, her eyes lowered towards the ground. "And I tried, in fact I'm still trying, to find out by whom. It's so hard to explain, you see originally it was all because of Drubenheimer's goodbye poem and–"

She explained. Once more. And Lisa listened, the frown on her face occasionally deepening, then becoming lighter again, until she finally looked more worried about Rosalind than herself. And Gabriel listened too, his eyes at times darkened by confusion he struggled not to show, then warmly focused on Rosalind again.

By the time Rosalind came to the part about finding Drubenheimer's supposed poem in the anthology, the three of them were sitting on Lisa's messy corridor, their postures expressing various degrees of weariness and fascination.

"I can't understand how I didn't recognise it. I'm supposed to be an expert in literature," Rosalind chastised herself.

"You can't possibly know every single poem in the world," Lisa tried to comfort her.

"Thank you," Rosalind said, accepting these kind words gladly yet with a lingering sense of guilt. After all, she had hardly been asked to identify Drubenheimer's plagiarism of some obscure 17th century Russian poet.

"I do find it worrying," Gabriel exclaimed, teasingly. "A bit like me trying to surf on, say, a washing machine."

Lisa shot him a nervous glance as if to say: "Not now!"

"You really are a little crazy, Rosalind," she began, carefully. "And I'm obviously not very impressed that you stole my key. But I do forgive you. I even understand you, I think. And it's not like I've always been entirely honest myself. In fact, I haven't at all."

Here she looked eagerly at an empty wall, to avoid Rosalind's and Gabriel's eyes.

"Anyway. As to you looking for a murderer, I told you I also had the idea that Mark might have been murdered, at some point. But then it was because of the poem I realised it must have been over for him. You know, I don't mean to rub it in, but it was actually in the *Guardian* that day. They mentioned that the poem was by Keats and…"

"I know," Rosalind interrupted. "But wait, you think he killed himself because of the poem?"

Rosalind almost found their crass differences of interpretations more shocking than the fact that she should have noticed her error much sooner.

"Yes. It was when I read his poem that I knew he really had committed suicide," Lisa explained. "I finally understood what must have happened the night Mark decided to die."

Gabriel lifted his left palm as if trying to stop them. His face was a little paler than usual. He looked a little overwhelmed, but the women were too engrossed in their talk to stop now.

"What do you mean?" Rosalind asked and couldn't help remembering Berlina's Rosebud joke.

"Nothing," Lisa replied, her voice becoming ever so slightly unsteady again. "It's only a theory of mine. But I can just picture how, the night of his death, Mark came home, drunk, and wanted to write a poem. Mark was a poet, at heart, Rosalind, and he should have followed his vocation. Instead, he was obsessed with narrative as a way to fame and that turned out to be his downfall. I wish I could explain! In any case, I imagine he came home late and felt suddenly inspired. He sat down at his desk, smiled, wrote down the words in his mind, this beautiful poem. He must have felt elated on completing such a good work. But suddenly, it dawned on him..."

"What?"

"It dawned on him that this wasn't his poem at all. So he ran and opened a book of Romantic poetry and—and realised his poem was by John Keats. You see, he did learn the poem off by heart for our presentation on Romantic poetry—Keats and Shelley—so many years ago and… "

Gabriel looked at his watch.

"I don't know," Rosalind mentioned, unconvinced. "Why would he copy an entire poem thinking it was his?"

"These things happen," Lisa said. "Composers hear songs in their minds and think they are divine inspirations when they actually heard them before. Writers come up with ideas which... Of course, this is only my hypothesis. I suppose we'll never know the full truth."

"You know," Rosalind found herself cutting off Lisa once

more, before she could stop herself. "To be honest, I don't quite understand why you keep on mentioning Drubenheimer's problems with narrative. Why do you emphasise his poetic vocation, if he was such a wonderful prose writer?"

Lisa fell quiet.

Gabriel took this as his cue to leave.

"I'm afraid I really have to go," he said, jumping to his feet.

The announcement instantly dispirited the two women. They might not have needed him to say much, but somehow his presence had given them energy.

"Take care," Lisa cried out and moved towards him, as if about to hug him, but her gesture awkwardly froze at a half-lifted arm.

"I'll see you soon, Gabriel. Thank you for stopping by," she added.

"Thank you for giving birth to me," Gabriel replied. "The world would have been a darker place without me. Don't you think, PhD?"

He looked at Rosalind expectantly.

"I'll see you soon," she said, first lifting her voice on "soon" as if turning it into a question, then forcing her intonation down again, making her sound like a rather unaccomplished singer. But it worked.

"Tomorrow?" Gabriel asked.

"Fine," Rosalind beamed once more.

Lisa smiled, although she looked oddly shaken.

"You call her," she instructed.

"Mothers!" Gabriel pronounced, evidently savouring the word. "You two keep on talking. I'll see myself out."

Then he disappeared, with a final wink at Rosalind. But her knees no longer went shaky. Her body knew that—after this brief and enchanting distraction—it was time to worry about Drubenheimer and his poem again.

"So what were we talking about?" Rosalind asked, but Lisa appeared not to have heard her. The woman stared after Gabriel longingly. She took a strand of her hair into her mouth and began to chew on it. Then she spat it out again and shut her eyes for at least ten seconds, drawing deep yet arrhythmic breaths.

"You asked me why I mentioned his poetic vocation when he was such a great prose writer," she said, without looking at Rosalind. "Do you really want to know?"

The second Rosalind had answered "yes" to Lisa's question, uncertain as to what exactly she had agreed to, all blood drained from the French teacher's face and she seemed about to faint.

"Are you alright?" Rosalind asked, worried.

"I think so," Lisa replied, heavily. "Why don't you go into the living room? Let me just quickly go and get something for you."

Rosalind wandered through Lisa's corridor and sat down on the floor of an almost empty room. There was the sound of bells again, high and low, hitting against the uncovered walls. What would happen now? Rosalind's neck stiffened. It would be nothing serious. It might even be something beautiful. Somehow she doubted this was true.

A few minutes later Lisa arrived, carrying a small box. Somewhat more composed, she sat down next to Rosalind.

"I've never told this to anyone," Lisa began and Rosalind shivered inwardly, trying to fight down a renewed sense of panic. There had been so many revelations; she had hardly digested any of them yet. What was to come now? "I told you, I often feel you've come into my life so I would finally have to unburden myself of all these secrets."

Lisa declared, staring at Rosalind intensely: "I'm the real author of Mark's books."

"I'm sorry?"

"I'm the one who wrote *Seabound* and *Story*."

It was like a person exploding in front of Rosalind. With a dead body inside. Both splashing their blood onto her.

Aghast, she stared at Lisa who stared at the floor.

"Have you never asked yourself," the woman continued, hoarsely, "how a mere French teacher could possibly afford to live in a building like this? Well, I haven't taught a French lesson for years. Mark and I had an agreement, Rosalind. I wrote his novels and he—he signed them with his name. We split the money and this is what I used to live. But now it's over! I haven't had the heart to tell Mrs. Drubenheimer the truth, yet. And Mark just left without a will, without thinking of my financial future. Not that I particularly care about money, but still. This was my only income. Anyway, I'll forgive him. He was very, very troubled. And no-one else knows about this. No-one except for you."

"What?"

Even though she still held the image of being splashed with two intertwined strangers' blood in her mind, Rosalind had at least been able to speak.

"I'm so sorry," Lisa said, looking pleadingly at Rosalind, as though seeking some form of comprehension or even forgiveness. "I so wish I had told you, or anyone, before. But I—"

Lisa's eyes became blurred by a thin veil of tears which almost made Rosalind cry too. Internal pictures of exploding bodies, corpses and blood became foggier and then started to fade.

"Please don't be angry with me," Lisa entreated her. "It was so hard on me, so hard on Mark and me. You have no idea how it hurt me sometimes. Living like this. Writing about my life, about Anne's terrible death," she pointed where the photograph of the violinist had stood, "my healing passion for the sea. Writing and writing, and never seeing my name in print. The feeling that there's never any real recognition for me. And I mean recognition in the most basic sense of the word. That people recognise you for who you are. That's what hurt me the most. I'm a writer, Rosalind. And nobody ever knew!

"In a way," Lisa carried on as if talking to herself, while Rosalind just sat there listening, glad that the woman's words drowned out her own thoughts. "You could also say Mark saved my writing. Things are never that easy, never that clear. It was another one of our pacts, like the one about Gabriel. He couldn't write and needed to be called a writer. I felt banned from becoming a writer, but I desperately needed to write. You know, it really seemed as if your father had put a curse on me with that letter! Anyway, Mark and I decided during one of our dangerous conversations that I would write and he would add a few corrections and publish everything under his name. This was the deal, and—apart from the recognition I craved— it set me free. Because this way, you see, it wasn't really me, Lisa, writing the novels. It was Mark, a Mark inside of me. And, once the books were out in the open, there was the real Mark to take the praise, but also the blame."

Lisa shot a quick glance at Rosalind who bit her upper lip so intensely, it was about to bleed. Rosalind felt dizzy. This woman was destroying Mark. This woman was the writer she had always wanted to meet. This woman-

"So this is why I always speak about Mark's talent as a poet. Because he was a poet at heart. Now to prove all this to you, I want to show you his real writing. For a while Mark tried to make me help with a very dubious plan involving contemporary classics, which I never quite understood. But this," Lisa handed Rosalind the box, "is the last project Mark worked on, when he went into this strange crisis and broke away from our pact. It was called…"

Rosalind touched her forehead. She knew it before Lisa had spoken it out loud. It was of course: *Accounts of a Muse*.

"You see, I've removed all but its folder from his studio," Lisa revealed. "I went there one last time as soon as the police had lost interest in it, put the anthology into a drawer, as if this too was part of our secret that needed to be hidden away from the world. Then I took the few texts he had written for his new novel. I worried people would find it and discover the truth about his—our—writing before I was ready, that the entire chaos would get even worse…"

"So this is what's in here?" Rosalind asked, still only understanding half of what she had heard.

Lisa opened the lid with unsteady hands and stared at the title for a few seconds. Then, in a moment's resolution, she took away the front page of the manuscript and looked at Lisa as if to ask for her permission to go ahead. The woman closed her eyes to assent.

"There isn't much," she added, opening them again.

Rosalind would manage. She would somehow stay brave. This woman was destroying Mark. This woman was the author she had always wanted to meet.

Rosalind started to read the first page. It contained another poem:

Make me infinitive, muse
For I'll be future tomorrow

As I was yesterday's past
And would-be conditional
If only I were,
The last of England's subjunctives

Make me infinitive, please
And let's be imperative, both
If you give me a moment
To be, be, be,
Like Hamlet
Yet doubtless
and infinitely more
infinitive

Because
To be
Is
Not to be
As there is no "to be"
Without being

A few more stanzas in a similar vein followed. Rosalind went through them quickly then lowered the paper in her hands.

"This was Drubenheimer's actual writing?" Rosalind asked incredulously, hoping that her shock had made her delirious; that tomorrow morning she would wake up and Drubenheimer would be the wonderful writer of *Story* and *Seabound* again.

"And who is this muse he is writing about?" she asked, very quietly, like someone completing an extremely difficult task.

Lisa shrugged.

"I don't know. Maybe his wife?" she suggested with a tone of resignation.

"It's very creative," Rosalind lied. It was by far the worst thing she had read in a long time. Of course, she was quite out of her depths with poetry. She never knew if something didn't make sense in a good or bad way.

"Rosalind," Lisa gently patted her shoulder. "Is this very terrible for you?"

Rosalind didn't answer.

"Do you think this is any good?" she asked Lisa instead, as if a lot depended on the woman's reply to that question.

"I'm not sure," Lisa admitted. "To be honest, not really."

She took the box away from Rosalind, started leafing through it and handed her another page.

"I like this one better," Lisa claimed, in an evident attempt to comfort her. "This one is quirky, in a way."

Quirky! That word alone made Rosalind envision blood again. It was an expression so evidently at odds with the author; for nothing about Lisa was "quirky" and it was difficult to imagine her sincerely associating the term with anything outstanding or even just good.

Still, Rosalind wanted to feel hopeful. Be hopeful. To save some fragment of an admiration she had been clinging onto for so long. Dizzily, she looked at the words in front of her:

All the world's a stage,
and we're but curtains in it.
They have their exits and their entrances,
But you, my muse, and I, have none.
And one man in his time plays many parts,
and we just write them down—or publish

And we fail at both.
Last scene of all,
That ends our strange eventless history,
Is mere oblivion.

This, too, was appalling. But she didn't say it out loud.

"What about your own writing?" Rosalind whispered, instead. "Are you writing as Lisa now?"

"I've been trying," the woman replied, sadly. "But so far it hasn't been working too well."

"All the world's a stage," kept on humming in Rosalind's mind as she walked out of the building in a haze. "And we're but"—what was it, curtains? Really? This was the extent of Drubenheimer's originality, what he had wanted to add to Shakespeare's eternal wisdom?

For the first time in a while Rosalind felt herself floating again. Everything seemed so unreal. So awful; so amazing. So–

A sneezing sound came from her bag. What now? Another sneeze. Had she finally lost her mind?

She started rummaging in her bag. It was her mobile phone. Othello must have played around with it.

She caught the phone on the third sneeze. "Hello?"

"PhD?" It was the voice she had most longed to hear. "Listen, I'm only calling because Lisa told me to. And because I could do with a little comfort, having just re-connected with my mother and all. Do you think you could provide some?"

"Didn't you say you had to work?" Rosalind asked.

"I did. But I called to say I'm not feeling too well. Which is kind of true, you know? It has been a bit much for me, after all," he confessed.

Rosalind stood outside Campden Hill Court. Right beneath the window Drubenheimer had been dangling from.

"Well, wait until you hear what I discovered now," she said. She could actually do with a bit of consolation herself. Then, some part of her she didn't quite control decided on a complete change of tone.

"As to comforting you," she heard herself add. "It depends on what it involves."

So she could do flirty speech, after all. Even under these circumstances.

"A bit of talking," Gabriel proposed. "This wasn't the original plan, but I'm curious and terrified what you have found out now. And stroking is good. You know, just generally touch. Sex, but this is optional."

Rosalind didn't reply immediately. She was a little shocked. At his daring. The fact that he called. That he cared. And had said "sex".

"We can go surfing on the Thames, instead," Gabriel offered and she could almost see the malicious twinkle in his smile.

"Stroking is fine," Rosalind said. "And we can take it from there. Just remind me, where do you live?"

"Very funny, PhD," he replied.

Chapter Sixteen

It was a cloudy day. Frank Waterloo sat down on one of the aluminium chairs in the café beneath his office window. A waitress came and he ordered a double espresso, to gather strength for the occasion.

The café was unusually empty. Frank Waterloo crossed his arms behind his neck, waiting for his drink to arrive. It was difficult to admit, but he somehow felt grateful towards Rosalind and her search. More than grateful. His daughter had impressed him. When she had him told out about Lisa Croydon-Bay being the actual author of Drubenheimer's work yesterday, deep joy had arisen within him. All's well that ends well. Mysteriously, almost as if by magic, his star-author was actually alive! Later on today, he would call Mrs. Drubenheimer, call off the ghost-writing project and start preparing her for a few more uncomfortable truths about her husband. He should probably recommend therapy, to soften the blow.

Well, he had ended up in a DIY family therapy session of his own, yesterday. After telling him about Lisa Croydon-Bay, his young Sherlock had felt empowered to also bring up the wet-nurse incident. Standing in the kitchen, opposite him, she had defended herself; argued that she had not been mad, hysterical or immature. That she had reacted in a comprehensible way, out of grief, trying to defend her mother.

He hadn't been fully able to understand her. But maybe

Rosalind was right. He had needed to kiss that woman, to gain back his own faith in life. But he should have seen straight away how difficult it must have been for Rosalind, finding him with somebody else. Someone who wasn't her mother. Even Suzy— the wet-nurse—had told him this. Straight after Rosalind had left, she had left him too.

Rosalind! He still grinned about him and Othello, secretly making her telephone sneeze. It had been the little boy's idea, because his nanny's phone had a permanent cold, too. It was almost a shame Rosalind had left this morning, to go back to university. His little girl…

Frank Waterloo's grin turned into a sad smile. His little girl? How the past assaulted him these days! He had even dreamed of his wife and own mother recently. In two oddly similar dreams Freud might have been enchanted with, they had been shouting at him; then he at them. Strangely, both times, he had woken up feeling sad yet a little more at peace.

The espresso finally arrived and Frank downed it in one gulp. As soon as his heart-to-heart with Rosalind had finished, he had called Lisa up and she had agreed to meet him, today. Not in his office. Right here, in this café. But what if she wouldn't show up at all?

Then he saw her walking towards him. The woman he remembered seeing at the funeral. Lisa Croydon-Bay. Author of *Story* and *Seabound*. Author of many critically acclaimed bestsellers to come. She wore a sunflower dress that may have been fashionable when his mother was born. Still, he was happy to see her.

He waved at her, cheerfully.

"You must be Lisa Croydon-Bay," he announced. His voice came out as smoothly as ever. "It's such a pleasure to meet you."

"Yes, I'm Lisa," the woman said shyly. "Thank you. And you must be Frank Waterloo."

Something in her voice made him guess she admired him. He felt oddly thankful for this.

"I am, indeed," he answered, laughing. "Please, do sit down. So, Rosalind tells me you're our star author." *Plus the mother of a secret son. Who would have thought?* "You had us all fooled."

Lisa blushed.

"Thank you so much. Yes, I wrote the novels that were published under his—under Mark Drubenheimer's—name."

The waitress delivered a delicious-looking chocolate cake to an elderly couple next to them, then came and took Lisa's order. She asked for a cup of herbal tea.

"Have some cake," Frank Waterloo insisted. He would eat some himself, but he felt somewhat nauseous again and his stomach hurt. But Lisa shook her head.

He hoped he could make her spill her entire tale, but she seemed terribly reticent.

"Well, you had us all fooled," he commented once more, ineptly. What was wrong with him?

She just smiled, stiffly.

"Congratulations," he tried again.

But she only nodded and waited for her tea.

When it arrived, she took a sip and evidently burned herself, even though she said nothing. She simply flinched and briefly looked him in the eye.

This encouraged him.

"So," he began. "I cannot begin to tell you how excited I was when I found out. And let me be straight. Can we make this public soon? Or perhaps once your next novel is done? Are you working on something else now?"

Lisa looked at her shoes. Unfortunately, he followed her gaze. They were of a dirty white, at least as old as her dress.

"Not yet," she acknowledged, very quietly. "I'm still very upset. And have been for a while."

Frank Waterloo laughed again, too loudly.

"I fully understand," he said. "Do take your time. But we need to get all sort of paperwork done. The contract, now under your name."

He grinned, happy to deliver his big news. He loved this phrase.

"Mrs. Croydon-Bay—or Ms., isn't it? You have just found yourself an agent."

Lisa stared at him. Frank Waterloo stared back. Something had gone wrong.

"I sent you my first novel many years ago," Lisa began, very quietly. "And you rejected it."

Frank Waterloo rolled his eyes to the ceiling. That story again. Author ego. Like the promising writer who had refused the ghost-writing project. Had they any idea how many manuscripts landed on his desk? That he often spent weekends and evenings reading them? That they had to be good to actually get published?

"Oh, did I?" he asked. He probably should say something about margins of error and *Harry Potter* being rejected numerous times before finding a "home" and his own tough luck of not recognising her potential in time. Yet he couldn't get himself to do it. He was tired.

"You did," she said, taking a sip from her tea and probably burning herself again. "It may have been routine for you, but it hurt me a lot. So I won't want your representation, thank you."

Frank Waterloo glared at her.

"You don't want what?"

This had never occurred to him. That she would reject him.

"You don't want an agent?" he asked. "You already know Flow will want to publish your next work. Is that it? You want to skip over one species in the food chain?"

He confused himself with his metaphor.

"You want to—"

He couldn't think of anything better. He felt out of his depth. What had he lost? How could he find it again?

Lisa had been sitting opposite him in silence, her eyes still lowered towards the ground.

"I hope I'll find another agent. Not you, Frank Waterloo. I know it may seem childish to you, but it's something that I must do. For myself. For all these years spent hiding away. I'm sure you understand."

She pronounced the last sentence almost in a whisper. It seemed difficult for her to tell him all this.

"Fair enough," Frank Waterloo said, trying to save his dignity. "I wish you good luck."

He got up and left a twenty pound note on the table.

"Now, if you will excuse me, I'm awfully busy," he declared. *I have to go and bang my head against a wall.*

He started walking away, but feeling a glance upon him, he turned around. There she was, this bizarre woman. Drinking her tea and smiling at him. Not quite triumphant. But deeply satisfied.

Rosalind let herself glide into the bath water. Even though she still felt tired from all her adventures and sore about her most recent discovery, her body couldn't help prickling with satisfaction. Finally she had returned to the island of peace, her own flat in the Midlands, determined this time to make her surroundings alive from within.

She breathed in deeply and identified the smell of her lavender bath oil, that of her own warm body and the cool spring air entering through the open window. The only sounds she could only make out were the gentle splashing of her feet inside the tub and, eventually, the slight crunching of shampoo being spread into her hair.

For two days, Rosalind had mostly remained in her London room, especially on Berlina's visits to her father. She had written a lot in her diary, where she had recounted and analysed every event that had occurred to her at least three to four times, desperately trying to make sense of it all.

Then there had been the talk with her dad. Rosalind smiled, immersed in warm water. After a lot of thinking and asking for Lisa's permission to do so, she had proudly told her father what she had discovered. About Gabriel; about Lisa actually writing Mark Drubenheimer's novels. He had seemed very impressed. Standing in the kitchen, his face had copied the look of eternal surprise of the priest at Drubenheimer's funeral. Still, he had claimed that he had suspected Mark Drubenheimer had a ghost-writer all along. Rosalind didn't believe him. But she just let him be.

Also, the expression "ghost-writer" didn't seem to describe the situation accurately. Lisa was no ghost. She was a woman, a body, a mind, a genius, perhaps—and one whose confidence her father had helped to destroy. Like the protagonist in *Story*, Lisa had lived in a fiction from then onwards. In a plot. A ploy. No wonder she had written that book. It must have been based on her own experience! The good thing was that, like herself, she appeared to be breaking free. Rosalind suddenly felt a lot like Lisa. Also treated too harshly by her father sometimes, unnecessarily put down.

To her great surprise, she had managed to take a deep breath and tell her father all of this, right there, in the kitchen. Calmly. With new confidence. And he had listened to her. Explained that he had a right to grieve in his own way. Then, the famous agent Frank Waterloo had smiled at her and, awkwardly, apologised.

Her dad! How lovely it felt to hear this.

But here she was now, back at home. She submerged the back of her head and massaged out the shampoo till the water turned white. She thought of Gabriel. They had spoken this morning before she had left, and he had promised to visit her soon. How exciting! She had seen him thrice more in London, including the day she had hurried to his flat right after her talk with Lisa. He had been both shocked and overjoyed that she was the actual author of the Drubenheimer novels. He claimed that, albeit irrationally, this improved the novels' quality for him and he would read them again. Once he had digested—or pretended to have digested—the news a little, they had made love, and love, and love! What a man! And *her* man. Was this even conceivable? How happy this made her!

They would travel back and forth on weekends, him coming to the Midlands, her going to London. She saw them talking, laughing, making love everywhere, in this very bathroom, at the train station, on the train, in his bedsit, in a hotel, on holiday in Sicily, in Fuerte Ventura, Australia...

He may not be the perfect man, but after all that had happened to her, Rosalind was tired of searching for supposed perfection in human beings. Also, she had understood something wonderful about him. He didn't enjoy reading, had no interest in writing, but—quite apart from a beautiful face and body—he had a lightness she loved. As if he embodied Lisa's message in *Seabound* that beneath life's suffering, everything was light. Maybe that was why he loved surfing so much. Gliding freely and joyfully on top of a wild sea.

With deliberate slowness Rosalind applied the conditioner, waited for two minutes, then turned on the water and started to rinse her hair. Small rooks of foamy liquid hurried down her face. The image of Lisa carrying a box appeared before her again, as it had almost continually over the past days, relentlessly haunting her.

How was this strange but impressive woman? Should she call her? Above all, should she ask if she could use the discovery for her PhD? Lisa would soon go public about her real identity. And once it was out in the open, she could write an entirely new and far more interesting article for a journal and a highly innovative PhD…

But really, this didn't matter so much to her now. She hoped more than anything that she and Lisa could remain friends, become even better friends. When Lisa had told her that she was the actual author of Drubenheimer's novels, Rosalind had become aware only very vaguely at first that her profoundest dream had, in some way, come true. Wasn't she the one able to work a writer's true magic; using language—as she had thought on reading Flaubert—like a bewitching musical instrument that made the entire universe sparkle with joyful relief because it felt caught and found out?

There was the chance that one day, separated by two cups of coffee (most likely with horrific taste), Rosalind Waterloo and Lisa Croydon-Bay would not only talk, they would think together. She would ask her why—and if—she believed in this profound goodness of life, despite so much evidence to the contrary. If she thought there was a life beyond stories and if one should seek it. She would ask her so much! And there was time still; there was time.

This made Rosalind smile. She felt enriched by her search, although it never led to a clear conclusion, at least not one she had expected to find. Yet now it was time to relax with a classic. Not that this was a particularly spontaneous decision: a book she had borrowed from her father's library already waited for her, placed on a folded towel on the floor.

Rosalind reached for it with her damp hands; it was the Subtlety Classics edition of *Mrs. Dalloway*. She felt vaguely nostalgic. This had been the book she had browsed through on her arrival in London, on the day she had first met Gabriel and started her search.

She opened the novel and instantly enjoyed the first page:

Mrs. Dalloway said she would buy the flowers herself.
For Lucy had her work cut out for her.

What a beginning! How lovely to think about flowers! In fact, she would skip the passages about Septimus and his suicide today. It would all be lovely, flowery and pure.

Satisfied with this decision, Rosalind flicked through the book searching for something that would suit her intentions. She came to a passage about Sally Seaton, Mrs. Dalloway's friend:

But all that evening she could not take her eyes off Sally. It was an extraordinary beauty of the kind she most admired, blonde and large-eyed, with that quality which, since she hadn't got it herself, she always envied—a sort of abandonment, as if she could say anything, do anything.

Rosalind smiled some more. She liked the whole thing about Sally Seaton in *Mrs. Dalloway*. The subtle yet powerful attraction between the two women. If only she had felt half the fascination for Mat over the past months, they might still be together. Maybe, if she had found a sort of abandonment in his nature, she could have abandoned herself to him. But it didn't matter now. She had Gabriel.

The water in the tub had turned cooler. Jumping a few paragraphs ahead, Rosalind read on:

Sally's power was amazing, her gift, her personality. There was her way with shoes, for instance. Mrs. Dalloway never knew which shoes to buy. Sally went out, picked high-heels, sandals—foot-wear of all colours which Mrs. Dalloway would have never dared to wear.

Rosalind started. Shoes? Was that what Sally's power, her gift, her personality boiled down to? Did Mrs. Dalloway love a woman because she had a way with shoes? And the SCASA of the world had let this pass? She knew that Virginia Woolf was—to an extent—famous for her sense of the mundane, the sensuality of it; but shoes? It was fine, of course, it was fine.

But was it?

Again, Rosalind told herself rather than actually thought, a classic had managed to surprise her. Again, she had been granted the private privilege of discovering a new angle to an immortal literary work. How wonderful. Except it wasn't. Rosalind was sure, getting surer, that something wasn't quite right. She felt a strange discomfort; she could swear she remembered differently. That the novel never praised Sally Seaton for her way with shoes. That she was never described in those terms, blonde and large-eyed. It just struck her as so odd, so unlike a character Virginia Woolf would create. This way, Sally Seaton almost sounded like a literary version of–

Rosalind's body shot out of the tub, flooding the light-blue tiles with water and foam. The revelation had come to her all at once, a spiral conceived in her mind. She could follow it, up and down, and strain her inner eye along its slithering turns. There had been too many surprises. Too many small miracles.

Standing next to the bathtub, she reached for the towel still lying on the floor and quickly wrapped it around herself. The copy of *Mrs. Dalloway* had become soaked in her hands. She looked at the cover again. There was the picture, the title and the glossy Subtlety logo. Still staring at it, she remembered Raskolnikov's all-important girlfriend in Crime and Punishment, the bizarre praises of Lucia's mother in *The Betrothed*. One was described as a girl with light caught in her hair and her eyes, the other, Agnese, as a woman of lasting beauty and charm who seemed to have special talents and gifts. And now a blonde and large-eyed Sally Seaton had a way with shoes!

Almost breathless with shock (for weren't the classics holy?), Rosalind recalled the receptionist at Flow who had been reading *Don Quixote*. "Some of the people at Flow used to work for Subtlety," the girl had said. But this was absurd! She could now picture the Dulcinea of this edition, almost certainly a woman with esoteric powers, fond of hypnosis and feng shui!

Rosalind hurried towards her computer and quickly

switched it on. She needed proof, she needed proof, she needed proof! Maybe, hopefully, she was wrong!

She wanted to start with *Mrs. Dalloway*, the obvious choice, because she was still clutching the wet copy in her hand. As soon as the computer was ready, Rosalind went on the internet. A few clicks and some wild typing later, she had the entire work on the screen in front of her, in a version Subtlety had not been able to tamper with. She started looking for Sally Seaton, for shoes.

This was what she found:

Sally's power was amazing, her gift, her personality. There was her way with flowers, for instance. At Bourton they always had stiff little vases all the way down the table. Sally went out, picked hollyhocks, dahlias, all sorts of flowers that had never been seen together—cut their heads off, and made them swim on the top of water in bowls.

Rosalind just stared. Flowers, of course. Flowers again. Sally Seaton had a way with flowers, not shoes! Yet this wasn't all: Her hair also wasn't blonde but black! Following a sudden intuition, Rosalind also checked the passages about Septimus she had read. She could hardly believe what she saw. The whole scene about the wife subtly trying to make her husband commit suicide was absent from the original. It was the doctor, Holmes, alone who made Septimus jump.

As though moving through a strange dream, Rosalind frantically searched for an online edition of *Crime and Punishment*. The day Drubenheimer died she had been surprised to find Raskolnikov's girlfriend mentioned on the first page. Now, all she had to do was read the electronic version's beginning to realise that it contained no reference to her, at all. Eventually, she did discover a brief allusion to a girlfriend, but it was much later in the book. And instead of being described as an angel, she was a weak and sickly creature, just as she had remembered.

In *The Betrothed*, Lucia's mother also turned out to be anything other than a woman with overflowing hair and sparkling eyes, but simply an elderly lady, neither particularly attractive nor important. She was a rather minor character.

To make sure she hadn't gone mad, Rosalind rapidly went through all the passages from *Madame Bovary* she had read. As she suspected, this edition alone had remained faithful to the original intentions of Flaubert's pen. Except for a few differences in translation, the two versions were identical. She had been right. It was only the Subtlety Classics, then. All novels had been falsified.

Even though Rosalind would have preferred to think about this first, imagine the circumstances, motives and ways of committing such a metaphysical act of destruction, her mind was completely blocked. There was no way she could simply think about it. She needed to act.

With a wild feeling, as though she were tumbling down a building on a rope, she walked towards the phone and was about to call her in the office, when another intuition told her to dial the number of her father's flat instead.

"Dad!" she cried out as soon as somebody picked up the phone.

"Hello? Bad Monster speaking, hello?"

It was Othello, playing with the receiver.

"Othello," she said, affectionately, as though his mere

existence might somehow pull her out of this bizarre dream. "Can I please speak to Dad?"

"Rosy!" Othello roared, joyfully. "I'm a monster."

"Boo," Rosalind shouted, "I'm terrified!" she added, quite truthfully.

Othello giggled and then a bang indicated that he must have dropped the telephone onto the floor. A moment later she heard her father tell him off and pick up the receiver.

"Hello?"

"Dad," Rosalind repeated, her heart beating so wildly she feared she would explode.

"Rosy, is that you? Did you get home alright, oh worthy human being, talented detective who found out the truth about Mark Drubenheimer without her cruel father's help or intervention?"

He sounded a little depleted, yet evidently struggled not to let it show.

"Yes, Dad, I'm home. And you're not that cruel, really. You only destroy a great author's and great daughter's self-esteem, occasionally," Rosalind said, happy about her sudden ability to imitate her dad's bizarre style of human interaction, especially given the dramatic circumstances of this call. "In any case, there is something important I need to ask you."

"Oh dear," Mr. Waterloo complained. "What's it this time? I mean, please, oh Rosalind, ask me everything, anything you need to know!"

"Well," Rosalind began. She suddenly craved for a cup of coffee, or two, or three. "It's about Berlina."

"About the most beautiful editor this planet has so far produced?" he asked. He was performing again. Probably—hopefully—for her.

"Do you know if she ever worked for Subtlety Publishing?" Rosalind asked, starting to bite her lip but then releasing the pressure her teeth put on the fragile flesh again.

Mr. Waterloo chuckled.

"Darling?" he shouted, away from the phone. "Did you ever work for Subtlety Publishing?"

"Yes," he said into the phone. "Berlina says she did. She used to work as an editor there. What is it, Berlina? Oh, that's why the company was so successful, she says."

"And do you know," Rosalind continued, bravely. "If she worked on the Classics edition, by any chance?"

"My daughter wonders," her father echoed, "if you worked on the Classics edition?"

Rosalind could tell he was slightly drunk. She wished she could have a drink too! Or two. Or three.

"Yes, she was," her father confirmed, then added: "You know, why don't you two speak? This is getting a little tiring."

Rosalind listened to the phone being moved about. She felt tempted to hang up, but didn't. Ignoring all hesitations had become a kind of habit, by now.

"Hello, my darling! Just give me a moment," Berlina greeted her. She heard her send her father away. "How are the charming Midlands?"

"Charming," Rosalind replied. She cleared her throat, nervously. Would she be able to do it? Confront the editor like this? "Berlina," she said very quietly, not out of shyness, but because she suddenly tried not to shout. "Can I ask you a question? I've been reading several Subtlety Classics lately and in many of them I came across characters who strangely reminded me of you."

"At long last!" Berlina exclaimed, joyfully. "You've finally caught me! It's such a marvellous coincidence, really. What do you think of my work?"

At long last? This was the last straw! The woman admitted to having falsified classics freely and cheerfully?

"Rosalind?" Berlina insisted, with exaggerated concern. "You're alright, aren't you? You do sound a little, well, shocked. What's the matter? You're not too conservative, are you, to see the value of updating classics a little? Or did you find my writing too drab? I've improved a lot since then, I promise you! So very much has changed."

"Conservative", "shocked", "classics", "much has changed"— Rosalind's mind threw individual words and phrases from Berlina's speech back at her, in no apparent order. Did Berlina also falsify contemporary classics now? Had she proposed herself as a model for the mermaid in *Seabound*?

"You know," Berlina meanwhile went on, "I do feel it gives those old books new life. And whoever reads them twice, in two different editions, to notice my slight and wonderful alterations? In any case, which ones did you read?"

"Let me think," Rosalind snapped, before she could stop herself. Her own voice came from afar. "I saw you as Sally Seaton, as Raskolnikov's dead girlfriend, as the mother in *The Betrothed*..."

"Is that all?" Berlina giggled. "When I made such a lovely Kitty in *Anna Karenina*? And the most enticing of sirens in *The Odyssey*?"

Rosalind took ten deep breaths before she was ready to take all this in. *The Odyssey*? Surely this couldn't be right. Surely Berlina must be joking again.

"You re-wrote *The Odyssey*?" Rosalind asked, almost trembling.

"Yes, and so what?" Berlina replied. "I also asked Drubenheimer to help me, the useless monkey. I tried to open a whole new Flow Contemporary Classics series with him. But that, obviously, didn't work. Ha! To think about the ghost in this Mexican classic by Juan Rulfo he tried to give my features. Despicable! You shouldn't be so protective of all these writers, my gorgeous. Also, don't you realise how humble I was? Only ever improving a side character, never one of the grand historical figures. Thinking about it, this hasn't really changed. Oh, my loveliest Rosalind. If only you knew! Well, you will know now, the moment has finally come. I've stopped writing myself into classics. I've become a writer myself! And my favourite subject is a very nice play-detective, a literature student, also known and appreciated by some as a 'sweet stalker'. Yes, I have almost written a whole novel! I thought that if that Croydon-Bay woman can write, then so can I! You'll love it, I'm sure. Especially because it'll prove that you were actually right, in a way. About Drubenheimer's death, I mean. But you'll see, you'll see. I've already asked your dad lots and lots about you. In fact, his tale of an agent deprived of a star-author makes up the subplot of my brilliant opus! But don't tell him yet, will you promise? Anyway, would you just be so kind as to send me your last diary entries? Then I can quickly work on the last bits and post the novel to you! And now I'd better get going, my muse! Your father tells me that dinner is ready. Alright then, my darling. Byeeeee!"

Chapter Seventeen

Gentle sunlight fell on the pond in the park beneath her little flat and, sitting on a bench opposite, Rosalind observed the patterns the dancing, gleaming rays created. Ducks quacked their cheerful call and response performance; children laughed all around her, lost in their play. She would have thoroughly enjoyed this moment, if it weren't for the surprise visitor comfortably lounging next to her. Berlina had arrived this afternoon, a month after their last talk, a parcel in her arm. As Rosalind had feared—and the editor proudly declared as soon as she had found her standing outside her flat—it contained the novel she had written, the work which apparently centred on her.

Of course, Rosalind had never sent her diary entries. It was terrible enough that her private thoughts had been abused in such a way. And yet, as soon as Berlina had said hello and asked her to come to the park, the editor had stated—beaming more convincingly even than the present sunrays—that "her brilliant mind" had been able to "make up for all the narrative gaps Rosalind's unnecessary reticence had created".

So now Rosalind sat next to Berlina wordlessly, hoping that the editor would do all the talking. Unfortunately, quite out of character this time, Berlina hadn't spoken much since her earlier declarations and was just seemingly happy to be there, holding the package in her hand.

Rosalind stroked her forehead, as if trying to massage some clarity into her feelings; her thoughts. She wasn't enraged with Berlina. Ever since her conversation with the editor the day she found out about the falsified classics, she had struggled to know what she felt. Rosalind had simply not found a pattern in her mind which gave instructions on how to react if one appeared in a novel. Not suppressing her emotions for once, she had felt extremely angry, yes, but that wasn't all. She was also a tiny, inadmissible bit grateful that someone had found her worth writing about, had attempted to turn her into a mysterious and memorable muse.

Perhaps, the message of Lisa's *Seabound* had once again proven true: good things could come out of bad ones. Berlina's bizarre and often highly reproachable actions had also made her feel special—even more so, or on a different, more metaphysical level than being with Gabriel. She now also "lived" inside a most precious thing, a book for the whole world to see, to touch, to read! Some of her fragile being had been captured on lifelessly lasting paper. And, somehow, this would push her further to create her very own, unique, Rosalind-life-plot, from now on.

Life really was quite complex. Darker as well as more beautiful than she had been able to see.

Meanwhile, the editor still sat there, smiling. This situation was getting increasingly strange.

"Don't you want to tell me why exactly you came?" Rosalind forced herself to prompt her visitor. "Didn't you say you'd send me this… novel by post?"

At last, Berlina turned towards her, with a dramatic but tender smile.

"I was hoping you'd ask me that question, my darling," she sang. "Any question, really! You see, I've prepared a little speech.

But since I'm now practising advanced receptive social skills—which means I'm supposed to listen and react rather than speak right away—I was waiting for you to say something first. You know, one can't just stop at hypnosis and communication with the dead."

"I see," Rosalind said, wearily. "So why don't you hold that speech, then?"

Berlina laughed and patted Rosalind's shoulder.

"Oh, Rosalind, I like this new assertiveness in you," she exclaimed, fluttering her eyelids and hurling her package onto Rosalind's lap. "So, here's my novel and here's my speech. I haven't learned it off by heart, don't worry, I'm also going to have to improvise a little. As an editor, now writer, I'm of course wonderfully good at this. You see, I have a way with words too!"

Berlina winked at Rosalind who, without having intended to, looked back at her reproachfully. Didn't she feel guilty about what she had done, at all?

"Well, my darling," Berlina went on, ignoring her glance. "I'm afraid it's all a bit complicated. Then again, you've heard so many complicated stories, I'm sure you'll be able to put up with just one more. So it turns out you were right and Mark was murdered. Self-murdered, as his German parents would have said. And I helped to murder him. In a way. You see, my lovely, as I once told you, I'm terrified, terrified of dying. I just so hate the thought of the world without me. Do you understand?"

Rosalind stared at Berlina. The editor had murdered Drubenheimer, too?

"Well," Berlina sighed playfully. "You don't seem to fully understand what I'm talking about, although you must do. Every so often, you must lie awake at night, wondering what death may be like and it must give you the most unbearable shock.

I find it dark, confusing and—quite frankly—unbearable! But then, my dear Rosalind, I'm a woman of many resources. And I realised one day that there was one solution, imperfect, yes, but still a lovely antidote for my fear. I'm talking about literature, of course, and writing! With a little bit of marketing savvy and luck, it can carry us right into eternity!"

Berlina pronounced "eternity" with an American accent again and shot Rosalind a challenging glance.

"You agree, don't you? Given the fact you are so in love with literature yourself?"

"But how is all of this related to the classics and Drubenheimer dying? I just don't understand," Rosalind said.

"Oh, just wait, my darling, wait," Berlina replied, evidently pleased that Rosalind had become more involved in their conversation. "Just hear me out. You see, I soon noticed that literature would be my only possible ticket to immortality. But there was another slight problem: I thought I couldn't write. I had this idea of being an enabler, a very noble task, really, but fairly useless when it comes to achieving endless life. I mean, could a few dutiful dedications by authors really be all that would remain of someone like me? No, Rosalind, no! Even you, who, how shall I put it, are a little more humble, cannot possible think so."

"Berlina, I really don't know, I would-" Rosalind ventured and looked at a cloud suspending the sun-beam dance on the lake.

"Well, my gorgeous," Berlina interrupted her, "you can of course be smug now and say you don't care, because you already are in a novel and at your young age! I did all of that for you. But whoever did it for me? I tried with my ex-husband at first, but he failed me. I told him to write a book about me and the useless man completely refused to do it. So I kicked him out and started falsifying classics instead. A marvellous idea, isn't it? Pure genius! It just suddenly occurred to me, in a flash of inspiration. That I would hitch a ride with the great, so to speak! And make the covers as nice and appealing as I could, which I've always had a real talent for. So this is what I did for a rather long time, and it worked astoundingly well. Everyone loves the Subtlety covers and by reading what's inside, everyone loves me! Now, I know that you don't approve of such things. Nor did I, in the long run. For I realised it wasn't enough. I wanted, I needed more! So that's when…"

"What?" Rosalind asked, bewildered yet by now trained to absorb very unsettling information rather quickly.

"That's when, once I had started working at Flow, I naïvely thought Drubenheimer was the man for me! First I wanted him to help me with my innovative re-workings of contemporary classics, but that didn't work out too well. I felt angry at first, but then I had the most brilliant of ideas. That he would write an entire, immortal novel about the most fascinating subject matter of all: Berlina Marrowing!"

For some reason, this made Rosalind smile; and interpreting this as a sign of complicity, Berlina joyfully patted her shoulder again and continued:

"Don't just smile, you may laugh out loud! To think how he fooled us all! Such a fake, Mrs. Drubenheimer's quite right. She's now in therapy, by the way. And taking piano lessons, again. Apparently, her widowhood will catapult her more deeply into music, as it has done for that American composer she is so obsessed with, Amy Beach. In any case, I asked him to write a novel about me and, once more, the man who cannot write declined."

"*Accounts of a Muse!*" It was Rosalind's turn to interrupt the editor. Slowly it all began to make sense. "You were the muse he was writing about!"

"Yes, my lovely," Berlina granted. "Which already tells you the next bit. That he didn't decline for very long."

"And how did you make him change his mind?" Rosalind asked, unable to maintain her reticence now.

"Well, you see, my sweet, I offered him more fame and more money and what not, but he refused because he claimed he was blocked. So I told him I loved blocked writers. That I could cure them with one of my wonderful methods. And this was how he accepted. Thinking, as one would think, that I can achieve miracles! We started having our 'sessions', as we used to call them, but all of that's really a bit tedious to remember. Not that our sessions were tedious. I mainly spoke about me! My qualities, my aspirations, my past, everything, so he could write about it! And then I told Mark to look into the mirror and say, 'I love myself and I can write critically acclaimed bestsellers' three times a day, so he'd think I treated him against writer's block. Well, unfortunately, it didn't work."

Unaware, Rosalind had started touching the wrapped up novel in her hands while listening to Berlina; she had even started scratching at the sealing.

"Hello?" Berlina called out to her, then blew into her face and giggled. "Are you still listening? Well, I gather from what Lisa told me recently, she now has a very young, nice agent, by the way; good, your father can do with a bit more rest— you read some of the unspeakably bad writing Mark composed as a result of our sessions. 'There is no bee without being', or whatever. Certainly none of it was about me. So the day he came into my office and read these things to me I was furious,

furious. But I also noticed that something was wrong and decided to find out more."

"More about what?" Rosalind asked. Everything Berlina told her sounded like utter madness. And it was this nonsense which, finally, helped her to make sense of everything that had happened, to Drubenheimer, to Lisa, to her.

"Well, more about the circumstances that led him to write such terrible poems!" Berlina explained, flushed with the excitement of sharing all this with Rosalind. "I told him we should go and have a drink. And I got him drunk, drunk, drunk the way I learned to do with my silly ex-husband. Then I attacked him, even made him cry. I let him feel how disappointed I was, that he didn't deserve his fame, that he was now clearly a failure. I must have somehow intuitively realised that this was his major weakness. I'm just so sensitive, you see? In any case, once I had weakened him this way, I pretended to be kind again and told him that I deeply admired and even loved him."

Here Berlina smiled at Rosalind cheekily, in evident admiration of her own skills of psychological manipulation.

"So by about five o'clock in the morning he was ready and confessed nearly everything, that drunk and silly man. I really think he had gone so far from his original dreams, he was secretly dying to unburden himself and be judged by someone. The human mind can't bear being a Drubenheimer and nothing else, in life. Once he had told me the whole ridiculous story, his many, many lies, I was an inspiring embodiment of composure and simply ordered him a cab home. And that's where my story ends really," Berlina declared and got up a little dramatically.

Rosalind jumped from the bench, the novel now safely clutched in her hands.

"But wait, how can you stop here?" she asked, a little too loudly. "You said you helped to kill him and-"

"Oh, my lovely," Berlina said and signalled that Rosalind should follow her. "It's nice to hear you're properly interested, at last. But there isn't that much left to tell. I was also a little drunk when I got home and still very angry. I felt so let down again! But then, at around six o'clock in the morning—I didn't even try to get any sleep, I was just pacing around my flat—I had the most miraculous, liberating idea. I would stop relying on other people's work for my eternity. I would write my own novel! I even had a working title, straight away. It would be *Editing Lies*. And it would obviously be about Drubenheimer's whole list of deceptions. He's famous enough. I knew there'd be a market for it! So when he came to my office completely hungover later that same morning, trying to find out how much he had revealed, I said something like: 'Dear Mark, I'm going to tell the world.' And he replied, sulkily and staring at me rather intensely: 'Then I'll kill myself.'"

Rosalind gasped, at which Berlina looked at her almost warmly and carried on in a gentle tone strangely at odds with her words:

"Well, yes, and you may blame me, but I didn't believe him. I thought he was trying to emotionally blackmail me, get some attention, you know, the whole 'I'm going to kill myself with two aspirins' package. And to show him I wouldn't let my emerging creativity be frightened away by him, I just told him not to be a baby."

Berlina's eyes filled with tears for a second, real tears that appeared to embarrass her. She pretended to be interested in the ducks and the playing children, quickly blinking them away.

"And so I visited Gabriel and wrote Mrs. Drubenheimer a letter, then told him about both."

"And so he killed himself," Rosalind said, very quietly, and felt sorry, in an entirely new way, for this man she had never met and knew so little about. "Especially after what Mrs. Drubenheimer had told him during their anniversary dinner!"

"Yes," Berlina acknowledged, gravely. Then she added, already cheering up again, "Well done about discovering that one, journalist! This was great news for my karmic record!"

She looked at Rosalind, sideways, to gauge her reaction. Rosalind cringed. So Berlina knew about Mrs. Drubenheimer's harsh, final words to her husband. Through her! She said nothing. Berlina spoke on:

"And, between us, I don't think Mrs. Drubenheimer's karmic record is all that tragic, either. I mean, she won't be reborn as a flying cockroach or anything like that. I believe, ultimately, the weight of Mark's many lies and deceptions finally got to him. He was always so eager to be admired and thought great. I suppose he just couldn't bear to think of the scandal, the shame. Not that I care very much. I do feel a little guilty. But then, to be honest, it was a great twist for my novel. Although a little uncomfortable for him, I suppose!"

"But what about me?" Rosalind asked, once more inclined to forgive Berlina's intrusions into her privacy for the sake of the attention she had given to her existence. They had reached the park exit and were standing opposite Rosalind's flat. "And what about his goodbye poem?"

"What poem? The one by Keats? I gave it to him during our first session to illustrate my fear of death! And that naughty man used it to accuse me, to make me feel remorseful about his death, I suppose. As to you, my lovely," Berlina's eyes filled with real tears, once more, "you were just a wonderful coincidence. A sign that I was on the right track! I'll never forget that day I met you in your father's kitchen, telling me that Drubenheimer had been murdered. What better thing could have happened to me? I had already decided that your father's story would be my B-plot. Berlina's B-plot, isn't that funny? By the way, he is a tiny bit angry with me at the moment. Don't be surprised, though, if we end up going on a romantic reconciliation trip somewhere, soon. But enough about him, back to you! You see, the main story was supposed to be about me. But then, when I met you, Rosalind Waterloo, I realised I was meant to be a humble side character again. That you deserved to be my protagonist, my muse! I decided I would follow your search and that would be my novel. I gave you that diary and read it the day you came to my flat and on many other occasions, when I just nipped into your room in St John's Wood. You write quite nicely, you know. Keep it up! But enough now, I'll have to catch my train back. Take care, my darling! And have a good read! Bye!"

"Wait!" Rosalind almost shouted, suddenly not wanting Berlina to go.

"No, my lovely, I'm afraid I really have too much to do. All these manuscripts, you know. And now I want to cause a post-mortem scandal and republish Drubenheimer's work under that woman's name. Actually, before I go, let me tell you just one more thing. I've changed my mind about something I once told you. That it's important to live every day as though it were your last. You see, my darling, I realised that's just a little too stressful. And also, quite honestly, no novels and a great many other things would ever get done this way. So now, having given the matter some thought and having talked it over with my handsome social skills trainer, I find imagining one has ten years to live ever so much more helpful. It means you'll have to find a balance between seizing the moment and a bit of long-term planning. So if you want a fulfilled existence, just repeat, in front of a mirror, three times a day: 'I have ten more years and today's the very first day'. It's so much calmer, don't you think? No stress and no hurry. A simple reminder that time is precious and short, that our 'fair creatures of hours' are counted. But now I am getting emotional, so let me go."

And having given her this strange piece of advice Berlina walked off into a glittering evening, leaving Rosalind behind with a parcel in her hand and a gentle, but cheerful, shake of her head.

Acknowledgements

Working with the inspiring team of Jacaranda—Valerie Brandes, Jazzmine Breary and especially my editor Laure Deprez—has been a wonderful experience. I would like to thank them warmly for their invaluable guidance, kindness, wisdom and, above all, for believing in this book!

Also, a big acknowledgement to all of those who read the novel at various stages and helped me along with their comments and encouragement, such as Ernesto Mestre, Helen Mee, Ruth Kitchen, Antonio Ramieri, Giuseppe di Salvatore, Sandra Gubo-Schlossbauer, Katia Meleady, Katja Heiden, Harumi Shimada, Anette Boudeken, Caroline Humer, Ingeborg Rehak, Sandra Moncayo, Miguel Cane, Irina Cornides, Constanze Veigel-Maruschke, Emma Brandon-Jones and Lotte Elwell, among others. Stefania Fietta deserves a special mention for providing crucial insight into the secret world of literary agents. On the whole, I would like to thank all of my friends—and this for me includes students and teachers—for their countless contributions and just for being such a lasting source of happiness for me.

The same holds true for my family. As to my "Mexican crowd", thanks so much to all of you, especially María Elena Soltero, Olivia Palancares and Santiago Enriquez. I am also extremely grateful to my parents Eva Chibici-Revneanu and

Bernd Chibici-Revneanu for their never-ending support, and to my sister Nicole and my brother Stefan.

Last but not least, thank you to the ones this book is dedicated to—my husband and eternal (writing) accomplice Gonzalo Soltero and my life's light, Ana Lucía—for pretty much everything.

About the Author

Claudia Chibici-Revneanu is a geographically confused Austrian, who lived a brief but happy time in Italy, a long time in different places in England and Wales (completing her PhD in Cultural Policy Studies at the University of Warwick), as well as in Mexico., where she lives with her husband and daughter. She currently works as a lecturer at the National Autonomous University of Mexico (UNAM) in León, Mexico. She has published poems, literary essays, translations and academic articles in different international magazines such as Celeste, Schreibkraft, olasciviles and The International Journal of Cultural Policy Studies. In 2000, she won the Austrian award for women writers Minna Kautsky. Her great passion is exploring the literary and musical creativity of women, which she does in her writing, academic work and as a mezzo-soprano, giving concert-conferences about women composers. *Of Murder, Muses and Me* is her first novel.